Laurie Gilmore is a No. 1 *New York Times*, *Sunday Times* and *Globe & Mail* bestselling author who writes small-town romance. Her first novel, *The Pumpkin Spice Café*, won the TikTok Shop Book of the Year award in 2024. Her Dream Harbor series is filled with quirky townsfolk, cozy settings, and swoon-worthy romance. She loves finding books with the perfect balance of sweetness and spice and strives for that in her own writing.

www.thelauriegilmore.com

instagram.com/lauriegilmore_author
facebook.com/lauriegilmoreofficial

Also by Laurie Gilmore

DREAM HARBOR

The Pumpkin Spice Café

The Cinnamon Bun Book Store

The Christmas Tree Farm

The Strawberry Patch Pancake House

The Gingerbread Bakery

The Daisy Chain Flower Shop

MAPLE HOLLOW

Big Bad Wolf

THE DAISY CHAIN FLOWER SHOP

Dream Harbor Series
Book 6

LAURIE GILMORE

HarperCollins*Publishers* Ltd
1 London Bridge Street
London SE1 9GF
www.harpercollins.co.uk
HarperCollins*Publishers*
Macken House, 39/40 Mayor Street Upper,
Dublin 1, D01 C9W8, Ireland

This paperback edition 2026
5
First published in ebook by HarperCollins*Publishers* 2026
Copyright © Laurie Gilmore 2026
Map illustration © Laura Hall
Laurie Gilmore asserts the moral right to
be identified as the author of this work

A catalogue record of this book is available from the British Library
ISBN: 978-0-00-876147-9

This novel is entirely a work of fiction. The names, characters and incidents portrayed in it are the work of the author's imagination. Any resemblance to actual persons, living or dead, events or localities is entirely coincidental.

Printed and bound in the UK using 100% Renewable Electricity
by CPI Group (UK) Ltd

All rights reserved. No part of this publication may be reproduced, stored in a retrieval system, or transmitted, in any form or by any means, electronic, mechanical, photocopying, recording or otherwise, without the prior permission of the publishers.

Without limiting the exclusive rights of any author, contributor or the publisher of this publication, any unauthorised use of this publication to train generative artificial intelligence (AI) technologies is expressly prohibited. HarperCollins also exercise their rights under Article 4(3) of the Digital Single Market Directive 2019/790 and expressly reserve this publication from the text and data mining exception.

To all the nerds out there,
we think you look hot in your glasses

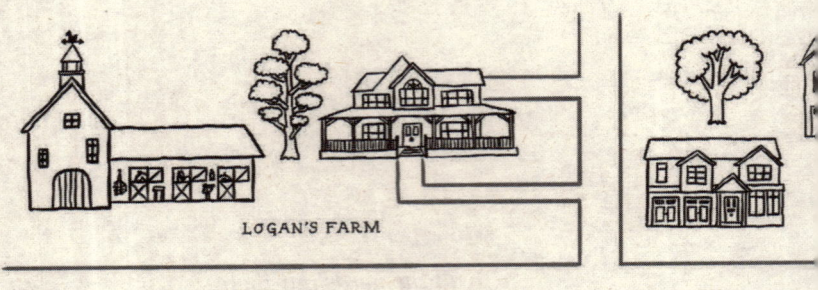
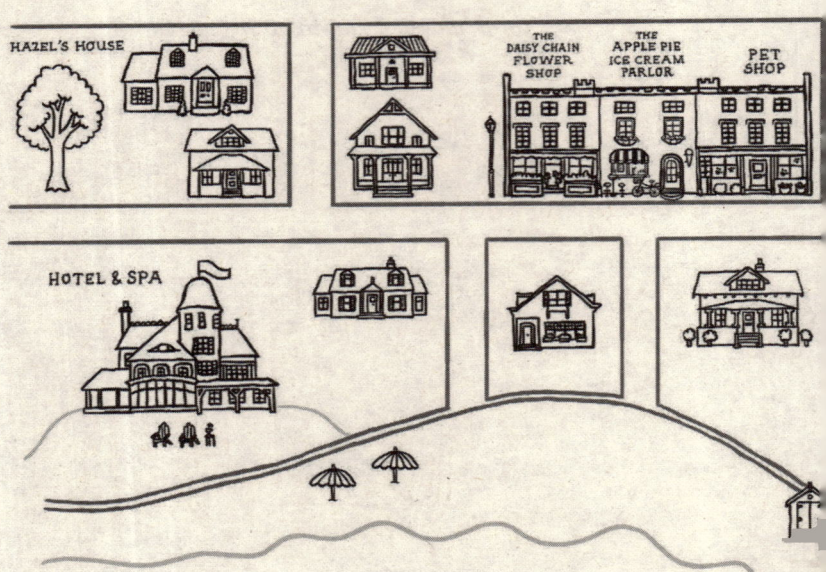

DREAM HARBOR

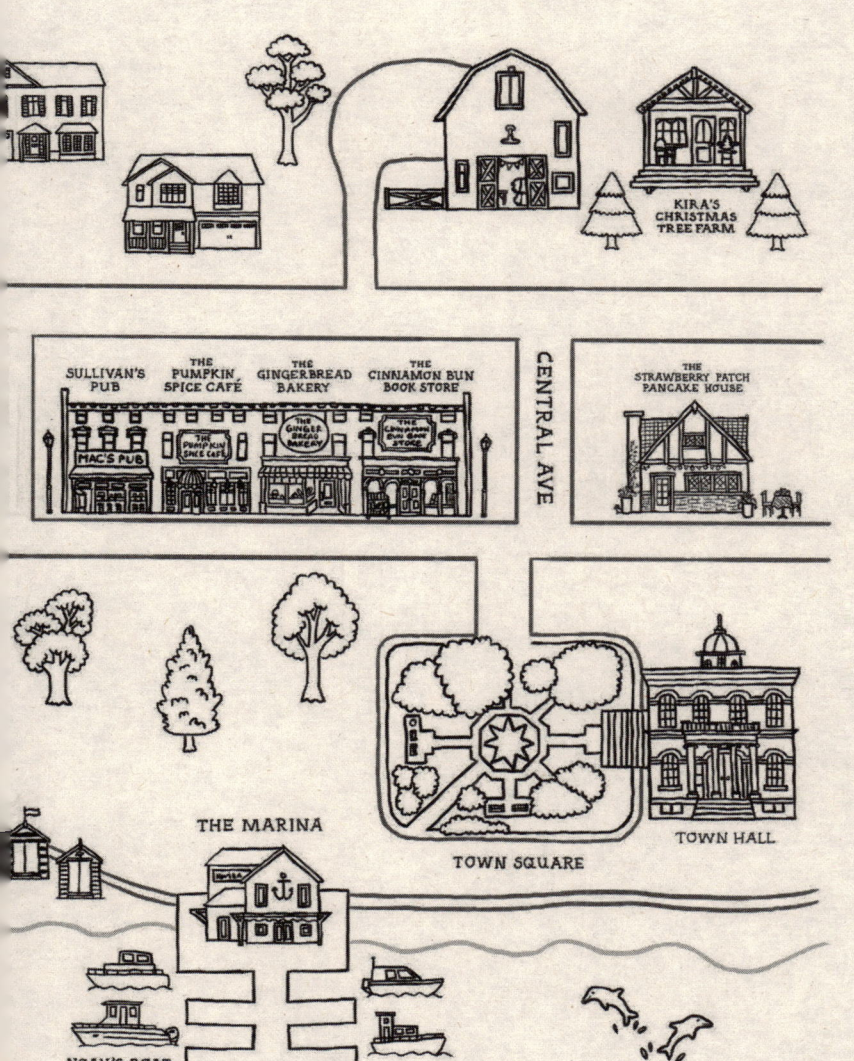

Playlist

DAISIES - Justin Bieber
that way - Tate McRae
Golden - Harry Styles
Home To Another One - Madison Beer
Feel Something - Clairo
lacy - Olivia Rodrigo
Wood - Taylor Swift
Vodka Cranberry - Conan Gray
goodnight n go - Ariana Grande
Already Over - Sabrina Carpenter
National Anthem - Lana Del Rey
I Think He Knows - Taylor Swift
we never dated - sombr
Risk - Gracie Abrams
Spring Into Summer - Lizzy McAlpine
Look At That Woman - ROLE MODEL
Paper Rings - Taylor Swift
Satellite - Harry Styles
Means I care - Tate McRae
Rein Me In - Sam Fender
House Tour - Sabrina Carpenter
So Easy - Olivia Dean
The Fate of Ophelia - Taylor Swift
undressed - sombr
Accidentally In Love - Counting Crows
Lover - Taylor Swift

Chapter One

Daisy Scott, current owner of The Daisy Chain Flower Shop, was just one Daisy in a long line of Daisies. Her mother was Daisy. Her grandmother was Daisy. The literal chain of Daisies went back for at least a hundred years. The women in her family passed down the name and the flower shop as diligently as they tended to their blooms. It was all very quaint, and she had quit fighting it years ago. But as far as Daisy knew, she was the first one to be cursed.

Not that she actually believed in curses, at least not at first. Mostly because it wasn't 1850 and she had a working brain. She had rejected the notion completely. Sure, three weddings she had done flowers for had ended in divorce within a year, but as far as she knew Jeanie and Logan were still going strong. Didn't that count for something?! And yes, she did have an ex-husband *and* an ex-fiancé, but there was no way her own unlucky love life was somehow rubbing off on to other people, right? That would be crazy.

The whole notion was crazy, and she wasn't even sure

the town would have cared if Mayor Kelly hadn't mentioned some foggy notion of a dream he'd had at a packed town meeting six months ago. He'd apparently seen a dark cloud hovering over the flower shop, and that was enough for the townsfolk to run with. Tales of her own sordid history and of the trail of broken relationships she left in her wake had been greatly exaggerated, and naturally, had spread like wildfire. Daisy had booked nothing but funerals ever since—with the exception of Jeanie and Logan's wedding—but that had been all Annie's doing. That woman could make anything happen. The mayor had felt terrible about her loss of business, and he'd been buying mixed bouquets every Saturday to make up for it. But a bouquet once a week did not make up for lost wedding revenue.

That man was a menace.

Still, she refused to believe she was actually *cursed*. She blamed small-town gossip and her own inability to pick a good partner for her current situation. Not a curse. But much like how she had tried to reject her name in the fourth grade, trying desperately to convince everyone to call her Jade, her denial of the curse didn't stick. In her head, or in reality.

And as she stood behind the counter of the shop with the early April sun streaming in through the stained-glass window above the door, leaving a kaleidoscope of colors on the worn wood floor, her ex-fiancé waltzed in with his new fiancée and confirmed once and for all the existence of curses.

A dark cloud, indeed.

Son of a bitch...

'David, hi!' *Well, that sounded far too perky. Tone it down, Daisy. You shouldn't be nearly that eager to see your ex.* 'What brings you in?' she asked, casually brushing petals and leaf bits off the counter from the giant funeral wreath she'd been working on.

This was fine. Totally fine that her ex, who she hadn't seen since the break-up and didn't even live in this town, was showing up in her shop on a random Tuesday afternoon. And that he was looking as handsome as ever; blond hair artfully sculpted away from his defined cheekbones and incredible jawline. *Totally fine.*

'Hey, Daisy.' Her ex, the man she had planned on spending the rest of her life with, tipped his head to the side as he looked at her. It was a pitying look. A look that said he felt sorry for her, like some horrible tragedy had befallen her. But the only tragedy was him dumping her a month before they were supposed to get married. Via text. And she really wished she could say she hated him. That she was over the whole fiasco. That it didn't cut her to her very core that he was already engaged again after only a year of them being broken up when she hadn't even managed to go on a single date. But she couldn't say any of those things.

Daisy wished she could be a 'Jade'. She wished her entirely black wardrobe transferred to her insides as well. But Daisy was actually still the little girl her mother used to dress in yellow dresses until the age of nine. Daisy was soft. Daisy was still in love with David. And she hated herself for it.

'Hi, Daisy! It's so nice to finally meet you! You have such an adorable shop,' the woman on David's arm cooed as she looked around at the stuffed-to-the-brim store.

Hailey.

Daisy only knew her name from the copious amount of internet stalking she'd done after she and David had ended things. Hailey, who worked in marketing for a firm in the city, was a Leo, loved brunch—and from what Daisy could tell—spent all her spare time at the gym or drinking matcha lattes and posting about it. Hailey, who had a much cooler name than *Daisy*.

Daisy would really like to hate her, too, but Hailey was smiling so genuinely as her eyes flicked from the refrigerated roses to the dried bouquets to the potted plants in the window, that Daisy was having a hard time with that one. She seemed nice. She was cute. Honestly, Daisy could see the appeal.

'It's nice to meet you, too. Uh … what brings you guys in?'

Translation: what the hell are you doing in my town and have you come into my store just to remind me of how shitty my life currently is?

Daisy's face hurt from the fake smile she'd contorted her mouth into. She absolutely would not let David's pitying look get to her.

Hailey looked up at David, beaming with perfectly straight teeth, and David, *Daisy's David*, smiled down at Hailey with hearts in his eyes. Daisy thought she might be sick. 'We are scouting wedding venues, and I remembered how quaint Dream Harbor was,' he said, as though this was all perfectly reasonable, as though he wasn't infiltrating *her* town, *her* life. 'We're checking out the inn this afternoon and The Christmas Tree Farm tomorrow.'

'They both look so lovely!' Hailey continued to beam, and Daisy's breakfast burrito rose higher in her throat.

'Of course, even if we get married in town, we'd find someone else to do the flowers. That would be a bit too awkward,' David said with a laugh.

'Right, of course, totally.' Daisy forced herself to laugh, too, but it came out as more of a bark. Hailey's eyes widened in concern at the sound.

This was surely a new level of hell. She didn't know what she was more upset about: her ex possibly getting married to his shiny new girlfriend in her hometown, or that she wasn't even going to get any business out of it. It was almost enough to make her choke out another insane laugh. Which, apparently, she did, because Hailey was looking like she was preparing to call the emergency room to have her checked out.

'Unless this all makes you uncomfortable…' David tipped his head again like he was looking at an injured puppy. 'I just figured it's been a year and we've both moved on…'

'Totally! Totally moved on!' Dear God, was she yelling? She seemed to have lost control of her voice. She did another hyena-esque laugh, and Hailey took a few steps back from the counter.

'I'm just going to browse over here…' she said, wandering away, but not before shooting David a look that clearly said she wanted him to take care of his mess of an ex.

'Look, Daisyboo.' David leaned closer, his toned arms on the counter, the smell of his expensive cologne overtaking the earthy smell of flowers.

'Don't call me that,' Daisy whispered, even as her heart leapt at the old nickname. She really was cursed. Cursed to pick men who didn't love her.

'Sorry, old habit.' He smiled that damn charming smile, the one that had fooled her into thinking he loved her. 'I just wanted to say, if this is too much, we'll leave right now… It's just that Hailey really likes this place … and I thought we could all be adults about this.'

'Of course she does. Everyone likes it here,' Daisy bit out, trying desperately not to let David see how miserable she was, how alone.

It was true. Everyone loved Dream Harbor. She'd somehow managed to forget that fact in the year she'd been away. The year she spent with David, moving into *his* condo, living closer to the city so he could be near *his* job, hanging out with *his* friends.

She'd forgotten how much she secretly loved this little shop, how much she missed her friends and seeing her parents and grandparents all the time.

Not that she'd admit it.

Not that it didn't still feel like she'd failed at something.

At love, mostly.

At being in a functional relationship.

She may have loved this shop, but it didn't change the fact that being back here just reminded her every day of what she'd lost.

The bell over the door jangled as a new customer walked in, giving Daisy a brief moment of reprieve. She recognized him from somewhere. The café, maybe? Or Jeanie's wedding! Elliot. That was it. The guy with the glasses who kept looking at her. Kinda like he was now.

Like a deer in headlights when Daisy caught his eye. But a cute deer, with a slight blush on his cheeks and rumpled hair like maybe he'd just woken up.

And Daisy didn't know if it was David's stupid handsome face, or Hailey's perfect gym-toned ass, or if it was the memory of the way Elliot had looked at her that night at the wedding, like maybe he wanted her, that made her do what she did next. It certainly wasn't any rational thought.

But when fighting a curse, maybe it was best to abandon rationality completely.

'Really David, it's fine with me. Like you said, we've both moved on.' Daisy smiled and waved at Elliot in the doorway. 'In fact, here's my new boyfriend now. Elliot, come say hi!'

Chapter Two

Elliot had been avoiding the flower shop for two reasons. Both having to do with the nearly frantic woman currently waving him over and calling him her boyfriend.

Daisy.

Lovely, soft Daisy.

Daisy, whom he'd spent far too much time thinking about ever since she'd arrived in town. He'd only been living here for a few months at that point, still wondering why he'd chosen this little town to hide out in. And then there she was, storming into a town meeting like she owned the place.

And he'd very nearly fallen in love with her.

A terrible habit of his.

Which was reason number one for avoiding the pretty little flower shop on Main Street and its pretty little owner. Elliot had moved to Dream Harbor to forget about love.

To avoid it entirely, if possible. After two years, he still hadn't been able to shake off the failure and heartache his divorce had caused, and he wasn't eager to try again.

He hardly knew Daisy. But he knew himself and he knew he had already developed an absurd crush on the woman based almost completely on the way she argued with everyone at town meetings and the way she looked in a tight black T-shirt. Like the one she wore now. Even with the faded, daisy-print apron she wore over it, he could see how it hugged all her curves.

Elliot swallowed hard.

He should not be looking at Daisy's curves. Daisy's curves were sure to lead nowhere good. At least, in the long term. In the short term, he was sure Daisy's curves would lead him to all sorts of amazing places.

But that wasn't the point, because the second reason he'd stayed away was a bit more insane but tied in with the first. Daisy was cursed. Not that Elliot believed in curses, but if town gossip was to be trusted, Daisy left a trail of broken hearts in her wake, and Elliot's was broken enough. He was fairly certain it didn't even work anymore, and so the issue of Daisy's black T-shirt was moot, really.

'*Elliot.*' Daisy's voice snapped his attention from her shirt to her face. Her eyes were wide, nearly pleading with him. She obviously wanted him to go along with whatever weird situation this was, but Elliot's thoughts were stuck on one thing. *She knows my name.*

Elliot had a tendency to blend in. To hide, his brother would say. He was just shy, his mother would insist. But Elliot wasn't sure it was either of those things. He was an observer. He liked to watch people, and he didn't feel a huge need to thrust himself into the action. Which most people seemed to find either creepy or boring.

But somewhere along the line, Daisy had learned his name.

And apparently now she needed him. 'Come over and say hi to David,' she said again, her volume increasing with each word. 'You remember David, *my ex*. I told you about him.' She raised her eyebrows dramatically like she was waiting for him to remember his line.

It was time to thrust himself into the action.

'David, right, of course,' he said, stepping up to shake the man's hand. 'So nice to meet you.' If there was one thing Elliot understood, it was the pain and embarrassment of running into your ex and their new person. He'd experienced it one too many times before moving here.

Daisy mouthed *thank you* over David's shoulder and scurried around the counter to stand next to Elliot. She grabbed his hand in hers, twining their fingers together, and Elliot had to swallow the startled sigh that wanted to escape his lips. It had been a long time since someone had held his hand. And Daisy's was so warm and small and perfect.

'I didn't realize you were seeing anyone,' David said, clearly still trying to piece together what was going on while Elliot tried to keep his shit together about a girl holding his hand like he was twelve.

'Yes, I'm seeing someone.' Daisy still sounded a bit unhinged, so Elliot gave her hand a gentle squeeze. She looked up at him with a surprised smile. 'I'm seeing someone,' she said again, rolling her shoulders back.

'Not everyone announces new relationships on social media, David.'

David frowned but Daisy charged forward, this time with her eyes on Elliot. 'His name is Elliot and he's a…' Her voice trailed off, and her eyes widened in panic. Okay, so she had learned his name but apparently, that was it.

'I'm an architect,' he said, turning his attention back to David and away from Daisy's amber-colored eyes. He didn't even know that was a real thing. Amber eyes. He shook his head. Not important right now. 'I'm working on a new design for the inn, actually.'

At the mention of the inn, the woman who was clearly David's new girlfriend, came hurrying back over to his side.

'Are they renovating soon? I would hate for that to interfere with our wedding day.' Her brow furrowed in concern.

'I guess you should probably look elsewhere, then,' Daisy blurted out and then immediately looked like she regretted it when the woman's frown lines deepened.

Elliot tried not to smile when he added, 'You know how these projects go; things will probably be a mess for a while. Personally, I would steer clear of the whole place.'

Daisy squeezed his hand in a silent thank-you, and Elliot hadn't felt this pleased with himself in a very long time. Possibly ever. Helping Daisy lie to her ex and his girlfriend might be his new favorite thing to do. He really needed to get out more.

'Right, well, we'll take that into consideration.' David's gaze flicked between the two of them like he still wasn't buying their little skit. Feeling bold, and high on Daisy's hand squeeze, Elliot removed his fingers from hers and draped his arm over her shoulder, tucking her tight to his side.

And if he thought holding her hand was life-altering, well, having her entire body pressed against him was another plane of existence all together. He *really* needed to get out more.

If she was surprised or put off by the move, Daisy didn't show it. In fact, she tipped her head to rest on his shoulder as though it was the most natural thing in the world.

David narrowed his eyes. 'When did you say you two got together?'

'About a month ago,' Daisy said at the same time Elliot said, 'Last fall.' Christ, even in fake relationships he wasn't on the same page as his partner.

Daisy laughed manically again, like she was coming undone. Elliot hugged her tighter as though he could keep her together.

'Has it only been a month?' he said with a laugh. 'You know what they say, time flies when you're having fun!'

'Right, but—'

'Don't you two have an appointment to get to?' Daisy cut David off before he could ask any more questions or dispute the use of that phrase in the current context, which admittedly made no sense.

'We probably should get going,' Hailey said, looking happy to take any excuse to get out of this awkward situation.

'I guess we should.' David gave them one last suspicious look before his fiancée dragged him out the door.

'It was nice seeing you two!' Daisy cooed. 'We should

double-date sometime! Don't be strangers! Y'all come back now…'

Daisy continued to call out insane goodbyes until the two were gone, and she finally slumped away from him and blew out an incredibly long sigh of relief followed by a bit of existential moaning.

Elliot stood quietly until she was done.

Chapter Three

When Daisy's brain was finished melting, she looked up and found Elliot still standing beside her. He seemed to be waiting patiently until her breakdown was over.

'I am so sorry about that.'

'I can't say I was expecting it,' he said with a lopsided smile.

Daisy groaned and ran her fingers through her shoulder-length hair. Of course, she hadn't washed it in days, and it was a stringy mess. Of course, David wouldn't have shown up on a day when her hair looked good. That would be too much to ask from the universe.

'I panicked.' She returned to her spot behind the counter and started sorting bits of ribbon. Elliot continued to watch her, waiting for her to go on. Maybe that was what had her being so honest. He seemed genuinely interested to hear whatever crazy words were coming next. 'It's just … they came in and they were so happy…

And I hated that. And I know that makes me some kind of bad person. But seriously, who just waltzes into their ex's hometown flaunting their new fiancée?! It's rude, frankly.'

Elliot let out a quiet laugh. 'I agree. *Who does that?*'

Daisy's gaze snapped to his and she couldn't help returning his smile. She'd be lying if she said she'd *really* noticed Elliot before. Sure, there was that moment at the wedding, but she hadn't really considered him at the time. She wasn't supposed to be considering anyone right now. She was supposed to be healing. She'd sworn off men entirely and was perfectly fine with her new celibate lifestyle. *Perfectly fine.* But being in such close proximity to him now, it was impossible not to notice his shy smile and his messy hair. The way his dark-rimmed glasses drew attention to his dark eyes and the way his cheeks flushed pink when she smiled back at him.

Maybe she should have listened to Annie at the wedding. Maybe Elliot was cute.

She shook her head.

No. Absolutely not.

'I'm sorry for dragging you into my web of lies.'

Elliot shrugged, another quiet laugh rumbling out of him. 'It made my day more interesting.'

'You're a pretty good actor.'

'It was a pretty easy part to play,' he said, his smile growing. Was Elliot the nerdy architect flirting with her? Did she like it?

Daisy's cheeks heated and a nervous flutter started in her belly. It had been a long time since she'd been flirted with.

'Well, thank you. It made this interaction slightly less terrible.'

'With any luck, we scared them away from booking the inn,' Elliot said with another shrug.

'We can only hope.' Daisy breathed out a long sigh. Just thinking about David being in town planning a wedding was giving her hives. How would she survive it if he stuck around? Weddings take forever to plan. He'd be here all the time! It had taken months for her to get to the barely functional place she was currently in. *Look at me, wearing real clothes and being upright!* Such progress! It had been nearly a year since she'd spent a full day crying. A few hours here and there, sure, but not a full day. But if David was around, if she had to see him, how the hell would she ever get over him?

She bit down on her bottom lip. Hard. She would not cry in front of this nice man who she had already accosted and forced to be her fake boyfriend.

She. Would. Not. Cry.

'So, you were married to that guy?' It was clear from the tone of his voice just how Elliot felt about her ex. Which didn't seem fair based on their five-minute interaction.

'No, just engaged. We never even made it to the married part.' *Not crying, not crying, not crying.*

'He's an idiot.'

Daisy's brows shot up, startled by Elliot's harsh words. She wasn't expecting them from his soft-spoken demeanor. 'You don't even know him.'

'I know he didn't marry you. Seems like an idiot move to me.' He held her gaze while he said it, and heat flooded Daisy's body.

'You don't know me, either,' Daisy whispered, surprised by how much his words affected her. 'I could have dead bodies in the basement.'

Elliot's lips rose in amusement. '*Do* you have dead bodies in the basement?'

'No.' Daisy narrowed her eyes at him. This conversation was going off the rails, and she didn't know how she felt about it. 'But you don't know that. I could be crazy. I could have driven him away with my constant nagging and insecurity. Maybe I always thought he was mad at me and I was always asking "are you mad at me" and he just couldn't take it anymore.' Oof, that was a little too honest. She swallowed the hot ball of emotion rising in her throat.

She had always felt like she was grasping with David, like she was trying so hard to hold onto something that just wasn't working. 'Maybe.' But Elliot shrugged again like he wouldn't mind if she asked him that a million times. 'But it seems to me, he should have made you feel more secure.'

Daisy opened her mouth in an automatic urge to defend David but maybe she didn't want to this time. Maybe it was nice hearing that the break-up wasn't all her fault. Maybe this was the first time she'd considered the idea that maybe if David had held her tighter, she wouldn't have had to grasp so hard.

'If you ask me, David had a beautiful, intelligent, funny woman and he let her go. Doesn't make sense to me, but what do I know? I couldn't keep my ex-wife happy.'

'You were married?' Daisy asked, mostly to avoid thinking too much about the *beautiful, intelligent, funny woman* part of the whole thing. Elliot couldn't be cute *and* say things like that.

'Yep. For five years before she decided I wasn't worth the trouble, I guess.'

The way he said it sounded so resigned, so sure that he was the problem that Daisy instantly felt defensive of him. 'She sounds like an idiot.'

Elliot's smile hitched higher. 'Sounds like we both have a type.'

'People who don't love us?'

'That's about right.'

'Bummer,' Daisy said even as she let out a resigned laugh. It was nice to finally have someone understand how she felt, someone who didn't try to placate her with soothing words about how things always work out the way they're supposed to. Was she *supposed* to end up alone? Thanks, universe and thanks, Aunt Jan, for pointing it out.

'I guess I should get my flowers and get going.'

'Oh, right, sorry! You didn't come in here just to play the role of fake boyfriend.' Daisy rolled her eyes at how stupid the whole thing was, but Elliot stopped her in her tracks again.

'No, that was just a fun bonus.' That lopsided grin was killing her, and every other thing out his mouth surprised her. Who the hell was this man? This guy who, until this very moment, had flown completely under the radar but was now in here and *flirting* with her.

Daisy's mind wandered to the feel of Elliot's strong arm around her shoulder, and she had to shake herself out of it. This man needed flowers, not to be sexually harassed. And she needed to stay far away from anything that looked like a relationship, fake or otherwise.

'What were you looking for?' she asked, clearing her throat.

'I'm not sure, really. My mom is going to be staying at the seaside cottages for a while, and I just wanted to make it feel homier.'

'Noah did a gorgeous job on those cottages. I'm sure she'll love her stay. But maybe a potted plant or two to breathe some life into the place? And maybe a flower arrangement for the table?'

'That sounds perfect, thank you.'

Daisy got busy with collecting things Elliot's mom might like and distracted herself from how much she liked being his fake girlfriend, even if it was only for a few minutes. But it was nice to be flirted with; it was nice to be looked at like she was desirable. It was really freaking nice to not feel like a lovesick loser for half a minute.

She was almost tempted to ask Elliot to keep up the charade. He could fill in for her body pillow and her plus one for all events moving forward…

'How about these?' she asked, pushing away her insane thoughts to have Elliot be her emotional support date for the foreseeable future. 'Succulents are always nice and low maintenance. And philodendrons are pretty hard to kill—plus they grow fast.'

'These are great.' Elliot added a colorful spring bouquet into the mix on the counter, and Daisy rang it all up.

'I'm glad I came in today,' he said, his shy smile back in place.

'Me, too. You really saved my butt.'

Elliot's smile grew and the blush rose on his cheeks. She thought for a second that he was going to comment on her butt, and then she really wouldn't know what to do, but he just nodded and gathered up his plants in the box Daisy had packed them in.

'You should come in more often,' she said as he turned to leave.

He smiled at her over his shoulder. 'Maybe I will. Thanks, Daisy.'

She watched him go, and against her better judgment she found herself hoping he would be back soon.

Chapter Four

'Tell me everything!'

Iris started talking as soon as Daisy answered the FaceTime call. It was late afternoon, and Daisy was about to close up for the day, but ever since Iris went on maternity leave just over a month ago, a call from her at this time of day was not unusual.

'Everything about what?'

Iris blew a strand of coppery hair from her face. Daisy could just make out the top of baby Owen's head where he rested on Iris's chest.

'I'm gone for a few weeks and I'm already out of the loop,' Iris whisper-yelled into the phone.

'What loop? I still have no idea what you're talking about. Also tip the phone so I can peek at those little baby cheeks.'

Iris moved the phone and Owen's sweet face filled the screen. Daisy let out a squeal. Her friend had made the cutest baby. At nearly four weeks old, he was all round rosy cheeks and soft, downy hair and he smelled like heaven.

'I heard you have a new man,' Iris said, her face returning to the screen, waggling her eyebrows suggestively.

'A new man? Ha.' Daisy continued watering her plants with one hand while she held the phone with the other. 'There is no new man in sight.'

Iris pursed her lips, not at all convinced. 'Well, I heard from Carol, who heard from Joe at the café, who heard from Jack at the inn, who had a wedding venue meeting today and he said that the groom was your ex and that you now had a new boyfriend.'

'What the actual hell?' Daisy jerked upright and poured water all over her shoe. 'Damn it,' she hissed.

'Daisy. Language. There is a baby present.'

Daisy rolled her eyes. She knew perfectly well the kind of language that came out of Iris's mouth. Iris would be lucky if Owen's first word wasn't four letters and not appropriate for church.

'Sorry, but the gossip chain is out of its mind. How did you even hear any of this? I thought you were out of the loop?'

'I'm still on the aerobics-ladies group chat, of course.'

'Of course. Well, there's no new man.' How was it possible that it had been only a few hours since Elliot left her shop and half the town already thought she was in a full-blown relationship?

Iris looked skeptical. 'Give me *something*, please. I've been trapped here with this baby sleeping on me all afternoon. I have to pee. I need a snack. My shirt is covered in breast milk and Archer took Olive out for ice cream after school. I have no one to talk to but a newborn. *Please* give me something to work with here.'

Daisy sighed, about to deny it again, but her friend really did look pitiful. And exhausted. She knew these first few weeks with the baby had been hard on Iris. The least she could do was fill her in on the hot mess that was her own life.

'David came in today with his new fiancée.'

'That bastard,' Iris gasped, her eyes lighting up with the gossip.

'I tried to be cool about it, I really did, but they looked so damn good together.'

Iris winced. 'How did you handle it? I mean, how did you feel seeing him?'

'Like my heart was ripped from my body and thrown into a blender and turned into some kind of heartbreak smoothie.'

'Wow. Graphic,' Iris joked but her face was full of sympathy. They'd known each other growing up, but they'd never really been friends in school, since Daisy had been a few years ahead of Iris. It wasn't until Daisy came home heartbroken and depressed that she and Iris got close. Iris had helped her mom out a lot with the shop while Daisy was gone, and it was so good to have her here while Daisy got her footing back. And now she considered Iris her closest friend. If anyone knew how rough this last year had been for her, it was Iris.

'This was the first time seeing him again, right?' Iris asked.

'Yep, since the day I packed up and left. So, it's been

nearly a year.' What a pitiful day that had been. She'd barely had three boxes worth of stuff at David's place. She'd wanted to think of it as their place, but had he ever thought of it that way? As she moved her few belongings out, it was painfully clear he hadn't. Just one more kick to the gut.

'And then he just shows up here with his new girlfriend? That's bullshit.'

'Iris, the baby.'

Iris glanced down. 'He didn't hear me. And besides, it *is* bullshit. What was he doing here?'

'He said Hailey liked the town and they wanted to look at wedding venues. He thought we could all be adults about it.'

'Ew.'

'Yeah. And they were all in love with each other right in my face, and it was disgusting. And then Elliot walked in...'

'Wait, the nerdy architect guy?'

'Yeah.'

'And...' Iris was practically vibrating. Daisy was actually concerned she might wake the baby.

'And I may have said he was my boyfriend, and he may have gone along with it, and there may have been some light flirting. Oh, and we held hands.'

'Held hands?!!' Iris squealed and Owen shifted. Her eyes went wide. 'You held hands?' she whispered. 'That's so cute.'

'It's not cute. It's insane.' Daisy put down the watering can and retreated to her stool behind the counter. Since her excitement this morning, the shop had been dead. It was pretty normal to not get too much foot traffic. It was doing events that kept her afloat. Events like weddings. Her calendar was usually filled with weddings for the spring and summer. But not this year.

The Daisy Chain Flower Shop was known for its floral wedding designs. It was what they did best.

Until now.

Until Daisy and her curse arrived back home and started messing things up. The first three weddings she was in charge of had ended in disaster. Word had spread and she hadn't booked a single one since—and the few weddings her mother had booked before Daisy got back to town had called and canceled. No one wanted to risk it.

She'd gone from bouquets and centerpieces to casket sprays and funeral wreaths. It was depressing in more ways than one.

'And it doesn't matter anyway because it was just a panic reaction and it's all done with now. So you can pass it back through the phone tree that I do not in fact have a new man.'

Iris was quiet for a minute thinking and stroking Owen's fuzzy little head.

'But what if you did?'

'What do you mean? I'm in no state to be dating anyone right now. I think I demonstrated that quite clearly by freaking the hell out when I saw David.'

'But what if it wasn't real?'

'Iris, I'm really going to need you to piece this together for me because I have no idea what you're talking about.' Except she kinda did. This sounded a little too close to the fantasy she'd had earlier today about keeping Elliot as her fake boyfriend for a while longer.

Iris winced. 'Ah, this kid just kicked me in the bladder. Inside or outside of my body, he just loves to step on my organs.'

Daisy laughed.

'Anyway, what I mean is, maybe having a fake boyfriend could be good for business.'

'Good for business, how?' Daisy had mostly figured it would be good for her loneliness.

'Everyone is so worried about your failed relationships. Why not give them a good one to talk about?'

Daisy frowned. 'And then what? Elliot and I stay together forever? Eventually we have to break up, and I'm right back where I started.'

'Maybe. Or maybe you can book a bunch of weddings this spring and by next year no one will even care or remember because some new, weird town drama will be happening.'

Iris smiled like she was very pleased with herself.

'That's insane.'

'Is it, though?'

'Yes.'

'But really?'

'It absolutely is. I'm not asking Elliot to be my fake boyfriend. How much of a loser can I possibly be?'

Iris rolled her eyes. 'You're not a loser, Daisy. No one thinks that.'

'Oh, right, I'm sorry, I forgot. They think I'm *cursed*. Much better.'

Iris winced at that. 'Not everyone thinks that.'

Daisy just stared her down.

'Okay, quite a few people think that, but you know how this town is. In a few months, they'll all decide there's a dead body buried at The Christmas Tree Farm.'

'That already happened.'

Iris's brow furrowed as though she was trying to remember. 'Hmm. Yeah, I guess you're right. But it doesn't matter.' She waved her hand and Owen's wispy blond hairs waved in the wind. 'Something new will happen and everyone will forget about you and your…'

'My what?'

'Your unfortunate taste in men.'

Daisy groaned.

'And the fact that it's now apparently rubbing off on other people.'

'It's not!'

'Look, you know I love you and I do not believe in curses, however, it *is* kinda weird that the wedding we did with all the white roses ended with the couple splitting two weeks later after that video of the groom with the maid of honor surfaced.'

'Oh, please! That is a classic trope. Happens all the time!'

'Okay, what about the couple that split up three months after the wedding we did with vibrant pink wildflowers because the groom decided he had a calling to be a monk?'

'That one was a little weirder…'

'And we did that gorgeous wedding with blue hydrangeas everywhere and then a few months in, the groom gets sucked into the manosphere and decides he wants his wife barefoot and in the kitchen the rest of her life.'

'I refuse to be blamed for the manosphere!'

Iris shrugged. 'Fair.'

'I think all these examples just prove that men suck.'

'Except this little man,' Iris said, running a hand over Owen's curled body.

'Of course.'

'Although at two a.m. he does kinda suck.'

Daisy laughed. She missed having her friend in the shop. She hadn't realized how much she'd been relying on Iris's help around here until she had Owen.

'And Archer's okay, too,' Daisy added and Iris smiled.

'Yeah, he's all right. And Elliot…'

'I don't think we have enough information to assess that yet.'

'He played along with your little lie. That's a green flag.'

'A man who lies?'

'A man who goes along with your crazy. I find it to be very important for a lasting relationship.'

Daisy laughed again and Owen started to stir.

'Well, I should go,' Iris said, her attention shifting back to her son. 'He usually wakes up incredibly angry and incredibly hungry.'

'Same.'

Iris shook her head with a laugh. 'Love you, Daisy.'

'Love you, too.'

'And think about what I said. It could be the perfect distraction to throw the town off this crazy curse business. You'll be booking weddings again in no time! And you could get a little action.' More suggestive eyebrow waggling.

'If it's fake there wouldn't be any *action*.'

'There could be, though. Fake relationship, real sex. That's a thing, Daisy.'

Daisy rolled her eyes but found herself replaying Iris's words over for the rest of the day. Combined with the memory of Elliot's hand in hers and his lopsided grin, the idea was starting to gain appeal.

Chapter Five

'Have you been eating enough?'

Elliot sighed. His mother had been in town for exactly thirty minutes, and she was already asking about his eating habits. She was eagle-eyeing him over her cup of tea.

'Every day, Mom. Usually multiple times.'

'You look gaunt.'

'Thanks so much.'

'Don't be fresh.' She pointed a finger at him but then relented and patted his cheek. 'I worry about you.'

The words *I worry about you* would probably be his mother's last words. They'd probably be printed on her tombstone. He shook his head, feeling immediately guilty for thinking about his mother's tombstone. Like most good sons, he assumed his mother would live forever.

'I know, Mom. Sorry.'

She was already ignoring his apology and staring at him again, studying. Assessing. Elliot's mother was *intense*. She always had been. Raising two boys on her own, she'd had to be. His father had died when Elliot was only a baby. It was no wonder she was a worrier. Elliot often thought it was a miracle he and his brother had survived, what with Caleb's tendency to do stupid shit like jump off the garage roof onto the neighbor's trampoline, and Elliot's desire to never leave his room. His mother had done a pretty darn good job of making sure they were both functioning members of society.

But sometimes she forgot that he was a thirty-two-year-old man, perfectly capable of feeding himself. This was her sixth visit since he moved here a year and a half ago. Six visits in eighteen months was too many. Especially when she was just here to check up on him.

'This is a cute cottage,' he said, changing the topic away from his apparent 'gauntness.'

'It's adorable. I just don't know why I couldn't stay at the inn.'

Elliot knew exactly why. He was working at the inn now. She'd stayed there during her prior visits but his mother staying at his current place of employment was not something he needed in his life. In fact, this entire visit wasn't something he was particularly looking forward to.

He loved his mother, but her fussing over him had exploded after his divorce. He had been a mess after Leigh told him she wanted to end things. He knew that. He had retreated from the world entirely. Stopped showing up to work. The renovation business he and Caleb ran together suffered. He knew it was bad. And for six months his mother and brother had done nothing but dote on him and worry about him and check on him.

It only made him feel worse.

So, he left the business, packed up his things and moved to Dream Harbor, a town he'd only been vaguely aware of but that seemed like as good a choice as any. He'd been buying and fixing up old houses and selling them when he got the job renovating the inn—a job he loved. And he started seeing a therapist. He was *trying*, and he actually felt reasonably competent again. Ready for a new relationship? Certainly not. But perfectly capable of feeding and caring for himself.

His family, however, was not convinced.

His mother was at least pretending she was here for other reasons. She'd said she wanted to come spend some time by the sea, ignoring the fact that she lived in Tampa, directly next to the sea. Coming to New England to *spend time by the sea* in April made no sense. It was still rainy and cold most days. There was snow predicted for Thursday! The cottages surrounding hers would probably be vacant until June, but Noah was doing him a favor.

She insisted, however, that she was not here to check on her baby boy. She just liked it here, she said. She'd probably come visit the town even if he didn't live here. His mother was a terrible liar.

His brother didn't even bother trying to lie. He still sent daily texts checking in on Elliot's mental health.

> How are you feeling today, El?

> Get out of bed today?

> I read an article about the benefits of daily sunlight.

> Answer me so I know you're alive.

> Elliot! Where are you?

And the worst one of all:

> If you don't answer me, I'll just have to drop by.

Which was something Caleb did every now and then, filling in the time between their mother's trips to town. The visits were always short and awkward. Elliot didn't love being reminded of how he'd bailed on the business they'd built together—not that Caleb ever brought it up—or how messed up he'd been after the divorce. He didn't love being reminded that Caleb had always been the strong one, the brave one. Caleb was big and hearty, and their mother probably never told him he looked gaunt. And these were absurd thoughts for a grown man, but it was hard to get over the wounds of childhood. Caleb had always been the one most likely to succeed at anything, really. Yet for a brief period in time, Elliot had felt like he had won at something. He'd gotten married. He had a house and a yard. It felt like, by some arbitrary metrics, he'd been in front for a while.

His marriage ending had only brought things back to their natural state, Caleb thriving and Elliot barely hanging on.

'I thought you'd like having more space,' he said, gesturing around the tiny house, trying to not be a complete ass to his mother despite his feelings about her being here.

The cottage was small, but it was still bigger than a hotel room. There was a cozy sitting area with two overstuffed chairs by the front windows, looking out at the sea; all new hardwood floors, and Noah had done the place in a cream and navy color scheme, accentuating the seaside New England vibe. Art from local artisans on the wall included a kitschy map of Dream Harbor and a fish made entirely of sea glass. The kitchenette had just enough space to cook and eat the day's catch (not that his mother had any intention of fishing while she was here) and the bedroom comfortably fit a queen-sized bed and a dresser. It was the perfect space for his mom. He knew she would especially love the front porch that Noah had added, complete with its two rocking chairs. Elliot had to hand it to him; the guy did a great job.

'And this way you have a kitchen.'

She smiled at that. 'True. Now I can cook for you.'

'Sure, that would be great.'

By the time they were sitting down to a meal with enough calories to feed a linebacker, his mother was ready to dive into the real reason for her visit.

'Have you been getting out?'

'I go to work every day,' Elliot said, shoveling another forkful of spaghetti into his mouth. He'd rather bulk up than rehash this conversation with his mom.

'You know what I mean, Elliot.'

She still thought of him as that little boy who would spend hours in his room, tucked away reading his history books. Or the man too broken to leave the house after his wife decided she didn't love him anymore.

He didn't know what it would take for his family to see that he was doing fine.

Okay, maybe not that fine.

Maybe he still spent too much time alone.

So, he wasn't thriving. But he was *okay*.

'I get out plenty.'

'You're dating?'

He squeezed his eyes shut. Of course that was what his mother wanted. That was what would convince her he was fine.

But Elliot didn't date. Not really. Far too shy in high school to ever ask anyone out, he'd fallen in love in college with the first girl who'd shown an interest in him and married her. Clearly, that hadn't worked out great. And he now spent his time mourning the loss of his marriage and the one person he thought he'd spend the rest of forever with. It hadn't been an easy adjustment for him. How was he supposed to go from planning to spend eternity with a person, to never seeing them again? It didn't make sense.

His morning with Daisy popped into his head.

Did pretending to be someone's boyfriend for a few minutes count as a date?

'I've gone on a few.' He looked down at his plate to avoid his mother's eye while he quite blatantly lied. But he couldn't take it! His mother's concern for him. It was too much. He didn't want to date. He didn't want the crushing disappointment of things not working out. Being alone was safer.

'That's wonderful!' His mother lit up. 'It's been a long time since the divorce, El. I'm so glad you're finally moving on!'

Moving on. How does one actually move on from the biggest devastation of their lives?

He cleared his throat. 'Yep.'

'What's her name?' his mom asked, leaning

conspiratorially across the table, like it was a secret, like they weren't the only two people in the tiny house.

'Uh ... Daisy.'

'Daisy!' His mother clasped her hands together over her heart. 'How sweet.'

Well, that was surely going to come back to bite him in the ass. Why the hell had he said Daisy?! He couldn't have just made up literally any other name?

'What's she like?'

'Um...'

How to describe the woman he'd formed a secret crush on a year ago but had been avoiding ever since except for this morning when he held her hand and now couldn't stop thinking about it?

'She ... uh ... owns a flower shop.'

'A Daisy who owns a flower shop? How perfect.'

'Yes.'

'And...'

'And ... uh ... she has brown hair.' *That sits just at her shoulder and looks like it would be silky to touch.* 'And brown eyes.' *More amber, really.* Not that he would ever describe someone's eyes as amber to his mother. 'And she's funny.' *She jokes about keeping dead bodies in her basement.*

'She sounds lovely! Maybe I'll get to meet her.'

Panic shot through his body.

'Well, it's all very casual still.' *She's clearly still hung up on her ex and so am I.*

'You don't want me to scare her off. I get it. But I promise I'll be on my best behavior.' His mom beamed at him across the table, and between the copious amount of spaghetti and the guilt from his lies, Elliot could feel the heartburn kicking in.

For someone trying to avoid relationships, he sure seemed eager to be in this fake one. And he would be absolutely mortified if Daisy found out… Although, maybe she owed him one?

Maybe one chat between Daisy and his mother could get her off his back for a while? Daisy had been more than happy to use him as a shield against her ex, so maybe he could use her to convince his mother he was perfectly fine. If nothing else worked, maybe seeing him with someone new would finally do the trick.

He might need to pop back into the flower shop after all.

Chapter Six

The evening town hall meeting was already in full swing when Elliot slipped in and took a seat in the back. Not surprisingly, Mayor Kelly was in the process of trying to get the crowd under control. Elliot had started attending these meetings a few months after he moved to Dream Harbor, thinking it would be a good way to learn about his new town and maybe meet some people, or that was what he told himself, anyway. And he'd been right. These meetings were a lively representation of the people who lived here. But sitting in the back corner quietly observing meant he hadn't exactly forged any real friendships. Story of his life.

'But it's not a wedding.' Daisy's voice cut through the din of the crowd. Elliot's attention snapped to where she was now standing, her hands on her hips.

'It's not a wedding, dear, but Beltane is all about *love* and fertility!'

That felt like a stretch to Elliot. Beltane was traditionally celebrated on May first, halfway between the spring equinox and summer solstice. As far as Elliot knew, it usually involved bonfires and warding off evil from the ancient Celts' herds. Not exactly a romantic holiday, if you asked him. Which no one had.

Although, the fertility component had some truth to it…

'And what are you worried about, Tammy? That your nonexistent cows won't get knocked up this year if I make the flower crowns?' Daisy said, and Elliot nearly choked. He laughed into his fist. Daisy had apparently done her Beltane research.

Tammy scowled.

'Now, if everyone could just calm down,' the mayor pleaded from the podium. 'I think Daisy should do the flower crowns like every year.'

'But you're the one who said the flower shop was cursed!' someone else yelled from the audience.

'I never said *that*. I simply said there was a cloud over the shop, but flowers need rain so it's very possible that the cloud was a good omen!'

The crowd just stared back at the mayor like he wasn't making any sense before returning to the debate at hand—whether or not Daisy's flower shop should provide the flower crowns for this year's Beltane festival. Because of course, this town had a Beltane festival. Elliot had been here long enough to know that these people would celebrate just about anything, even an ancient ritual that had no real bearing on their modern lives.

'For what it's worth,' Jeanie piped up, 'Logan and I are still happily married, and Daisy did our wedding flowers.' She held up her and Logan's linked hands.

'That's because you had those lucky underpants Estelle gave you,' Marty pointed out.

'We did *not* use those,' Logan grumbled.

'It's really all beside the point,' Daisy said, 'I'm not cursed. There's no such thing as curses and even if there were, flower crowns for Beltane have nothing to do with weddings!'

'But they have to do with love,' Tammy said, continuing to argue.

'Sex maybe, but not love,' Daisy snapped back. 'And you already blackballed me for Valentine's Day…'

'Again, *love*, dear.'

Daisy huffed. 'What about your nephew's baptism brunch? I heard that you bought flowers from Bakersville's Blooms.' Her hands came to her hips as she faced Tammy head-on.

'Well, we can't have a baby getting cursed!'

Daisy growled in frustration.

'If it helps, my Great-Uncle Lenny is ninety-eight. We don't expect he'll be around much longer,' Isabel piped up from the back.

'Gee, thanks,' Daisy gritted out. 'And what about Mother's Day? Are you all going to avoid the shop for Mother's Day, too?'

The crowd shifted uneasily in their seats.

'We love our moms, Daisy,' Mac said, apologetically.

Annie glared at him. 'We will be attending the Mother's Day flower-arranging workshop, don't you worry,' she told Daisy, and Mac winced.

'Right, of course we are,' he said.

'It's really just love we're worried about. We're not

trying to hurt you, Daisy, but you haven't exactly been lucky in love, no offense,' Tammy added.

Daisy's face fell in defeat. She had no retort for that one, and it was the first time Elliot had ever seen her back down from a fight. It was like she *believed* what Tammy was saying. She really thought she was cursed—unlucky, bad at love. Elliot knew exactly how she felt. And that was what had him springing into action before he knew what he was doing.

'I find that anytime you have to finish a statement with *no offense*, it generally means you're being offensive,' he said. He was standing now, not quite sure when that happened, and the entire room had turned to face him.

'Who the hell is that?' Norm said.

'That's Elliot,' Annie said. 'Hi, Elliot!'

He waved weakly. What had he gotten himself into?

'Elliot's new to town,' Annie said, explaining to the group.

'Not actually *that* new,' he said, probably only making matters worse. 'Been here for about a year and a half.'

Everyone looked surprised, including Annie, whose blonde eyebrows rose dramatically. 'Really? How did we not know?'

Elliot shrugged. 'Not sure, but I've been here.'

'That can't be right.' Annie looked truly horrified now, like she'd completely dropped the ball in failing to notice his exact day of arrival.

He shrugged again. 'I was here when The Christmas Tree Farm reopened.' He'd even gone and picked out a tiny tree and decorated it himself. It had been wildly depressing.

'Really?!'

'Yes, really. I was here when the diner was renamed.' His favorite pancakes were the 'Noah'. He was a big fan of blueberries.

The crowd looked truly shaken by this information, like an intruder had infiltrated their ranks and no one had noticed. It wasn't great for Elliot's self-esteem, but he powered on.

'I just wanted to say that Daisy *is* lucky in love. We've been dating for a month now.' He held her gaze when he said it and watched as her eyes widened in horror. Uh-oh … he may have misread the situation, but the crowd had already latched on to this new piece of information.

'I knew it!' Carol said, triumphantly. 'I told you all they were dating.'

'You're dating?' Annie looked even more upset about this development than she had about Elliot being in town for over a year. 'How did I not know about this?'

'We … uh…' Elliot glanced at Daisy again who was looking only slightly less like she might run straight out of the building.

'See, Daisy isn't cursed,' Jeanie piped in. 'She's dating Elliot.'

'Why are we even talking about this?' Logan grumbled from beside her.

'I don't know,' Jeanie stage-whispered back. 'But people seem very invested.'

'Of course we're invested,' Kaori said, speaking on behalf of the book club gathered around her. 'We need to know if Daisy's flowers are safe.'

Daisy rolled her eyes. 'Safe?! Of course they're safe. They're *flowers*.'

'Potentially cursed flowers.'

'They're not cursed,' Elliot said, struggling to get back on course. 'Daisy's flowers are perfect, and so is she.'

The crowd stilled.

Daisy was looking at him again, a new expression on her face. One he couldn't quite read. Was it pleasure painting her cheeks pink or anger?

She cleared her throat. 'Right,' she said, snapping her attention from Elliot and back to the crowd. 'We're dating. Not that it should matter, but we are. So, there you go, you can all go back to worrying about your own love and sex problems and leave mine alone.'

Daisy plopped back down in her seat.

'It's settled,' the mayor said, looking like a child who'd been chastised. 'Daisy will do the flower crowns just like last year and there will be no more talk of a curse.'

Judging by the grumblings around him, Elliot highly doubted that the town was done with their curse-related speculation, but he was too busy thinking about the word *sex* leaving Daisy's lips. Fake relationships didn't include sex, right? Definitely not. That would be…

Elliot did not let himself finish that thought.

Because that would not be happening.

He'd only done what he'd done to help Daisy out. And to help himself, as well. They both would benefit from this situation. He could get his mother to stop worrying about him for five seconds, and Daisy could turn the tide of public opinion about her business.

Win-win. Assuming Daisy wasn't pissed at him.

And just because it had been over two years since the last time he'd had sex, and that he'd kind of almost forgotten about it entirely until Daisy's tight black tops and the sound of the word leaving her lips, did not mean ... anything really.

This was fake.

A show.

And sex had always been very real for Elliot, never something he'd been able to do casually. It was all or nothing for him and surely this whole thing with Daisy was nothing.

Just a friend helping a friend.

He would just have to keep reminding his suddenly revived libido of that fact.

Chapter Seven

The mayor was apologizing to her again, but Daisy wasn't really paying attention. There was only one person she wanted to talk to, and Elliot hadn't filed out of the town hall building yet. Or if he had, she'd missed him entirely.

She really hoped she hadn't missed him. Clearly, they needed to talk.

What she was going to say when they did talk, she didn't know yet. Was it kind of him to stand up for her during the meeting? Yes. Should he have made this crazy decision on his own? Probably not. Did she actually think this was a good idea? Nope. Not at all.

But was she going to go through with it anyway?

Well, he had called her *perfect*.

'I told you, Dad, you can't just say things like that. This town takes it all too seriously,' Hazel was saying to Mayor Kelly when Daisy tuned back in.

'You're right. Sometimes I forget the power I wield here.'

Hazel rolled her eyes at her father, but Noah nudged him playfully on the shoulder. 'With great power comes great responsibility.'

'So true, Noah,' the mayor said, in all seriousness, and Daisy couldn't help but laugh.

'It's fine. It's really not your fault,' she told him for the millionth time. Even though it really wasn't fine. The mayor's dream had added fuel to the curse fire, but him feeling bad about it really didn't help her at all. The important thing was, she'd kept her spot selling flowers at the festival. They were always a big hit, usually selling out, and without that money, she wouldn't be able to pay her bills this month. Things were getting desperate at the flower shop.

Hence, the reason she hadn't completely rejected Elliot's plan. If it got the town to shut up about this damn curse and got some weddings on the books, then maybe she should consider it.

'Oh, hey, there's your new boyfriend,' Noah said with a grin, pointing to where Elliot was walking toward their little group.

As they all turned to stare at him, Elliot looked like he wanted to run in the opposite direction, but to his credit, he didn't.

'Hi, everyone,' he said, coming to stand awkwardly beside Daisy. His hands were tucked in his pockets like he wasn't quite sure what to do with them, and a furious blush had worked its way to the tips of his ears.

Daisy looped her arm through his, taking charge of the moment. Elliot had done enough of that for the evening.

It was her turn. If they were going to do this fake-dating thing, they might as well be convincing.

'Hi,' she said, tipping her face up to his. 'Thanks for rescuing me in there.'

His blush deepened. 'Any time.'

Hazel cleared her throat. 'So ... you two...'

'Uh, yeah,' Daisy pulled her attention from Elliot's shy smile to the overly interested group in front of her. 'It's all pretty new so we were ... uh ... keeping things quiet.' She felt bad lying to her friends but if too many people knew the truth, this would never work. And what would everyone think if they learned she'd faked an entire relationship? She shuddered at the thought.

'Guess that's over now.' Hazel winced. 'The crowd was a bit hostile tonight.'

Daisy shrugged, refusing to let everyone get to her. 'Spring fever has them all rowdy again.'

'It was very brave of you to out yourself to the whole town, Elliot,' Hazel said. 'It's not easy being anonymous here. I would have held onto that for as long as possible.'

'You're too cute to be anonymous, Haze. Everyone would notice you right away,' Noah said and Hazel pretended to roll her eyes, but she was smiling too hard to really pull it off.

'Not that you're not cute,' Noah said, turning to Elliot. 'And obviously, *I* knew who you were.'

'Uh ... thanks. You're cute, too?' Elliot said with a laugh, and Daisy felt oddly pleased that he was getting along with her friends, like that mattered, like they were a real couple.

'How's your mom enjoying her stay?' Noah asked.

'She loves the house. You did a great job with the reno.'

Noah beamed. 'Thanks, man. That means a lot coming from a professional like you.'

'You saw the potential and ran with it. Putting on all new cedar shakes was a great call. Very classic New England.'

Hazel leaned into Noah's side, giving him a little nudge and a smile that so clearly said how proud she was of him. Daisy thought Noah might burst with happiness. Which was lovely for him, but Daisy had a fake relationship to orchestrate. Or end. She wasn't sure which.

'She especially loves the small porch you added.'

'I thought that would be a big hit,' Noah said. 'A great spot to sit out and look at the water.'

'For sure. I caught her out there all bundled up yesterday. It will be gorgeous in the summer.'

'Agreed,' said Hazel, coming up on her toes to kiss Noah's cheek.

'Thanks for opening it up early,' Elliot said.

'Of course. Let me know if she needs anything. Fresh towels, more coffee, a fishing buddy. Anything. We aim to please.' Noah grinned.

Elliot laughed and nodded in thanks, and the conversation petered out. Or at least paused for enough seconds to give Daisy a chance to tug on Elliot's arm and ask him to walk her home. They needed to talk and get their stories straight before they spent any more time with other people.

By the time they were alone on Main Street, away from the milling crowd in front of the town hall, Daisy could breathe a sigh of relief.

Which she did, and then immediately turned and whacked Elliot on the arm. 'What the hell was that?!'

He looked back at her, shocked and rubbing his arm. 'What was what?'

'That little display at the meeting! You told the whole town we're together! Are you insane?'

'You just thanked me for rescuing you!'

Daisy threw up her hands in frustration. 'That's because we were in front of people!'

'Look ... I ... I just thought...'

'You thought what?' she hissed, walking off again. Elliot followed, his long strides quickly catching up to hers. 'You thought you would just decide that we should be together? Just like that?'

'Not ... I mean ... not for real...'

When she glanced at him again, he looked truly stricken. And she almost felt bad about that. Almost.

'I know you're not from around here, but these people are crazy and now they all think we're together and...' Daisy groaned loud enough to elicit another startled look from Elliot.

'I thought it would help,' he said. 'I thought it would help get everyone off your back. It felt right at the time. I thought we had an understanding, but you can feel free to fake break up with me. If you want.'

She stopped. He looked so damn sincere.

'We can't just break up now! That will only add more evidence to the growing pile that I am cursed in all things love.' Shit. She hadn't even really considered that. Elliot had backed her into a corner.

He winced. 'But you would be the one doing the breaking up this time. Maybe that would be okay?'

'No, Elliot. None of this is okay.' Her business was floundering, she had two failed relationships under her belt—and now she was trapped in a *fake* relationship. How does that even happen?

'Then let me help you,' Elliot said from behind her. She'd taken off walking again, but Elliot was keeping up. Unfortunately. 'Let me help you show the town you are perfectly capable of being in … love.'

Daisy stopped short, and Elliot nearly ran into her, skidding to a stop and narrowly avoiding her body. She looked up at him, feeling sad in entirely new ways. She didn't want to fake a break-up with Elliot. He was already feeling like a kindred spirit, a fellow broken-hearted soul. Even if his current move had complicated things for her.

'But I'm *not* perfectly capable of being in love.'

'Me, neither,' he said with a shrug like it was a small thing to be broken in this way. 'That's the fake part.'

Daisy blew out a long sigh, considering her options.

She could leave town but there was the pesky problem of having nowhere to go. And that she actually liked it here.

She could tell everyone to go to hell and make funeral wreaths, exclusively, for the rest of her life.

Or…

'This might work,' she said, and Elliot's mouth hitched up in one corner like this pleased him, just a little. 'If people see that I'm able to have a functioning relationship, maybe they'll get this whole curse idea out of their head.'

'Right, and after spending an afternoon with my mother

fretting over my lack of social life, I think this could help me, too.'

'Oh, yeah?'

'Yes. She is beside herself that I haven't dated anyone in two years.'

'Two years?' Daisy tried and failed to keep the shock out of her voice.

'Aside from a few disastrous blind dates.'

'Yikes.' Daisy winced. 'Sorry.'

'I think yikes is the appropriate reaction.'

She couldn't help but laugh. 'I am sorry, but I like that this helps us both. A mutually beneficial endeavor.' She did like that. It somehow made the whole thing feel less … icky. It wasn't her fault this damn town was obsessed with her love life, and it wasn't Elliot's fault his mom was worried about him. They could help each other meet everyone's absurd expectations while protecting themselves from the pain of a real relationship.

It might *actually* be the perfect plan, after all.

'Very romantic,' he said, dryly.

Romantic was the exact opposite of what Daisy was going for. This was a business deal. 'Now, Elliot, I think you know we failed at romance so we might as well create a situation where we can both be successful.'

He watched her for a beat. 'Of course.' He nodded and Daisy breathed a sigh of relief. He understood. He saw how this plan would help them both. He had his own reasons for fake-dating her, and they weren't based on real feelings at all.

That was important.

No real feelings from either of them was integral to the plan.

They walked on in silence, passing The Gingerbread Bakery and The Cinnamon Bun Bookstore. Music streamed out of Mac's pub as they walked past. She was sure plenty of townsfolk went straight from the meeting to Thursday karaoke night, but she was more than happy to walk on by tonight. She didn't really feel like mingling with the people who saw her as a cursed mess.

A new litter of kittens stared at them from the window of the pet shop and Daisy stopped to put her hand on the glass.

'Maybe I need a pet.'

'To scare away the curse?'

'Maybe. We're not entirely sure how this curse works. Maybe a cat would do the trick.'

'I've always been more of a dog person.'

'Do you have one?' Daisy asked, turning back to look at him. This was obviously important information to have about her fake boyfriend.

Elliot sighed and ran a hand through his mop of hair. 'I did.'

'He passed?' she whispered, already dreading the answer about this poor sweet dog she didn't know.

'No, my ex kept him.' He shrugged like he was used to life disappointing him.

'That's shitty.'

'I told her to. It just made sense. She kept the house, too.'

'Jesus, Elliot. What did you keep?'

He squinted like he was thinking about it. 'The wedding china.'

Daisy slapped a hand over her mouth to keep in the highly inappropriate giggles bubbling up in her throat. 'What the hell are you going to do with your wedding china?'

Elliot's mouth tipped into a grin as more laughter escaped Daisy's lips. 'Well, I smashed some of it. That was pretty fun.'

She was full-on cackling now as they stood outside the pet shop in a golden puddle of light from the streetlamp.

'You did?!'

'It was a particularly bad night, but the smashing helped.' He laughed. 'And now I eat my cereal out of one of the surviving bowls every morning. They're ivory with pale blue roses.'

'That sounds lovely.'

'It makes me feel very fancy.'

Daisy shook her head with another laugh and grabbed Elliot's hand, pulling him one more shop down.

'Well, here we are.'

'You live at the flower shop?' Elliot sounded surprised.

Daisy sighed. She did, in fact, live at the flower shop. 'There's a small apartment in the back. It isn't really supposed to be a permanent solution but when I had to move out of David's apartment … this is where I ended up.' Luckily, her parents hadn't rented it out to anyone else in a long time.

Moving back in here had not been a good day for her. Too bad she hadn't thought to smash something. Maybe that would have helped.

She thought she had escaped the little flower shop of her destiny. She thought her mother was going to have to find someone else to take over. Maybe Iris. Maybe a new flower was going to run this place. She was going to be the Daisy that broke the chain.

But life had other plans. *David* had other plans. Maybe she *was* cursed. All signs were starting to point in that direction. Her fiancé left her. She was forced to come back home. Forced back into her little Daisy life, like it was all meant to happen this way. Not that she'd managed to make a life anywhere else. Everything she knew was here. Everything she loved.

She'd given it all up for David and then he'd given up on her.

Just like that.

She shook her head. 'So, do you want to come in? We can talk about how we're going to do this. You know, set some guidelines.'

'Guidelines?' Elliot sounded amused and Daisy watched the corner of his mouth kick up. It was fun, this game they were playing, the secret they were telling. Things didn't have to be romantic with Elliot, but maybe they could be fun.

'Yeah, we should get our story straight. You know, our history and things we should know about each other. Like do you have any allergies? I don't want to feed you something that ends up killing you.'

'This is the second time you've made a joke about being a killer, Daisy, and honestly, I'm starting to get nervous.' Elliot's smile grew. He was so weird. She liked it.

Daisy laughed. 'Come on,' she said, pulling him inside. 'Let's talk. I promise not to kill you.'

'Sounds like something a killer would say.'

'You got yourself into this situation, buddy.'

'Wow, way to blame the victim.'

Daisy scoffed. 'I'm just saying, you volunteered for this fake-boyfriend gig without really knowing me. It's possible you'll agree with my exes by the end of this.'

'I doubt it.'

They'd stopped inside the small, dark space that was her apartment. Elliot was suddenly very close to her.

She tipped her head up and found him gazing at her from behind his dark frames.

'I like your glasses,' she said because the closeness of him was making her brain short-circuit.

Elliot smiled. 'Thank you.' Still so close. So warm and close and she could reach up and press her hands to his chest and just…

Woah.

What the hell was that?

Too long without human contact. That was it. It had been too long since Daisy was this close to a man. Any man. It had nothing to do with Elliot and his sexy glasses.

Sexy?!

Daisy, get a grip.

She cleared her throat and abruptly turned away, flicking on lamps as she went. 'Cup of tea?' she asked. 'Or something stronger, maybe?' She could certainly use something stronger. 'Sorry I don't have any fancy china to serve it in.'

'Tea is fine. Any mug will do.'

Good, she would make tea. Something to do with her hands and her brain. Appropriate things.

'Make yourself at home.' Even as she said it, she knew it

was absurd. There was exactly one place to sit in this sad little apartment, and it was at the tiny café table she had found on the side of the road. It barely fit in the corner with its two chairs. The only other furniture in the room was the murphy bed, currently still up in the wall. She may have moved back, but she hadn't exactly made this place home.

The apartment she'd been renting in Dream Harbor before moving into David's city pad wasn't available when she got back, and her finances weren't stellar after waitressing for a year, so finding something new didn't go great. This spot behind her parents' shop was the best she could do. And she hadn't felt like decorating.

'Thank you,' Elliot said, folding himself into the tiny chair. He looked ridiculous, but he just smiled at her before she turned her back again and put the kettle on in the miniscule kitchenette.

By the time she sat down across from him, she was totally embarrassed by the state of her life and was about to suggest they call the whole thing off when Elliot caught her gaze again and smiled.

'I'm glad we're doing this,' he said. 'I know it's kind of silly but'—he shrugged—'I don't have many friends here. So … this is nice.'

Damn it. Damn Elliot and his earnestness.

It *was* nice.

'You're right. I'm glad we're doing it, too.' If anyone wouldn't judge her tiny apartment and her sad heart, it would be this man who had to leave his home and dog behind. Elliot understood her.

'Great.' He lowered his mug as though he was ready to get down to business. 'So, what foods would kill you?'

Daisy threw back her head and laughed.

Chapter Eight

Two cups of tea and half a package of Oreos into the night, and Elliot couldn't remember the last time he'd talked so much or *wanted* to talk so much. Daisy seemed to bring it out in him. She made it easy. Going on dates had always felt like a performance, and one he'd never been good at. It was why he had been so relieved to be in a long-term relationship.

But now that they really were 'performing' a relationship, all the pressure was off. He didn't need to impress Daisy because it was all fake anyway. He could just be himself.

'Okay,' she said, leaning back in her chair. 'Let's see, we've covered how we met.' Didn't even really have to lie for that one. They met at the flower shop, of course. 'Allergies.' Easy, none. 'Pets,' she said with a frown. Unfortunately, none on all fronts for that one. 'Favorite books.' *The Book Thief* for him and *The Witch of Blackbird Pond* for her. 'And family history.' Daisy was an only child and her parents still lived in town. Her mom helped her run the flower shop.

'Actually, shouldn't I know your parents' names?' he asked, taking another Oreo and dunking it in his tea.

Daisy winced like she was dreading that question.

'My dad's name is Allen. And my mother's name is Daisy.'

Elliot smiled. 'Same as you?'

'Yes, same as me.' Daisy did not seem nearly as amused as he was. 'Same as my grandmother as well.'

Elliot's eyebrows rose of their own volition. 'You're *all* named Daisy?'

She sighed like it was the worst fate she could imagine. 'Yes, we're all named Daisy, we've all run this flower shop. For like generations. It's … it's … ridiculous really.'

'I think it's cute.' He was fully grinning now. An entire family made up of Daisies? And they all ran a flower shop? It was something out of a fairy tale.

'Of course you do,' she said, her scowl deepening.

'What does that mean?'

'Everyone thinks it's cute!'

'And you don't like being cute?'

'Cuteness is for kittens and babies and little girls. Not grown women. Not people that want to be taken seriously. Have you ever heard of a CEO named Daisy? Or an astronaut?'

'Do you want to be an astronaut?'

'No! But that's beside the point. I just…' She sighed again. 'I just thought I was getting away from this name and this shop and this life and … I got sucked back in.'

'You don't like it here?' He hated to think that she was

unhappy here in this little town that he'd grown to love, even if they'd barely noticed he was there.

She looked up at him with her amber eyes, and he wanted to tell her she was wrong, that she wasn't cute, she was beautiful.

'I like it here fine.' She shrugged. 'I just thought things would turn out differently.'

'I get that.' He was supposed to still be living in his three-bedroom house with the attached garage, the one Leigh had insisted on so they wouldn't have to walk outside in the winter to get to the car, and the fenced-in yard for his dog, Sam. God, he missed that dog. He wasn't supposed to be sitting in the back of a flower shop, sipping chamomile tea and eating cookies, in an apartment that smelled like roses with a woman he wasn't supposed to have a crush on.

But he was finding that he was glad he was here.

She gave him a small smile that lit up his chest, and he was even more glad the universe had deposited him here.

'Doesn't it get confusing, though?' he teased. 'All having the same name?'

Daisy sighed again and scrunched up her face like she really didn't want to answer that question. She spoke so fast, he barely understood her next words. 'My grandmother goes by June, and my mother goes by May.'

Elliot couldn't help the laughter rising in his throat.

'Don't you dare.' Daisy pointed at him. 'Don't laugh.'

'They go by their ... birth months?'

Daisy's eyes rolled toward the ceiling. 'Middle names that happen to be birth months.'

'Daisy June and Daisy May?'

'Yes.'

'And what's yours?' he choked out, barely able to control his mirth.

She looked him dead in the eye and said, 'November.'

'Daisy *November* Scott.'

'Maybe I will kill you after all.'

He held his hands up in surrender. 'I like it!'

'Shut up.'

'It's very sophisticated,' he said, fully laughing now and Daisy cracked a smile as she crumpled up a napkin and flicked it at his face. 'Like the name an astronaut might have.'

Daisy shook her head, laughter tumbling from her lips. 'I don't actually want to be an astronaut.'

'Okay, you don't have to be.' He grinned at her.

'I like running the flower shop.'

'Good.'

'Sorry I got grumpy on you.'

'You can be grumpy whenever you want.'

She paused, her laughter fading as she watched him. She ran a finger around the rim of her mug, and Elliot tracked its path with his gaze. He thought he might like to be under Daisy's finger like that, traced, touched.

It had been so long.

'Thanks,' she said, biting into another cookie. Crumbs stuck to her bottom lip, and Elliot imagined wiping them away with his thumb. Maybe he would press into the plushness of it, maybe he would follow with his mouth—

He shook his head.

'So, you never tried going by November?'

'It doesn't really roll off the tongue.'

Do not think about Daisy's tongue. Or yours ... licking off those crumbs...

Elliot shifted in his seat.

'And it's not really something you can coo at a baby.'

'Little Novie?' He teased, trying desperately to get back on track here. This was *fake*. He was not starting a real relationship with Daisy. He wasn't equipped to start a real relationship with anyone.

And then Daisy crinkled up her nose in that cute way that he'd already grown to like too much, and he lost the thread all over again. His brain was telling him this was fake, but his body was feeling very real things about Daisy at the moment.

She twisted apart her Oreo halves and, God save him, she licked the cream with one long swipe of her tongue. Elliot swallowed hard. Had Oreos always been so erotic?

Why had his dick chosen *now* to awaken from its two-year slumber? Why not on that date his mother had set him up with the daughter of an old friend ... he couldn't even remember her name and at the time he certainly hadn't felt like licking anything off of her. Or with that woman he'd met on one of the few times he'd attempted to go to the gym. She was dressed in practically nothing, and he could not have cared less.

It was like his sex drive had left when Leigh decided to end things and now it had decided to storm back in. How inconvenient.

'What about you?' Daisy asked, breaking through his thoughts. 'What's your middle name?'

It was his turn to hesitate, which made Daisy lean in across the table, her eyes glinting with excitement.

The position also caused her to press against the table, the top curve of her breasts rising above the neckline of her tank top, and Elliot had to look up to the heavens for strength.

'Ooh, it's a bad one, isn't it?'

He shrugged, still not looking at her. Luckily, she thought it was just embarrassment about his name and not the inconvenient rise of lust rushing through him. 'It's not great.'

'Tell me.'

'I don't think it'll come up.'

'I told you mine! You have to tell me.'

'Okay, fine.' Elliot sighed, bringing his gaze back to hers. 'It's Milton.'

'Ha!' A laugh burst from Daisy's mouth. 'Little Milty!'

'Absolutely not!' he said, but Daisy was laughing too hard to hear him and soon he was laughing again, too. It felt good, laughing with Daisy. Like he was finally breathing again, *living*, after so long being dormant.

'Novie and Milt, those are some pretty weird pet names,' Daisy said between giggles.

'Should we have pet names?'

She nibbled her bottom lip, looking at him thoughtfully, like she was deciding what she might call him if they were in a real relationship. 'Like what?'

'Sweetie?' he ventured. He and Leigh had never had pet names for each other. Was that some kind of red flag he should have noticed from the beginning?

'My grandma calls me that.'

'Honey?'

Nose-crinkle.

'Babe?'

'I'm not sure we can pull off babe...'

'Pudding, pumpkin, baby cakes?'

Daisy was giggling again and he loved it. That sound, the way her whole body participated, her cheeks flushing pink. *Beautiful.*

'Maybe we skip pet names?' He couldn't imagine calling Daisy 'love,' or 'sweetheart,' or 'darling' and not mean it. He would start to mean it. And then where would they be?

'Agreed. I think that's for the best.'

They were smiling at each other over the table and an alarming thought flashed through Elliot's mind.

I could get used to this.

He could get used to talking late into the night with Daisy, laughing and joking with empty mugs and cookie crumbs between them. And he realized what he was doing. It was just like when he met Leigh in college, and he'd been so *relieved* to find someone to be with, to share things with, to have a buddy, that he'd latched onto her and never let go. He'd married the first girl that paid him any attention, and in the end, it had been the wrong choice. *He* had been the wrong choice for *her*.

Isn't that what Leigh had said when she announced that she wanted a divorce? That they'd rushed things, gotten serious too fast, that she regretted not dating more in college? While he was so happy to never have to worry about being alone again, his wife was wondering who else was out there.

And here he was doing it again, fantasizing about spending the rest of forever with a woman he barely knew. A woman who was here with him for exactly one reason and that was to save her business. He needed to remember that. Daisy had her own share of heartache, and he was sure she didn't want to add more. He was sure she wouldn't choose him under normal circumstances. She wouldn't have chosen him for this fake relationship, either, if he hadn't been the one to walk into her flower shop at the exact moment her ex did. It was all just an accident. She would have grabbed whoever had come into the shop that morning. It had just happened to be him.

'I should probably go.' He stood and Daisy followed him the few feet to the door.

'What about PDA?' she said.

He turned abruptly at her question, and they nearly crashed, her hands landing softly on his chest. He felt the touch down to his bones.

'PDA?'

'Yeah,' Daisy said with a shy smile. 'Public displays of affection. I just meant, should we … do that?' She dropped her hands from his body like she was embarrassed they were still there, and he could breathe again. Just barely.

'Uh … I'm not…' He could breathe but not think. Not about anything other than her hands returning to his chest. He *ached* at the thought.

'We don't have to,' Daisy rushed in to say. 'I just thought we should discuss it first. You know, like if we should hold hands or anything like that.'

'Holding hands is good,' he said too quickly, but Daisy's smile grew.

'Okay, great. Holding hands is on the table.'

He reached out and she slid her fingers through his. Shit,

he was so screwed. Because as soon as her hand was in his, he was fantasizing again. Wishing he could have more.

'We could probably hug … you know … when we run into each other out in the world.'

Elliot swallowed hard. 'Right, hugging would be a normal way to greet each other.' He restrained himself from pulling her in, from pressing her against him right now.

'Kissing, though…'

Kissing Daisy. Just the thought was killing him.

'…that probably wouldn't be necessary,' she finished, her voice breathy, her eyes flicking to his mouth.

'Probably not,' he rasped.

Her gaze locked on his in the soft glow of her apartment.

'I should go,' he said again.

'Right, of course.' She gave his hand a squeeze before letting go. 'Thanks for being my fake boyfriend.'

Fake. He winced a little at the word. He hoped Daisy didn't notice.

'Gotta break that curse, right?' He forced a smile.

'Right.'

'Goodnight, Daisy November.'

'Goodnight, Elliot Milton.'

'I still don't think that's going to come up in conversation.'

Daisy grinned. 'Oh, I'll make sure it does.'

He waved goodbye to the sound of her laughter.

This was going to hurt later, but it was the best night he'd had in a long time.

Chapter Nine

Elliot had just finished up a meeting with Mary and Joseph, the owners of the inn, and yes, he had seen the irony the first time he met them. When he told his mom he was working on an inn for Mary and Joseph, she'd thought he was joking. Unfortunately, they weren't joking at all when they added new specifications for the main house during their meeting, and now he needed to update the plans, again, but it would all be worth it when it was done.

Renovating a historic building of this size and scope was his dream job. The inn had been around since 1801, according to his research, and had consistently hosted guests since then. The main building had gorgeous pillars and two levels of porches out front. It was a classic New England colonial with low ceilings and wood beams in the small lobby, and a sitting room complete with a big, cozy fireplace. The twenty-four guest rooms had various levels of historical accuracy as they'd been redone at different times over the years without a lot of attention paid to the age of the building. The carriage house, also original to the property, was being used as an event space, probably what Daisy's ex had been up here looking at with his fiancée.

Unfortunately, the whole property hadn't been well maintained through the years, and the repairs hadn't always made sense with the original style. He'd like to have a serious discussion with whoever decided to carpet the lobby and cover over the brick fireplace with river stones more appropriate for a hunting lodge than an inn. But those were easy fixes, more design than structural.

The main part of his job so far had been redesigning the motel-style rooms that were added to the inn in the 1970s. They'd been tacked on to create more rooms for guests, but they didn't match the style or the quality of the rest of the inn. Not to mention the new modern spa that had been added just a few years ago. As it stood now, the whole property was a hodgepodge of time periods and styles. It was Elliot's job to make it all make sense.

He loved it.

After spending years working on old houses with Caleb, alongside his architecture studies, he was thrilled to work on something like this, something that was all his. He'd been working on his designs for months, and it was nearly time to break ground. Or it would be, if Mary and Joseph stopped changing their minds and adding to the scope of the project. Today, they were discussing the possibility of converting the sunroom at the back of the inn into a breakfast room. Elliot assured them that adding breakfast to the inn's offerings was a great idea.

Assuming that room was structurally sound.

Something he now had to get a structural engineer out here to assess. The room had essentially been used as a greenhouse for years. If it was going to accommodate humans, he had to make sure it was safe.

But that was a task for tomorrow.

On his way out, he stopped at the front desk nestled under the main staircase to chat with Jack.

Jack, who was always impeccably dressed without a hair out of place, was a fellow Dream Harbor transplant. He'd moved to town a few years before Elliot, and he was one of the few people in Dream Harbor who knew Elliot existed. Without Jack, Elliot was pretty sure the inn would have completely fallen apart by now. Jack knew every guest that checked in, he made sure everyone was treated like a VIP, and he was the main reason Elliot got hired. Apparently, he'd seen some of the houses Elliot had worked on nearby and was a fan of his work.

At this point, Elliot was here so much, he and Jack had struck up a friendship. Or at least, Elliot hoped he could consider Jack a friend.

That would be nice. He needed a friend that he wasn't fake-dating.

'Hey,' he said, swiping a muffin from the basket Jack kept at the desk. Lemon poppyseed and clearly from The Gingerbread Bakery. Absolutely delicious.

'Those are for guests,' Jack said, half-heartedly swatting his hand away. 'And for people that don't keep secrets.'

'What secrets?'

'Oh, I don't know. How about that you've been dating the cursed florist for a month now and haven't mentioned a word about it, and I had to hear it from her ex of all people.'

Jack ran his palms down his floral-printed vest, smoothing out the already immaculate fabric, clearly insulted by this oversight.

Elliot sighed.

'I thought we were friends,' Jack said, accusingly and that was what did it. If Elliot had actually managed to make a friend, he certainly wasn't going to lie to him. Making friends as an adult was nearly impossible. He was pretty sure he'd only made this one by hanging around the inn so much, thinking and planning and sketching.

And Jack was here. And kind. And a little bit nosy, always asking Elliot about his plans, peering over his shoulder at his drawings. And he had a vest for every season, which Elliot found charming.

It was friendship by forced proximity, but Elliot would take it.

'It's not real.'

Jack rolled his eyes. 'It hasn't been that long. Of course it's not really serious yet.'

'No.' Elliot shook his head and lowered his voice. 'It's not real at all. We're just … pretending.'

Jack's eyes went wide. 'You're pretending?'

'Yes.'

'To date.'

'Correct.'

'You and Daisy are *fake-dating*?!'

'Shh!' Elliot hissed. 'No one else knows.'

Jack liked that. He smiled and leaned in toward Elliot conspiratorially. 'So why are you fake-dating the cute florist?'

'Well … it started when that ex of hers came into her

shop and I just kinda happened to be there ... and one thing led to another and now—'

'And now you're proclaiming your love for her at town meetings!'

Elliot flushed with embarrassment. 'That's not exactly what happened.'

'It doesn't matter what *actually* happened. It's what everyone is saying happened and everyone is saying you were very gallant and you came to her rescue when the rest of the town was ready for a witch-hunt.'

'That's definitely not—'

'Doesn't matter.' Jack waved away his protests. 'The important question, dear Elliot, is why not date the lovely Daisy for real?'

Elliot opted to shove more muffin in his mouth and pretend he didn't want to talk with his mouth full instead of answering the question that he'd been rolling over in his mind all weekend. Why not date Daisy for real? He'd had such a nice time with her after the town meeting, and he hadn't stopped thinking about her since.

But it was very clear that Daisy wasn't interested in him as anything other than a convenient shield from the town's judgment. Which was fine. He was using her, too, to keep his mom from staging some kind of dating intervention.

Any time his thoughts had wandered into why-not-date-Daisy-for-real territory, Elliot reminded himself that this whole thing had started because Daisy wasn't over her ex. She'd been so horrified to see him, in fact, she'd roped Elliot into being her fake boyfriend. And then he'd done the same thing back to her.

Their relationship, real or fake, was based on desperation.

Not a great start.

No, dating Daisy for real was not an option.

'She's pretty,' Jack went on when Elliot was still silent.

'She's more than pretty,' he blurted out and Jack's smile grew.

'I agree. She's also funny and smart and doesn't let anyone give her any crap at those meetings.'

'I know,' Elliot sighed.

'So why not go for it?'

'I just got out of a marriage…'

'Two years ago.'

Crap. Apparently, he'd already filled Jack in on the timeline of his heartbreak.

'I'm not ready…'

'To be happy?'

'I just…' Elliot trailed off because Jack was clearly not listening anymore. Gabe, the gardener/handyman/Jack's crush, had just walked in the door covered in grass stains with a low-slung tool belt around his hips. Elliot was pretty damn straight, but he could see the appeal. Gabe looked … confident. Competent. Elliot would love to feel the way Gabe looked striding into the inn with a screwdriver in one hand and a stepladder in the other.

And now he had an answer for Jack.

'Why not ask Gabe out?' he said, and Jack nearly choked. He smacked Elliot on the arm.

'Shh! He will hear you!'

Elliot laughed. 'Okay, so, you've been drooling over him for months. Ask him out.'

Jack glared at him. 'No way.'

'Why not?'

'He's clearly out of my league…'

'That's bullshit.'

'I just…' Jack sighed. '*Look* at him, he has heartbreak written all over him.'

'Exactly,' Elliot said, leaning his elbows on the front desk, mimicking Jack's pose as they both watched Gabe climb the ladder to change out a bulb in the chandelier hanging in the middle of the sitting room off the lobby. 'You're afraid. Which is the same reason I will continue to fake-date Daisy. We are cowards.'

That was the truth of it. Elliot was not ready to try again, with anyone and certainly not with a woman who had no interest in him.

'Am not,' Jack muttered even as he frantically started stacking business cards on the desk as soon as Gabe glanced in their direction.

Elliot waved hello and Gabe smiled back.

'Well, all I know is I cannot survive another failed relationship, so I will stick with my fake one, thank you very much. Oh, and he's coming over here.'

'Shit,' Jack hissed as he fumbled the business cards, and they scattered all over the desk and floor.

'Hey, Jack,' Gabe said with a bemused smile as Jack shoved the cards aside with one clean sweep of his hand. Half went fluttering over the keyboard, a few landed in the muffin basket.

'Oh, hello, Gabe. I didn't see you come in.'

Elliot stifled a laugh, and Jack jabbed him hard in the ribs.

Gabe's smile grew as he ran a hand through his hair. It looked effortlessly messy but somehow fell right back into place. Perfectly mussed. *How did he do that?* Elliot wondered while Gabe talked to Jack.

'So do you want me to change the lights out back today as well?'

Jack blinked. Apparently, he had also been hypnotized by the hair.

'Uh ... right ... yes. That would be great.'

'Will do. Anything else?'

The question hung in the air between them and Elliot suddenly felt like he should leave but before he could slink away Jack said, 'Muffin?' And shoved the basket toward a surprised Gabe.

'Um ... thank you.'

'You're very welcome. Gotta keep your strength up!'

'Right.' Gabe flashed them one more slightly confused smile before taking his muffin and leaving.

'What was that?' Jack blew out a long breath. 'I'm an idiot. "Gotta keep your strength up"? With muffins? What the hell is wrong with me?'

Elliot offered a few firm pats on the back in comfort.

'I don't know, man. That was pretty rough.'

'Thank you so much for your support during my time of need.'

'I'm sure it's fine. He seemed pleased about the muffin.'

Jack groaned. 'This is not how any of this is supposed to go! Doesn't this guy watch romcoms? I move to a small town and now I'm supposed to get the rugged, flannel-wearing guy!'

'Don't you need to like trip and fall and spill your drink

on him or something for that to happen?' Elliot offered with a grin. He'd watched plenty of those romcoms with Leigh. He knew how it went. Big-city girl (or in this case guy) meets small-town guy, they crash into each other in some kind of silly scenario, spend some time hating each other, and then inevitably fall in love. It was all so simple, so appealing.

Did he still watch them now to ease his anxiety and because it was comforting to see things work out? Yes, yes, he did.

'Oh, shut up, you're the one fake-dating the small-town florist. And you know what happens next don't you?'

Of course he knew, but he asked anyway. Maybe he'd feel better if someone else said it. 'What happens next?'

'You fall in love for real. It happens every time.'

Elliot's stomach flipped. Nope, not better. Still panicking. Because even if there was a chance they would fall in love, he knew all too well that those movies weren't real, that after the happily-ever-after there was still so much life to live. And there were no guarantees that the happiness would last forever. It didn't for him and Leigh.

'Not this time.'

Jack rolled his eyes. 'Okay.'

'I'm serious. I'm just doing this to help Daisy get the town off this whole curse thing.'

'Right-o.'

'Really.'

'Okey-dokey.'

Elliot sighed. 'I know you don't believe me, but neither Daisy nor I are looking for real relationships. We're just doing this to get everyone off our backs. Daisy gets more business, and my mother will return to Tampa happy and finally leave me alone.'

'Whatever you need to tell yourself, bud,' Jack said, returning Elliot's not at all comforting pat on the back.

'I'll ask Daisy out for real when you ask out Gabe.'

Jack stared him down, and for a minute Elliot panicked that he was about to call his bluff.

'Be careful,' Jack said, jabbing a finger into the center of Elliot's chest. 'One day I might actually do it.'

'Well, let me know when you do. I have to go.'

'Say hello to Daisy for me,' Jack said with a wink.

'Try not to stare at Gabe's ass all day,' he fired back.

Jack gasped dramatically and Elliot laughed.

'Bye!'

'Goodbye forever, Elliot! We are no longer friends!' Jack called behind him, but Elliot could hear the laughter in his voice.

'See you tomorrow, Jack!' he said with a wave, heading out into the warm spring sunshine. He had to get to the library.

Alex from the bookstore had agreed to meet him there so he could pick their brain about town history. He'd learned at various town meetings that Alex, while one of the younger residents of Dream Harbor, seemed to know an awful lot of its lore. And after going down some inn-history rabbit holes, Elliot wanted to know more.

Alex was already there when Elliot arrived, sitting at a table by the windows surrounded by several small stacks of books. Their short lavender hair was bright in the sunshine.

'Hey, Elliot,' they said with a smile when he approached.

'Hi, thanks for meeting me.'

'Always happy to help a fellow history buff.'

Elliot slid into the chair across from Alex, ready to dive in. He never got tired of this, digging into the past, uncovering how people used to live, wishing he could go back and see it with his own eyes.

'So, this is a particularly fun one,' Alex said, pushing a thin book across the table.

Elliot picked it up, turning it over in his hands.

Dream Harbor History. Pretty straightforward.

'A former mayor wrote that back in the nineteen-thirties, and it's filled with bizarre stories,' Alex said, their face lit up with the same excitement Elliot felt. 'I'm not sure how accurate anything is, but it's certainly an interesting look into one of our illustrious leaders.'

Elliot flipped it open to a dog-eared page in the middle, reading a few paragraphs before he realized what he was seeing.

'Wait a minute, this mayor thinks he's clairvoyant.'

'Yep!' Alex said with a laugh.

'And so does our current mayor…'

'It's a whole thing, actually. Multiple mayors throughout the years have claimed to have premonitions, dreams, future-telling abilities. There was even one that read people's tea leaves as a side hustle.'

'You're kidding.'

Alex shook their head. 'I would never joke about this.' They were grinning and Elliot couldn't help but laugh.

'That's wild.'

'That's Dream Harbor for you.'

Elliot was still chuckling when Alex passed him another book. 'This one has more about the inn. It was one of the first buildings in town and it's one of the few original buildings still standing. The flower shop is one of the others.'

'Really?'

Alex nodded. 'That string of buildings—The Daisy Chain Flower Shop, the ice cream parlor, the pet shop—they've all been here from the start. Right around the middle of the eighteenth century. Of course, it housed different businesses at the time.'

Elliot looked at the page Alex had opened to. An old black and white photo of Main Street from about sixty years after the town was founded was in the center of the page. It was probably one of the first photographs of the town but Main Street looked eerily familiar, other than the dirt road and horses. And there it was, the building that would become Daisy's flower shop. He wondered if Daisy would want to see this. If she'd want to hear about what he'd found.

He might have to visit the flower shop and find out.

Chapter Ten

Her mother was rearranging the flower shop again.

'Mom, I put those there for a reason.'

Her mother, Daisy May, put a hand on her hip and huffed a breath to blow the wispy hairs away from her face. She was wearing the same daisy-print apron she'd worn since Daisy was a little girl, the one Daisy had been wearing just the other day. She was left with a plain black one today.

'But they're blocking these smaller plants in the back.'

'Am I in charge of the shop now, or what?' Daisy snapped back.

'Fine, fine,' she said, throwing her hands up in surrender. 'God forbid I try to pass on some of my hard-earned wisdom.'

Daisy sighed. 'Just move the damn flowers if you want to.'

Her mother was supposed to be retired. When Daisy moved back to town with nothing but a shattered heart and puffy face from crying all the time, they'd decided that she should take over day-to-day operations. Her mom was clearly trying to make sure she had a purpose and a reason to get dressed every day. It worked. Having the shop to run had kept Daisy going.

But her mother's version of 'retired' involved checking in on the shop at least a few times a week. Most of the time Daisy didn't mind, but lately she felt like she was failing at everything and having her mom here just stressed her out, like having someone witness her failure made it that much worse.

'You're in a bit of a mood today, Daisy-girl. Do you need me to bring over more of those selenite crystals? They're supposed to be excellent for sleep.'

'I'm sleeping fine. And crystals don't help with sleep. They're just rocks.'

Her mother snorted. 'Tell that to your father. I put a bunch of clear quartz around the house, and his memory is better than ever.'

'Was Dad even having memory problems?'

'No, but I certainly don't want him to start!'

Daisy rested her head in her hands where she was leaning on the counter. She did not have the patience for her mother's particular brand of quirky today. She'd just gone over their books for the fourth time this week, and she didn't know how they were going to keep the lights on this month. Could she make shopping for flowers in the dark a new trend?

'Do you have any crystals that will earn us more money? Because that's what we really need,' she mumbled, getting back to adding more calla lilies to the casket spray for the dearly departed. Isabel was right. Her ninety-eight-year-old great-uncle had taken his leave of the earthly plane two days ago. And The Daisy Chain Flower Shop had been his family's first stop.

Daisy supposed she should be grateful.

'Oh!' her mom snapped her fingers. 'Good idea! I should get us some citrines. That would help.'

'It definitely won't help, Mom.'

'My little skeptic.' She patted her hand like being skeptical was a tragic quality to have. 'Are you worried about the curse?' Her mother lowered her voice to a whisper.

Daisy lifted her head from her work. 'There's no curse.'

Her mom opened her mouth to argue but apparently one look at Daisy's face had her changing her mind. 'Okay, love. But I'm still going to bring over some citrines and maybe some amethyst, just in case. They couldn't hurt anyway!'

'Sure, Mom.'

What she didn't tell her mom was of course she was worried about the curse. Worried that the town would never let it go. If she didn't start booking some weddings, she was really screwed. The whole shop was screwed. She was on the brink of letting down generations of Daisies. Daisies who'd survived the great depression, a world war, and the invasive rose fungus of 1987, and now the whole damn business was going to go under if she couldn't get her love life under control.

It was absurd.

Speaking of absurdity and her love life, her fake boyfriend came walking through the door at that exact moment and Daisy was not at all prepared for him to meet her mother.

'Um … hi,' he said, freezing in the doorway, clearly expecting her to be alone. This was a test. The first time they'd encountered each other out in the world in front of someone else since they officially decided to do this, and of course it had to be in front of her mom.

'Hey, Elliot,' Daisy said, dropping the lilies and coming around the counter. Her mother's face lit up at the name. Daisy had had to tell her mom about him after the whole Elliot-proclaiming-their-relationship-at-the-town-meeting situation. She was sure to hear about it from someone, and Daisy figured it might as well be her.

'Oh, *this* is Elliot!' Beaming at him, she held out a hand. 'I'm Daisy's mom, Daisy May Scott but you can call me May.'

Elliot stepped further into the shop and took her hand. 'It's so nice to meet you, May.' His gaze flicked over her shoulder at Daisy while her mother went on about how she was so happy to hear that they were dating.

Daisy just shrugged and Elliot gave her a lopsided smile.

'I'm glad we're dating, too,' he said.

'Such a sweet man,' her mom cooed. 'I have a really good feeling about you two. What's your star sign, Elliot?'

'Uh … my star sign?'

'Yeah, you know, for example, Daisy is a Scorpio.'

'I'm not sure…'

'When's your birthday? If you know the time and location of your birth, we can also get your moon and rising signs, that would really help…' Her mother was already pulling out her phone to look at her horoscope app when Daisy practically hip-checked her out of the way.

'Nope, not right now, Mom.'

'Okay, just your birthday then.' Her mother was relentless when it came to the zodiac.

'September second.'

'A Virgo!' her mother crowed. 'An earth sign. You two will get along great.'

'Oh ... uh ...good?' Elliot smiled at Daisy again like he'd accomplished something by being born in the correct month, which was total nonsense, but she had to admit it was pretty cute that he was pleased.

'Okay, Mom, that's enough for one day. Don't you have to go pick up Dad from racket ball?'

'That's right! I nearly forgot.' She pulled off her apron, looking forlornly at Elliot, just dying to dig more into his whole astrological chart. Luckily for Daisy, her parents had gone down to one car when her dad retired and now her mom had to take him to his weekly racket ball games. Thank God for her dad's dedication to the sport.

'We'll have to talk more next time, Elliot,' her mother said, taking his hand and giving it a squeeze.

'Definitely. I'll ask my mom for my birth time.'

'Perfect!' Her mother shot her a vindicated smile. Daisy just rolled her eyes. But man, if Elliot was her real boyfriend he was definitely nailing the 'delight her mother' portion of the relationship. David had never been a good sport about her mother's astrology interests.

Plus, he had been a Gemini. A horrible match.

'Sorry about that,' Daisy said when her mom was out the door.

'Sorry for what? She's great.'

'She can be a lot sometimes.'

Elliot shrugged. 'I liked her.'

Daisy cocked her head, studying him, trying to make sense of a man that was so sweet. Surely, there was something wrong with him. She wondered what it was. What secret red flags was Elliot hiding?

Maybe he didn't eat carbs? No, she'd seen him eat cookies.

Maybe he didn't like animals? No, he loved dogs.

Maybe he left dirty dishes in the sink overnight? Oh, no, wait, that was her. Hmm…

He shifted a little on his feet. They were still standing in the middle of the flower shop, the late-day sun filtering in green through the leafy hanging plants in the window. Even this late in the day, Elliot looked like he'd just woken up: his hair a floppy mess on his head. Daisy had the sudden and strange urge to run her fingers through it.

'What is it?' he asked.

'I just … you're so agreeable.'

'Um … thanks?'

'I'm having a hard time figuring out why your wife left you.'

Elliot flushed red to the tips of ears. Daisy clapped a hand over her mouth with a wince. 'I'm so sorry. That was a really shitty thing to say. I didn't mean for it to come out that way.'

'It's okay.' He shrugged, that shy grin returning. 'Let me know if you figure it out.'

Daisy laughed. 'Will do.'

'So, I had a thought. Something that might help with uh ... business.'

'Is it us making out in front of the town hall?' Oops ... that just kinda slipped out. It was possible that not having sex for so long was making Daisy's brain not function at full capacity.

Elliot's eyes widened behind his glasses, his ears turning even redder.

'I'm open to trying that,' he said, his grin growing and Daisy flushed hot everywhere. 'But I was thinking more about flowers for the inn.'

'Oh?' Daisy shook herself off. *Focus, Daisy*.

'Yeah, I was there today, and Jack had muffins from the bakery, and I was thinking it would be nice if he had flowers at the front desk as well. He could put some in the sitting area in the lobby—and we're hoping to turn the sunroom into a breakfast area, so maybe some flowers for the tables? You'd need to keep them replenished somewhat regularly. It could be a decent amount of...'

He didn't get a chance to finish his sentence before Daisy threw her arms around his neck and hugged him.

'Elliot, that's brilliant,' she breathed.

'Oh ... uh ...good.'

She was so thrilled by this idea, this keep-the-lights-on idea, that she didn't realize he wasn't hugging her back. Until his arms wrapped around her, firm and solid and warm, and he was hugging her back. She noticed the heck out of that.

Daisy couldn't help the sigh she gave; she couldn't stop herself from tucking her face into the side of his neck. She breathed him in, and she could feel him doing the same.

He smelled like soap and sunshine. She wanted to burrow into him. She wanted to live here pressed against him.

She wanted…

Uh-oh.

'Sorry,' she said, disentangling herself from a stunned-looking Elliot.

'That's … don't be.'

He looked so flushed and mussed. Jesus, why did he look like they'd done so much more than hug? She scurried back behind the safety of the counter, keeping the big scarred wooden surface and several dozen calla lilies between them before she could do something crazy like fling herself at him again.

'That's a really good idea. Thank you,' she said, tucking her hair behind her ear in an attempt to compose herself.

'You're welcome.'

He continued to stare at her until her face heated all over again.

'Did you need anything else?'

Elliot blinked. 'Oh, right. Yeah. I actually found some history about the shop… Uh, your shop. It's one of the oldest buildings in Dream Harbor. Did you know that?'

'No, I mean I knew it was old, but not really the specifics.'

'I could tell you more about it. I found some old photos when I was doing research for the inn, and I just thought you might like to … uh, see them.' He shook his head like he was being ridiculous. 'But if you don't want… You know what … you're probably busy. I'll just head out.'

'Elliot,' she stopped his sudden progress toward the door. 'I'd love to see them.'

When he turned back, his smile did something to her heart that she refused to accept.

Her heart was an idiot.

Her heart had led her astray too many times.

She was *not* doing this again. She fell hard and she fell fast, and look where it had left her. Two times she'd found the love of her life, and two times they'd found someone else.

It didn't matter that Elliot had a cute smile or that maybe she needed sex more than she'd previously thought. It didn't matter that he was a good hugger or that she had yet to find a single red flag.

She was not going to latch on to Elliot like some lovesick barnacle. He was her friend. He was a nice guy helping her out.

He was a giant history nerd that wanted to show her some old pictures.

That was it.

'Maybe there's something in there that will help break the curse,' she joked.

'You're not cursed, Daisy.' He was serious, earnest, when he said it. But this curse was feeling more real every second she stood here looking at Elliot and wishing she could bury her face in his neck again.

Daisy *was* cursed.

But she was going to fight it this time.

Chapter Eleven

Elliot didn't get a chance to argue with Daisy about her not being cursed before Iris entered the shop, with a tear-stained face and a wailing baby in a stroller.

'Iris. Oh, my gosh, what's wrong?'

Daisy dashed out from behind the counter to put a comforting arm around her friend.

'Nothing ... I don't know. Everything?' Iris sniffed.

'Honey, you're crying. What's going on?'

Iris wiped her eyes, pushing the tangle of red hair away from her face. 'I was just out for my daily mental health walk with Owen. Obviously, that's going super well,' she said with a watery laugh. 'And we passed the shop and I was thinking about how I should start up my classes again soon, but then I thought about how I can't even get him to stop crying today and ... I don't know, Daisy, how will I ever be a normal human again?'

She was crying again and so was the baby. Daisy rubbed

circles on her back, glancing up at Elliot as though he could be some help here.

Unfortunately, postpartum emotions and newborns were not things Elliot knew anything about. But he was willing to try.

'How about you go make Iris a cup of tea and I'll man the shop,' he said. 'And … uh … the baby.'

Both women turned to look at him like he'd lost his mind.

'You'll just be right back there,' Elliot said. 'And I'll be here with Owen. We'll be … fine.' He looked down at the fussing baby. Owen seemed even less convinced than Iris, who was now pushing the stroller back and forth in the shop, getting Owen to stop his more boisterous cries, but he certainly wasn't happy.

'Maybe that's a good idea,' Daisy said, hesitating at first but seeming to come around as she talked. 'Just for a minute. You can have a little break and you'll feel better. Come on.'

Iris eyed Elliot as he took over pushing the stroller.

He tried to give her a reassuring smile even as he doubted his entire plan. He may not know much about babies, but he knew a lot about having big, devastating feelings. He knew what it was like for the world to feel too much sometimes.

'Just a short break,' he repeated. 'We'll be right here waiting.'

With one last sniffle, Iris shuffled off with Daisy to the back of the shop and her apartment, and Elliot looked down at Owen.

'Hello, there,' Elliot said, and the baby scrunched up his

face and made an angry squawking sound. 'Hmm. Maybe you're tired of being trapped in here.' He reached in, and after several intense moments of squawking escalating to full-on cries as Elliot tried to extract him from the high-security baby seat buckle, he lifted him out, and Owen was free.

Owen's body immediately curled up, turning himself into a tiny ball. Elliot held him to his chest, supporting his little head with one hand and his little bum with the other. He was so small. And yet so full of rage. He was still crying and squirming against Elliot, so Elliot began to walk, taking slightly bouncy steps around the shop, shushing and whispering to his new cranky buddy.

'I get it man, life is tough out here,' he said and Owen seemed to agree with another loud cry. 'There's a lot to be upset about.'

'But there's good things, too.' He patted Owen's back with a steady rhythm, and the baby started to settle.

'Right, that's a good man,' Elliot whispered. 'Plenty of good things, like your mom. She obviously loves you a lot so you should probably give her a bit of a break.'

Owen made a little snorty pig noise that Elliot chose to take for agreement.

He'd pictured himself like this once, rocking a crying baby—his own. He figured it would be something he would do one day. He always thought he'd be a dad, but it hadn't happened.

He cleared his throat. 'And I'm sure your dad is great, too. It's nice to have one of those. And I hear you have a sister. You two will get up to a lot of fun someday.' More snorts and wiggles.

'If that's not enough for you, there's … um … sunny days, and the way dogs look when they smile. There's ice cream. You'll like that. There's flowers and big fat bumble bees covered in pollen when they fly out of one.'

Owen let out another angry grunt, and Elliot adjusted his patting.

What else could he tell this new little human he could look forward to? What were the things that kept Elliot getting out of bed in the morning, even in those dark days after Leigh signed the papers, when he wanted nothing more than to disappear?

'There's the taste of a tomato fresh from the garden sprinkled with salt … um … the sound of rain on the roof while you're tucked inside reading, driving with the windows down singing at the top of your lungs.'

There was something new getting Elliot out of bed these days, and he thought he could probably confide in Owen. Babies were good at keeping secrets.

'And one day you might meet someone who becomes your new favorite person and then hearing them laugh becomes your new favorite thing.'

'Wow, Daisy, I didn't know your fake boyfriend was so poetic.'

Elliot turned at the sound of Iris's voice, who was apparently feeling better enough to tease him. Daisy was looking at him with a curious smile on her face.

'I was just … trying to convince Owen that maybe the world isn't so bad,' he said, feeling his face heat. How long had they been listening and exactly how pathetic had he sounded?

'A noble endeavor,' Iris said with a chuckle. 'And how's it going so far?'

'Not great,' Elliot admitted, right as Owen squirmed against him, burped, and released a stream of spit up right over Elliot's shoulder and down his back.

Iris clapped a hand over her mouth, clearly trying not to laugh. At least he was providing her with some comic relief. 'Oh, no, Elliot! So sorry! But at least that explains why he's been so cranky today.' She rushed over yanking spit cloths from her diaper bag and patting them against Elliot's back, which only caused his shirt to stick to him and pressed the warmth of regurgitated milk against his skin.

'It's fine, really.' He squirmed away from Iris's help, still holding a now sleepy and content Owen. 'And what makes you say I'm Daisy's fake boyfriend?' Was it that obvious already? Did they just not make sense as a couple and everyone could tell?

Daisy was definitely out of his league, but he was hoping they could fake it at least for a little while…

'It's okay,' Daisy said, snapping out of her dreamy staring and coming over to them. She ran a hand over Owen's soft head. 'I told Iris. And she won't tell anyone.'

'Right, your secret is safe with me.' Iris smiled. 'Oh, except I totally already told Archer.'

Daisy rolled her eyes. 'Of course you did.'

'He won't say anything! You know he doesn't have the Dream Harbor gossip gene like we do.'

'I don't know. I think there's something in the water and he's been here a year now, ingesting all that Dream Harbor gossip-y-ness.'

Iris laughed. 'Keep your conspiracy theories to yourself, Daisy. I have enough problems.'

'You! I'm the one that everyone thinks causes marriages to break up!'

'It really sounds absurd when you say it out loud.'

'I know!'

Elliot smiled to himself as he rocked Owen and listened to the two friends talk.

'Maybe you two need to hold hands and dance around the fire at Beltane. We'll tell everyone it's a love-curse reversal dance or something,' Iris suggested.

Daisy was giggling now, and Elliot was right. Her laugh was reason enough to get out of bed every day.

'That sounds like a nightmare. Doesn't it, Elliot?' She turned to him with a big grin, and he would jump over the damn fire if she wanted him to but decided not to voice that thought. Judging by the look on Iris's face, she might actually think that would be a great idea.

'Yeah, maybe we just go together? But without the public dancing part.'

Daisy held his gaze, her cheeks rosy from laughter. 'Are you asking me to Beltane, Elliot?'

'I … uh … yes. It's what a boyfriend would do, right?' He swallowed hard, even when it was fake, he wasn't great at this. 'And Iris is right; it would help sell our story to the town.'

Daisy's smile dimmed slightly, but she nodded. 'Definitely. We'll show them how fake-in-love we are and if any night would break a curse, it's gotta be Beltane.'

Iris's gaze flicked between the two of them, and Elliot had to look away from Daisy's sweet face, or he was sure he was going to give away how much he wished this wasn't fake.

'Riiight ... okay, well, give me my baby back. I'm feeling at least partially sane again.'

Elliot handed over Owen, already missing the weight of him on his chest.

Iris snuggled her face against his chubby cheek, like she'd missed him in the few minutes she'd been away. 'Thanks, you guys. I guess I really did need a break.' She laid him back in the stroller and then gave Daisy a kiss on the cheek.

'Any time,' Daisy said, and Elliot wanted to agree. He'd be happy to hold Owen again even if meant being covered in spit up, but Iris barely knew him, and he didn't want to overstep. Iris was Daisy's friend not his, but this fake relationship had already thrust him into Dream Harbor life, more than living here for over a year had.

Apparently, dating the florist really got you noticed.

'That was very sweet of you,' Daisy said once Iris and Owen were on their way again. 'To hold Owen like that.'

Elliot shrugged. 'He's a good guy.'

Daisy laughed. 'He spit up on you.'

'It happens.'

'Lupita should be here soon to take over for the afternoon. Do you want to show me what you found out about the shop when she gets here?'

'Sure, sounds good.'

Her eyes flicked up to his, a shy smile on her face. 'You looked really cute holding a baby, by the way.'

Elliot swallowed hard. *He looked cute?*

Daisy thought he was cute.

This was life-altering information.

'I don't think I can take credit for that. Owen is a very cute baby.'

'The cutest,' Daisy agreed with a little smirk, stepping closer. She smelled like springtime, like leaves and earth and honey. Like life. 'But you are also very cute.'

Elliot had always hated his tendency to blush, and he felt it now, the red seeping into his cheeks and ears. He hated it until Daisy ran one delicate fingertip over the outer edge of his ear and whispered. 'It's cute when you blush, too.'

He felt that fingertip over his entire body. He wanted it everywhere. He wanted to pull Daisy to him and breathe her in, to taste her, to *have* her.

He'd never felt anything so strongly in his entire life.

But he didn't have time to react before Daisy was moving past him, rearranging the bouquets by the window. He blew out an unsteady breath. What the hell was that?

He'd been attracted to his wife, he'd loved her, but his feelings for Leigh had always been more ... measured. His feelings for Daisy were turning into something he didn't recognize. Could he like and respect this woman and want to ravage her at the same time? And when the hell had he started thinking words like *ravaged*. He stood stunned in the middle of the shop for far too long before he propelled himself back into action.

'Maybe I'll just go home and change my shirt and come back in an hour?'

'Perfect. How about we meet at the café?' Daisy said, not looking up, her own cheeks pink like maybe she'd surprised herself with her comment as much as she'd surprised him.

And she'd sure as hell surprised him.

'Sure,' he said, heading for the door still feeling stunned and a bit giddy, Daisy's touch lingering on his skin and her words replaying in his mind.

It's cute when you blush.

Life-altering.

Every time he left this flower shop, it felt like he was a new person. Maybe there was some magic at play here after all.

Chapter Twelve

Daisy had passed the shop over to Lu for Tuesday evening's spring-wreath-making class, and Elliot had changed his spit-up covered shirt and now they were sitting together at The Pumpkin Spice Café. It seemed safer than being together in Daisy's tiny apartment again. Between Elliot's above-average hugging skills and the way he looked rocking baby Owen, Daisy's feelings for him were more confused than ever.

Actually, that wasn't true.

Her feelings were becoming quite clear.

She was attracted to Elliot.

She glanced across the table at him to confirm. His brow furrowed as his gaze flicked from where his laptop was opened to some old copies of the *Dream Harbor Gazette* to his phone, where he was googling some of Daisy's relatives, to a dusty old book of town history he'd found at the library. Okay, so he was a giant nerd (was that a red flag?), but he looked hot in those glasses and the way his damn hair refused to stay in place was really doing something for her.

Yep, attracted.

And it was highly inconvenient. She wasn't supposed to be attracted to her fake boyfriend. Elliot looked up and caught her staring at him. His cheeks immediately turned pink in that adorable way they always did, and Daisy had to repeat her mantra all over again.

Done with relationships.

Done with love.

'Sorry,' he said, his cheeks flushing deeper. 'This is probably boring you.'

'No! Not at all,' Daisy assured him, focusing back on the article he'd pulled up on the screen. 'I had no idea the flower shop was such a town institution.'

'The building itself is over two hundred years old. And you can see in this early photo here, that stained glass above the door is original. Which is remarkable really.'

'I've always liked those windows.'

'They're gorgeous and very rare to find in such good condition. Especially here in the US.'

'Was it always a flower shop? I thought my grandma said our family opened the shop in the nineteen-twenties.'

'That's right. Before that it looks like it was an apothecary of sorts.'

'Like for potions and stuff?' Her mother would just love that news.

Elliot chuckled. 'Herbal remedies, I guess you could call them.'

'I wonder if they would have sold something to break a

love curse,' she muttered, taking a sip of her smoothie. It was good, filled with local strawberries.

The Pumpkin Spice Café wasn't busy this time of day. They'd be closing soon, and Jeanie was working her way through the room, wiping tables. She smiled at Daisy as she went by, her gaze flicking between her and Elliot. The café owner's dark brows rose in question, and Daisy gave a little shrug in return. It was harder lying to everyone than she thought it would be.

She liked Jeanie. She didn't want to lie.

But the more people who knew this was fake, the more likely the truth would come out. Daisy just needed to fake it for a few months, tops. And then she could set Elliot free and go back to her self-imposed single life. The one designed to keep her safe from further heartbreak or humiliation.

'Oh, here's what I was looking for,' Elliot said, clicking a few more links. 'Here's a picture from the early days of your family's shop. It was just called *Daisy's* at the time. Apparently, they did flowers for the mayor's wedding, and that really launched the business. They were very well known for weddings.'

Weddings. Ugh. Right from the start, apparently.

Daisy peered at the grainy, black and white photo. A few people stood smiling out in front of the shop, relatives of hers, presumably. One woman stood out, though, mostly because she wasn't smiling. She looked miserable, actually, dressed all in black and staring straight at the camera like she would rather be anywhere else.

But that wasn't the only thing that made her stand out.

'She looks exactly like ... me.' The resemblance was so

strong that goosebumps raised along Daisy's arms. She sat back in her seat, needing some distance between her and the past staring at her through the computer screen. 'That's spooky.'

'It's uncanny, right? Do you know who she is?'

Daisy shook her head. 'No. I can ask my grandmother. She might know.'

'She's clearly a relative.' Elliot shut his laptop and started gathering his books, noticing that Jeanie was about ready to lock up. 'You two could be twins if it wasn't for the hundred-year age gap.'

'Yeah,' Daisy said, her voice faint. It wasn't so much the fact that she had the same face as that woman, it was more the misery she saw in her eyes. Was that how Daisy looked? Did she give off an air of tragedy so strong that it was clear to everyone she was cursed? And what happened to this poor ancestor of hers?

'You okay?' Elliot's gentle touch on her lower back brought her attention to the present.

'Oh, yeah, fine. Just thinking about … you know … history,' she finished lamely.

'That's how I spend a lot of my day,' he said with a quiet laugh.

'Do you need to do all this research for the inn renovations?'

'That's always how it starts,' he said as they headed for the door. 'I like to restore old buildings to their original glory. It's usually why I'm hired.'

'Are you good at it?'

'I like to think so, yeah.'

The smile he gave her then was different from the shy

one he usually flashed. This one was confident, like he knew how good he was at his job.

Oh, no. Confident Elliot was even more attractive than shy Elliot.

Damn it.

'I bet you are.'

They were standing just outside the café now, Daisy's face tipped up to his.

He cleared his throat. 'Thanks for letting me bore you with that.'

'I wasn't bored.'

'Maybe we can do it again some time?'

More time sitting in close quarters with Elliot? Daisy's mind wandered to quiet library tables and cozy café corners, to heads bent together and hands on knees, on thighs, to darkening evenings like this one where they stood so close together and it would be so easy to ... lean in.

She swallowed hard.

'Sure. It would be good for people to keep seeing us together,' she said, and the reminder of their arrangement sent Elliot's confident smile slipping, just a little.

Maybe she *was* doomed to be as miserable as the woman in the photo. Maybe that Daisy had been just as screwed up in love as she was.

'Right. Definitely.' Elliot stepped back. The moment turned awkward, and Logan pulling up in his beat-up pick-up truck didn't really help.

'Hey,' he said with a nod, through the open window.

'Jeanie's on her way out,' Daisy told him, and thankfully she appeared from the alley beside the café.

'Daisy, Elliot, you're still here! I wanted to ask what you

two were studying.' Jeanie went to the driver's-side window on the truck and leaned in for a kiss. Logan happily obliged and envy shot through Daisy like ice through her veins. She'd thought she had that. She thought she'd found her person. *Twice.*

And she'd been wrong. All the nights she'd spent crying over David came roaring back to the forefront of her memories. Did she really want to go through that again? Definitely not.

'Just town history,' Daisy told her, swallowing down her emotions. 'Elliot was filling me in on some details about the flower shop.'

'Oh, neat!' Jeanie said. 'Anything interesting?'

'You're not the first person to think the café was haunted,' Daisy said, remembering the little tidbit she'd found in that weird town history book.

'Really?'

'Yeah, it used to be a hat shop, and the owner swore that a ghost named Sally was scaring his customers away.'

'No way!'

'But I guess his business was going under and he just needed someone to blame.'

Jeanie laughed. 'Wow, anything else?'

'Daisy has a family member with a striking resemblance to her,' Elliot said.

'Do you know who she is?'

'Not yet,' Daisy said, really not wanting to think any more about her sad relative. Or her own sad life for that matter.

'My grandfather's pretty interested in town history and my grandmother knows everything about everyone so'—

Logan shrugged—'if you want to pick their brains, I'm sure they'd love it.'

Elliot's face quite literally lit up.

'That would be incredible.'

Logan chuckled. 'I'm not sure incredible is the right word, but it could be interesting. Feel free to come up to the farm anytime. You ready?' he asked, turning his attention back to his wife.

'Yep,' Jeanie replied cheerily and when Logan got out of the truck to come around and open her door for her, Daisy wanted to curl in a ball and cry.

'Bye, guys!' Jeanie called, oblivious to the emotions swirling through Daisy. She gave a weak wave back and was left alone on the sidewalk with Elliot, the setting sun painting Main Street in gold and pink.

How romantic.

'Walk you home?' Elliot asked.

'I live three buildings down. I think I can make it alone.' Daisy was fiddling with the zipper on the black hoodie she'd thrown on over one of her ubiquitous black T-shirts. Something had clearly upset her, he just wasn't sure what it was.

'I know, but who knows what dangers you might face at this time of night.' He tried to joke, and Daisy's mouth lifted in a reluctant smile.

'It's six o'clock.'

'I hear it can get rowdy in Dream Harbor at dusk.'

She just shook her head, still fighting her smile and

started walking. Elliot fell into step beside her. He felt silly when they landed in front of the flower shop thirty seconds later.

'What happened?' he asked.

'What do you mean?'

'You got sad.'

Daisy avoided his gaze, running her fingers through her hair. 'I'm sad a lot, Elliot. I just don't always show it.'

'Me, too.'

She looked up at him, and he wanted to cup her face in his hands and run a thumb over the delicate skin on her cheeks. But he tucked his hands in his pockets instead, not wanting to overstep, not sure what Daisy wanted from him.

'You never talk about your ex-husband.'

She shook her head, her gaze leaving his face and finding her black Converse sneakers interesting instead. At first, he thought she wouldn't answer, that maybe he'd intruded on things she didn't want to tell him, but eventually she said, 'Matthew. We were together in high school. He was my best friend at the time. We thought it would be fun to get married, run off together. So, we eloped when we were eighteen, got hitched at the city hall in the next town over.'

Her laugh was more sigh than laughter, and Elliot's heart ached for her, for what he knew must come next.

'We were married for just over a year. My parents let us live in the back of the shop. We fought all the time. We didn't know how to be adults, let alone *married* adults. It was a stupid mistake.'

When she looked up, there were tears in her eyes.

She wiped them with the back of her hand, trying to laugh again.

'It turns out being married is a lot harder than going to prom together and skipping school to make out. We were dumb kids.'

'But you loved him.'

'Yeah.' Her answer was a whisper.

'And it hurt.'

'Yeah.' Daisy sniffled and wiped her face with the sleeve of her sweatshirt. 'It took me a long time to get over it, to move on and then I met David and I thought … I thought okay, this is the real thing, you know? We were adults, making adult decisions to live together and be together and then he just … he just … changed his mind.' The sniffles were becoming full sobs now, and Elliot couldn't take it anymore. He pulled Daisy toward him, and she burrowed her face in his chest as his arms wrapped around her.

'And I felt so stupid. Like, how did I not see it coming? How could I not know that he was falling out of love with me? And then I had to move back into the same shitty apartment I lived in with Matty, and it was like my terrible decisions had come full circle. It's like I was moving backwards. Like I was stuck.' Her voice was muffled as she spoke into his tear-dampened shirt. He was going through shirts fast today, but Daisy was pouring her heart out to him, and he wanted to offer something in return.

The woman crying in his arms wasn't exactly the heartbreaker the town had made her out to be. He knew David had been the one to end things, and now hearing Daisy's story about her marriage, well, he felt silly for avoiding the flower shop for so long.

'Leigh was the only woman I ever really dated,' he blurted out. 'She made the first move, and I was just so *happy* that I didn't have to. So relieved. When she asked for a divorce, all I could think was that I'd be alone forever now, that I wasn't at all equipped for dating or finding love or doing any of this all over again. I'd had my chance and I blew it.'

He'd been confessing to the top of Daisy's head until she pulled back to look at him.

'That's really depressing.'

A surprised laugh escaped him, and Daisy gave him a teary smile in return.

'When we were looking at that picture of my relative, I was thinking that maybe she was like me. That she'd had her heart broken, too.'

Elliot nodded, resisting the incredibly strong urge to plant a kiss on the top of Daisy's head.

'I wonder what happened to her.'

'Maybe we could do some digging and find out.'

'You just want an excuse to look at some more dusty old books,' she teased.

'Guilty.' *And to spend more time with you.*

She pulled away, dabbing at his wet shirt with the sleeve of her sweatshirt. 'Sorry about that.'

'Don't worry about it.'

Daisy looked up at the sky, wiping at her face again. She spoke with a sigh. 'No, really, I'm sorry. Good thing this is fake. Imagine doing that to someone you were actually dating? Getting tears and snot all over his shirt?'

Elliot glanced down at his shirt. 'I didn't realize there was snot. You should definitely be sorry.'

Daisy's laughter filled the quiet street, but when her gaze met his again she was serious.

'Thank you, though. For that. For letting me get that all out.'

Elliot shrugged even though he wanted to say he was more than happy to hold her while she cried.

'Anytime.'

'Any time I want to use you as a human Kleenex, I can?' Her teasing grin was back, brighter because it came after the darkness.

Elliot smiled. 'Owen already used me as a spit-up cloth today, might as well pile on.'

'You're a good guy, Elliot.'

'Uh ... thanks.'

'And I don't think Leigh was your one chance.'

'You don't?'

Daisy shook her head. 'No. I think there's hope for you.'

Elliot's heart picked up speed. Hope for him with ... her?

'You do?'

'Yeah,' she said with another smile before opening the door to the shop. 'And maybe this whole fake relationship thing will help you practice for the real thing.'

His hopes fell. 'Practice?'

'We'll get all the awkwardness out now and then you can go and date someone for real. Just think of me as training wheels.'

'That's not how I think of you at all.'

She paused but didn't ask how he thought of her. 'Training wheels. And then when you're ready, you get rid of the training wheels, and you can ride for real. Whoever you want.'

'I don't want to … ride anyone else.'

'I know you're not over Leigh, but you'll get there. And then maybe you will want to *ride* someone else.'

God, he wished she would stop saying it like that. All he could think of was Daisy on his lap riding him until those eyes weren't sad anymore, until she was whimpering for entirely different reasons than crying over her shitty ex.

It wasn't Leigh he was thinking about at all.

And that startled him.

'And what about you?'

She shook her head. 'You know what they say, Elliot. Fool me twice… And I've been fooled enough times. I can't do it again.' And then she turned and went into the shop, leaving Elliot standing alone feeling confused and a little bit sad and far too horny.

Chapter Thirteen

Daisy was sitting with her grandmother at the pancake house, a plate of strawberry pancakes and two cups of coffee between them. She was showing Grandma June the old picture that Elliot had discovered. It had been a few days since she'd embarrassed herself by sobbing into his chest and she hadn't talked to him since. She was sure that when he signed on to be her fake boyfriend, he hadn't thought it would include emotional outbursts and so many tears.

But she also hadn't been able to stop thinking about her doppelgänger. And what might have happened to her. She'd even been dreaming about her, but at the risk of sounding like the mayor she was keeping that to herself.

'So do you know who they are?' Daisy asked as her grandmother squinted at the picture on her phone.

The pancake house was buzzing around them. It was early on a Friday morning, and the usual breakfast crowd was in for their pancakes and coffee. Her grandmother had

had to stop at three other tables on their way in, to say hello and catch up on the town news. In the last hour, Daisy had learned that Mac and Annie had been caught making out in the back of the pub like 'a couple of teenagers,' that the alpaca, Harry Styles, had gotten loose again and was found on the side of the road munching on wild flowers, and that the substitute water aerobics instructor couldn't hold a candle to Iris.

It had been a very informative morning.

'Can you make it bigger?' Grandma June asked, passing the phone over their sticky plate. 'I can barely see it.'

Daisy zoomed in and handed it back. Grandma squinted at the picture and then her face lit up.

'Oh, my! Well, that's my daddy there. Look how young he looks! My goodness!'

Daisy smiled at her grandmother's delight. She was fully made up today like she always was whenever she left the house. Her favorite string of pearls adorned her neck, and she'd recently gotten her hair done in her signature, platinum blonde. She looked lovely. Daisy, in contrast, looked (and felt) like an emo teenager, in her black hoodie and black jeans. All she needed was some dark eyeliner, and she'd be all set.

It was possible she needed a new look.

'What year was this?' her grandma asked, still studying the picture.

'The caption says nineteen-twenty-seven.'

'Incredible,' Grandma breathed. 'And there's my mother next to him.'

'Was she a Daisy, too?'

'Oh, no. The name comes from my father's side. My

mother's name was Lydia, and my goodness, was she a stern woman.'

'Really?' Daisy couldn't imagine any woman in her family being stern. Her mother and grandmother had always been fun and silly. Growing up, Daisy's life had been filled with plenty of after-hours dance parties, giggling with her grandma until chocolate milk came out of her nose, and giving her mom more atrocious 'makeovers' than that woman deserved.

She'd somehow forgotten about all of that lately. She'd let herself get bogged down by her failed relationships with men and had forgotten the beautiful relationships she had with her family.

'Yes, very. She had high standards and she was hard to please, but she loved me in her own way.' Grandma June looked up with a smile. 'She was young in this photo. Must have been barely nineteen.'

'And they were already married?'

'Oh, yes. It was a different time, of course.' Grandma sipped her coffee placidly while Daisy thought of her failed first marriage. Maybe teenagers were more mature back then. As much as she'd cried over her marriage to her first love the other night, she knew it never would have worked out. She'd gotten over Matthew a long time ago. It was only the second failure with David that had brought all those memories back up again.

'And who's this?' Daisy asked, pointing to the one person in the photo she was most interested in.

'That's my Aunt Daisy! Daddy's sister. She never had any children, so the name passed on to me.'

'And what happened to her?'

Grandma shrugged. 'She lived and died like the rest of them.'

'Yeah, but why does she look so sad? Did something particularly tragic happen to her?'

Grandma was looking at the phone again. 'I guess she does look sad.' She shrugged again. 'She was in her thirties by the time I was born, and I was just a child, so I don't really know. I guess she was always rather somber. Wore a lot of black. I remember that.' She pointed at Daisy with a laugh. 'Just like you!'

Daisy frowned and snatched the phone back. 'That's it? That's all you remember about her? She didn't get accused of witchcraft by the townsfolk or anything?'

'Daisy, it was the nineteen-twenties. No, she didn't get accused of witchcraft.' Grandma shook her head. 'You really should have paid more attention in history class, dear.'

'Well, *something* must have happened to her.' Maybe Daisy was losing her mind or having too many bad dreams, but her Great-Aunt Daisy had become an oversized tragic figure in her imagination. And the fact that they looked alike wasn't helping. It was like if she could figure out what was wrong with her aunt, then maybe she could figure out a fix for her own problems, too.

'She ran the shop with my dad. I know that. And I know she never married or had children, which I suppose would have been hard on her as a woman in that time. But that's all I know.' Grandma patted Daisy's hand. 'Sorry, love. Wish I could tell you more but it's all so long ago.'

Daisy sighed. 'That's okay, Grandma. Thanks anyway.'

'Now, where's that cute waiter? I could use some more

coffee.' Grandma June looked around the diner, ready to flag someone down to refill her cup.

'You mean Archer? He's the chef not a waiter.'

Her grandmother scoffed. 'This is a diner, sweetie. He's not a chef anymore.'

Daisy laughed. 'Don't let him hear you say that.'

'There he is!' Grandma waved to Archer, who had just emerged from the kitchen with baby Owen strapped to his chest in a baby carrier.

'What can I do for you today, June?' he asked as he approached their table.

'Just a refill please, darling.' Grandma smiled sweetly at Archer.

'Oh, now he's *darling* … a minute ago he wasn't even a real—'

'Oh hush,' Grandma admonished, shooting Daisy a warning glare. 'Just the coffee is fine, dear.' She batted her eyelashes at Archer, and Daisy stifled a laugh.

'Coming right up,' he said with a smile.

'Lord, he is so handsome,' Grandma whispered, loud enough that Daisy heard Archer chuckle as he walked away. 'The coffee isn't even that good. I just come in to get a peek at that man walking away.'

'Grandma, you're married!'

'For sixty long years, like I could forget it. But there's no harm in looking.' She winked at Daisy and Daisy just shook her head, feeling more like her great-aunt than her grandmother. As long as she'd known her, Daisy June had always been wild, and she'd married a sweet, quiet man just like Daisy May had.

A man kinda like Elliot…

Nope, Daisy was not going down that road. It was bad enough she was physically attracted to Elliot, she wasn't going to let his personality win her over, too. Daisy was not going to get attached to her fake boyfriend.

Archer returned to their table with a pot of coffee and refilled their cups while lightly bouncing to keep Owen fast asleep.

'Is it bring your baby to work day?' Grandma asked.

'Iris started taking Olive to school on Fridays, so Owen has been coming with me. It gives the girls some alone time.'

'That's sweet,' Daisy said, happy that they'd figured out a way for Iris to spend more time with Olive. She knew it had been worrying her, balancing the new baby and a little girl that still needed plenty of attention.

'How are you two handling everything?' Her grandmother really did have that Dream Harbor nosiness down pat.

'It's been ... a learning curve,' Archer said with a rueful smile. 'But we're figuring it out.'

'I'm sure you are.' Grandma beamed at him. 'There's just nothing like a man holding a baby.'

'Down, Grandma,' Daisy whispered, but Grandma June ignored her.

'You tell Iris I said she's a lucky woman.'

Archer's smile grew. 'Will do. Anything else I can get you ladies?'

'I think we're all set. Thanks, Archer.' Daisy took out her wallet to pay, but Grandma June slapped it away.

'None of that,' she said. 'I know you don't have a dime to spare.'

Daisy sighed as Grandma passed her card to Archer, and he left to ring them up. 'It's not that bad.'

Grandma scoffed. 'How many weddings do you have booked for next spring?'

'So far ... none. But there's still plenty of time!'

'We usually book a year out...'

'I *know* but what can I do? If people aren't hiring me...'

'Break this curse, that's what.'

'Grandma, you don't actually believe I'm cursed?' But of course, her grandmother believed in curses. This was the woman who wouldn't let Daisy kill a spider in the house because it was bad luck and insisted on blowing cinnamon through the front door on the first day of the month for prosperity and wealth. Huh, maybe Daisy needed to get some cinnamon.

'I believe in good publicity, and this is not working in our favor.' The way her grandma waved a hand in Daisy's general direction, as though *the thing not working in their favor* was all of Daisy, was hurtful to say the least.

'I'm trying.'

'How?'

'I'm pitching an idea to the inn. I was thinking we could do monthly flower arrangements for the lobby. At least until construction starts...'

'That's something. And what else?'

Daisy sighed.

'I ... uh ... I have a new boyfriend.'

'Oh?' Her grandma's eyebrows rose, as though she hadn't already heard this little piece of gossip. Grandma June had always liked to hear things straight from the source.

'And it's going really well.'

'It doesn't matter how it's going, love, as long as everyone *thinks* it's going well.'

'What are you suggesting?' Did her grandmother somehow know it was all fake? If anyone could sniff out a fake relationship, it would be Grandma June.

'Just sell it, is all I'm saying. Make sure this town thinks you are so in love that hearts are flying out of your bottom! Make them believe that The Daisy Chain Flower Shop is the most romantic spot in town! Sell them the dream, Daisy. It doesn't matter if it's real.'

Well, damn. That was a lot to unpack. She had no idea her sweet little grandma was so … ruthless. Apparently, you don't run a successful business for all those years without a bit of an aggressive streak.

'Okay. I will sell it.'

Her grandmother smiled, once again the doting grandma. 'That's a good girl. I know you can turn this around.'

Daisy wished she had half as much faith in herself as her grandmother did.

Chapter Fourteen

Elliot had spent the first half of his morning assuring his mother that she would get to meet his new girlfriend soon, and the other half explaining to Joseph and Mary that he couldn't remove that pillar in the lobby because it was load-bearing and the whole damn roof would come down without it.

They were not pleased.

And now he was stuffing his face with muffins at the front desk with Jack. Again. Pretty soon, his mother would not have to worry about his 'gauntness' at all because he would have gained two hundred pounds from stress and muffins.

Except, he wasn't actually that stressed about his mother's demands. He was used to those. And he was very used to clients having insane ideas about what was possible for their projects. What he was actually upset about, if he was being honest with himself, was that he hadn't heard from Daisy in days, and now he didn't know where they stood or if they were still doing this whole fake relationship thing or if she was upset with him for some reason or if—

'Why don't you just text her?' Jack asked, after Elliot sighed for the fiftieth time since he'd joined his friend. He had texted her. A very casual, *Hey, everything all right?* Daisy had read it and hadn't answered in two days. And for two days he'd been wondering why.

'I did. She didn't respond.'

'Hmm.'

'*Hmm*? What does that mean?'

Jack shrugged. 'I don't know … that just doesn't seem like a great sign.'

'That's what I'm saying!' Daisy's silence had felt like a pretty clear message that this whole little charade was over. And that upset Elliot more than he would care to admit.

He certainly wouldn't be admitting it to Jack.

'You could ask her in person.'

'I can't just keep going into her shop—'

Elliot stopped mid-sentence when Jack gestured toward the front doors where Daisy was juggling several large flower arrangements. They both rushed around the desk to help her.

'Thanks,' she said as they took the flowers from her. 'I thought I could get it in one trip. Probably should have made two. Make sure Mary sees these. We spoke on the phone, but she wanted me to do a trial run.' She was speaking mainly to Jack, and Elliot could see the moment she realized she should acknowledge him, that as his girlfriend she would definitely acknowledge him.

'Elliot!' She hesitated and then wrapped him in an awkward hug. Especially awkward because he still held a large flower arrangement in one hand. 'I'm so glad to see you ... sweetie.'

Sweetie?

'Uh ... right. Me, too ... honey.'

He could hear Jack snickering behind him.

'I thought of you while I made these arrangements,' Daisy said. Her voice was far too loud for the quiet lobby. 'I think they came out really ... *romantic*.'

A couple seated by the fireplace glanced in their direction, confused by the volume of Daisy's voice.

'What are you doing?' Elliot whispered.

'Just play along,' Daisy hissed back.

'Jack already knows.'

She pulled away, suddenly, leaving Elliot regretting mentioning that fact. If he hadn't, they might still be hugging. 'He does?'

'Yep,' Jack said with a smug smile. 'But you were very convincing, *sweetie*.'

'Oh, shut up.'

'I thought we decided on no pet names,' Elliot said, still reeling from the feel of Daisy pressed up against him.

'You told Jack?'

'Well, you told Iris.'

'I will take it to my grave!' Jack called as he placed one of the arrangements on the mantel. He smiled at the confused guests. 'We're just working on a little play.'

Daisy squeezed her eyes shut like she was regrouping.

'Okay, that's okay as long as no one else knows.'

Gabe appeared from the second-floor guest rooms, pausing halfway down the stairs. 'Hey, Jack. Could you come up here a minute? We have an issue in one of the rooms. Looks like we might need to get a plumber out.'

'Oh, of course.' Jack smoothed down his pastel plaid vest and went to follow Gabe, but not before glancing over his shoulder at Elliot. His smile was a mix of excitement and terror at being alone with Gabe. Or maybe at whatever plumbing issue he was about to find. Elliot gave him a thumbs-up for encouragement.

By the time the two men had climbed the stairs, Daisy had pulled herself together and had a new look of determination on her face.

'I think we need to go on some dates. To be more … convincing,' she whispered, glancing over at the couple by the fire who no longer seemed to have any interest in them. Daisy tugged him by the arm back to the front desk anyway. 'We need to be seen *together*.'

Together.

'Okay, what did you have in mind?'

'Well, we're still on for Beltane, right?'

'Wouldn't miss it.'

Daisy tapped a finger against her lips as she thought. 'I guess I haven't actually dated in a while…'

'What did you used to do with David?'

Her frown made him sorry he'd asked. 'Mostly whatever he wanted to do, which toward the end wasn't much. Probably should have been a red flag. One of many.'

'Right, I forgot David's an idiot.'

The way her frown slowly morphed into a smile was Elliot's new favorite thing.

'What's your perfect day out?' he asked, eager to get this conversation on track. If he was going to fake-date this woman, he was going to do it properly. No more bringing up her exes.

'My perfect day out?' She tucked her hair behind her ear as she thought about it. Her hands were half covered by the sleeves of her black sweater today. It was oversized and made her look smaller than usual.

'Yeah, what would *you* choose to do? And then I'll just come with you and make heart-eyes at you the whole time.'

Daisy laughed but Elliot knew it would be far too easy to follow her around and pretend he was in love with her. He was a hopeless fool.

'I guess we could … go wander around the bookstore?' There was hesitation in her voice, like she'd suggested this idea before and been shot down.

'If you think I'm going to be scared away by books, you are very wrong.'

'I forgot who I was talking to,' she said with a teasing smile.

'I'd be happy to carry your books,' he added. Her gaze caught his, and for a split second he thought maybe he saw something there that wasn't fake, that maybe in another life, one in which they hadn't had their hearts so thoroughly broken, he and Daisy could be something real.

'And then grab some takeout from Mac's and bring it to the beach for a picnic?'

'Sounds perfect.'

'We could go on Saturday when a lot of people will be out, plenty of exposure.'

'Right.' Plenty of exposure for their fake-date. Because as much as he liked Daisy, neither of them were ready for the real thing.

'And it will be good practice for you,' she said, turning away and grabbing a muffin from the basket.

'Please don't start talking about riding bikes again.'

Daisy giggled. 'Okay. I do really appreciate you doing this for me. I know it's silly, but I am hoping it helps. My grandmother says it's all just marketing.'

'I'm happy to be a marketing ploy, but you will have to meet my mom someday. And then we'll be even.'

'Deal.' Daisy stuck out her free hand, and they shook on it.

'Can I ask you something?'

'If it's about my past relationships, then, no.'

'I think we've covered all that. I'm just wondering… Why all the black?'

Daisy laughed. 'Oh, that. Do you not like it?'

'I like it. It suits you.'

'And my depressing personality?'

'No. It brings out your eyes.'

'My eyes?' She stopped in her tracks on her way to throw out her muffin wrapper and turned back to face him.

'Uh … yeah. They're this unique amber color. And something about the lightness of your eyes compared to the darkness of your clothes just makes them … pop.'

She was smiling at him now. 'Elliot, you've spent a lot of time thinking about my eyes.'

He could feel his face flushing. 'Not that much time.'

Her smile grew. 'Okay.'

'It's really just that one observation.'

She raised an eyebrow like she didn't believe him, but she at least answered his question. 'My mom used to love dressing me in these frilly dresses when I was little. Usually, bright yellow or bubblegum-pink or baby blue. It was a lot. Add that to my name and I used to get teased.'

'Teased for wearing bright colors and being named Daisy?' Elliot was incredulous.

'For being a flower.'

'Wow.'

'Yeah, kids are the worst. And wildly uncreative in their insults. Anyway, in fourth grade I demanded to pick out all my own clothes, and I chose all-black. I tried to change my name, too, but it didn't stick.'

'To what?'

Daisy rolled her eyes like she didn't want to say. 'Jade.'

He couldn't help his grin. 'You thought Jade was a better name than Daisy?'

She was picking at the sleeves of her sweater, but she answered him from behind a curtain of hair. 'Cooler, yes.'

Elliot inched closer, nudging her shoulder with his. 'For what it's worth, I think you're cool.'

'Well, you're a giant nerd so I'm not sure that means a whole lot.' She glanced at him with a mischievous smirk and he laughed.

'Wow, harsh.'

'Anyway, I'm not going to stop now. I like black.'

'It's very versatile.'

'And it brings out my eyes,' she teased, batting her eyelashes.

'Remind me not to compliment you anymore,' he grumbled, but was secretly delighted that she was smiling again.

'No way! I like compliments and I like watching you turn pink.'

She booped the tip of his nose and laughed.

'What's so funny?' Jack asked, returning from his errand alone.

'Elliot's ability to change colors,' Daisy said, grinning at him.

'And Daisy's resistance to wearing any,' Elliot shot back, and Daisy feigned offense, slapping a hand to her chest as she gasped dramatically.

Jack's gaze flicked between them. 'You two have a weird way of flirting.'

'We're not flirting,' Daisy said, a bit quicker than Elliot would have liked. 'We're practicing.'

'Right,' Jack said with his own little smirk. 'I know how this movie ends.'

'How are things with Gabe?' Elliot asked, derailing whatever Jack was going to say about fake relationships always ending in real ones. At least on the Hallmark channel.

'Big development! He asked if I was going to Beltane and I said yes and he said great, I'll see you there!'

'Oh … that's … great?' Did that mean Gabe had asked him out or just compared plans? Maybe Elliot did need to practice.

Daisy smacked his arm like he should understand just how big this news was. 'It's really great, Jack. You know how things get at Beltane!'

'I know!' Jack practically squealed.

'How do things get? You guys are making me nervous.'

'It's just…' Daisy trailed off, no longer meeting Elliot's eye. Now she was the one turning pink.

'It's when everyone hooks up,' Jack supplied, gleefully.

'Hooks up? What is this some kind of pagan orgy?'

Daisy spewed muffin crumbs from her mouth while Jack burst out laughing.

'Calm down, Grandma!' he said. 'If you had pearls, you'd be clutching them right now.'

'I wouldn't.' Elliot huffed. 'I just thought this was like a family affair, a wholesome Dream Harbor event not some kind of…'

'Pagan orgy?' Daisy said, barely holding in her laughter, one arm wrapped around her middle and the other wiping muffin crumbs from her lips.

'Right.' Elliot felt lightheaded.

'It *is* a family affair. Very wholesome. During the day…' Jack grinned. 'After dark things get a little wild.' He waggled his eyebrows suggestively.

'It's why we have so many January babies in Dream Harbor. Nine months after Beltane…' Daisy added with a shrug, like this was all perfectly normal.

'Wow.'

'But don't worry, Elliot,' Daisy said, patting him on the back. 'All you have to do is be my date. Hold my hand and hang out with me. I'm not expecting you to knock me up or anything.'

Elliot swallowed hard.

Daisy grinned and ran a finger over the rim of his ear. 'Pink again,' she whispered before turning to leave. 'I have to get back to the shop. Thanks for the business opportunity, Jack!'

'Bye, Daisy!' Jack called as Elliot stood there watching her go, wondering what he'd gotten himself into.

Whatever it was, he was having a hard time regretting it.

Chapter Fifteen

The next day, Daisy and Elliot were on their first official date, browsing the stacks of books at The Cinnamon Bun Bookstore when Daisy heard a sound that made her blood run cold.

'Wait,' she hissed, grabbing Elliot's forearm before he could leave the aisle they were currently perusing.

'What is it?' Elliot froze, turning back to her. He looked cute today, slightly less disheveled, like he'd tried to get his hair in order. They'd spent the last half an hour just sipping their coffees and looking at books, side by side in the stacks. Every once in a while, Elliot's arm would rub against hers or he would peer at her over the top of the book he was holding and smile at her. It was peaceful and comfortable and … Daisy was pretty sure no one had noticed them except for Hazel.

But now, it was time for them to perform.

She had to sell it.

She was not *cursed* Daisy, not unlucky in love, not a

person who caused marriages to break up with her bad vibes.

No, she was Daisy in love. Daisy in a perfectly healthy and functional relationship who now channeled all those romantic feelings into her work and sprinkled love around like some kind of Goddamn cupid ... okay, she might need to tone it down a tad...

She shook off the anger at her situation. That wasn't going to do her any good right now.

'The book club is here.' Daisy could hear the distinct sound of Jacob laughing and Nancy trying to call the meeting to order. If they needed to convince anyone in town that they were in love, it was these romance-reading fiends.

'Okay...' Elliot waited for her to explain, clearly not understanding the gravity of the situation. 'And that's bad?'

'No, it's good.'

'If it's so good then why are your fingernails digging into my arm?' he asked, with a lopsided smile.

'Oops.' She loosened her grip, rubbing her palm over the place on Elliot's forearm where she'd left little crescent moons with her nails. It was a nice forearm ... long, lean muscle leading to a big hand with strong fingers...

'Daisy?'

'Right. Sorry.' She pulled her hand away, letting Elliot's arm drop back to his side. 'I meant it's good because we need more people to see us together and the book club will spread the news far and wide.'

'Great.'

'Yeah, but we need to be really convincing. They'll be able to sniff out a fake from miles away.'

'Daisy, they're just a book club.'

'Ha. Said by a man who is clearly not from around here.'

'So, what's the plan?' Elliot tucked the books he was carrying under his arm, an amused smile on his face.

'How about...' Maybe they didn't actually need to put on a play in front of these people. Maybe they could just ... hint at it. Create the illusion.

Daisy stepped closer and Elliot's eyes widened. She reached up and ran her fingers through his hair, mussing it up. It was thick and coarse between her fingers.

'What are you doing?' Elliot asked, his voice dropping low.

'Messing you up a little bit to, you know ... *suggest* what we might have been doing back here.'

He stared at her for a breath, his pupils blown wide and his cheeks flushed red, and she didn't move away, keeping her fingers tight in his hair. She tugged a little and a quiet groan left his lips, the sound reverberating through Daisy's entire body.

'Fair's fair, then,' he said, setting the books aside. His arms came around her as he gently pulled the hair tie from her hair. When he ran his fingers through the strands, her breath came out in a shaky staccato.

'Elliot.' She hadn't meant to moan his name, but it had been so long since anyone had played with her hair. His jagged sigh blew across her cheek.

He tugged her closer until she could feel his rapidly beating heart against hers. Her arms were wrapped around his neck now, his fingers still twisted in her hair. If anyone came around that corner, Daisy was sure they'd be convinced as hell that something very real was going on between her and Elliot.

So much for illusion.

She let her forehead rest on his sternum as he continued to mess up her hair. She pressed closer, her face tucked in the crook of his neck, and she had the insane urge to lick him there, to run her tongue over his fast-beating pulse.

Elliot hissed a pained breath when Daisy rocked her hips toward his. He dropped her hair.

'I think that should do it,' he said, his hands on her shoulders, holding her back.

Daisy blinked. She cleared her throat. 'Right. Good. That's good.' Elliot stared back at her looking completely wrecked. 'Very … suggestive.'

He nodded. 'Very.' He certainly looked like they'd been up to something back here in the stacks, and if Daisy's racing heart and flaming cheeks were any indication, she probably did, too.

'Okay, let's do this.' She grabbed his hand, and together they emerged into the center of the bookstore where the Dream Harbor book club was set up for their meeting. They were not so busy, however, to miss Elliot and Daisy holding hands and looking incredibly guilty.

'Oh, look,' Jacob cooed. 'It's Dream Harbor's latest lovebirds.'

Nancy, Linda, Kaori, Isabel, Jeanie and Mac all turned to look at them, their eyes lighting up immediately. Daisy felt like a little mouse being sized up by the house cat. How much would they toy with her?

'What have you two been up to, today?' Mac asked with a knowing smirk.

'Books,' Daisy blurted out. 'Looking for books.'

'Together? How sweet,' Isabel said, her gaze running

over their red faces and mangled hair. Maybe they'd been too convincing. Daisy felt exposed. Nothing she and Elliot had just done had felt fake.

But she remembered her mission. Her shop.

'We just love to be together,' Daisy said, gazing up at Elliot and nudging her elbow into his side.

He blinked. 'Uh ... yes, we um ... can't seem to get enough.'

'Wow,' Kaori said, from her perch on a stool by the window. 'We didn't realize things were so serious between you two.'

'Very serious,' Daisy said.

'It's nice to see you so happy,' Nancy said, her shrewd gaze still flicking back and forth between them.

'Is it?'

'Of course, dear. That's what we all want for you.'

Daisy forced a smile. She held back the words bubbling up in her throat. If Nancy really wanted her to be happy, she would have referred The Daisy Chain Flower Shop to her niece, whom Daisy happened to know was getting married in six months.

'Well, we are *very* happy.' She didn't realize how hard she was squeezing Elliot's fingers until he gave a gentle squeeze back. She loosened her grip and peeked up at him. He winked at her, and she couldn't help the way her forced smile turned real.

'Is the shop open today?' Mac asked, pulling Daisy's attention back to the group.

'Yeah, Lu is there all day.'

'Why, Mac? Buying flowers for Annie?' Jacob teased.

Mac just grinned like he couldn't be happier to buy his

girlfriend flowers. Maybe if the town was filled with a couple hundred Macs, then Daisy's store would survive. 'Of course.'

'What'd ya do?'

Mac scoffed. 'I didn't *do* anything. Can't I just buy my girl some flowers?'

Jacob crossed his arms over his chest, staring Mac down until the other man confessed. 'Okay, I may have beat her at cards last night.'

'Ha! She really hates to lose, doesn't she?'

'She really, really does.'

The book club descended into a conversation about whether or not Mac should always let Annie win for the rest of forever, but Daisy was tuning them out. She'd take any business she could get at this point, even if it was due to Mac's poor decision-making and Annie's inability to lose gracefully.

'Should we go?' Elliot's words tickled her ear as he leaned down to whisper to her.

'Yeah, let's get out of here.'

They'd done what they needed to do. At the very least, they'd been seen looking like perverts who maul each other between the bookshelves. That seemed like as good a place to start as any.

Before they could sneak out the door, though, Jeanie called them back.

'Wait! Estelle and Henry really want to help with your town research. Are you going to come up to the farm?'

Daisy hesitated. She was definitely still curious about her great-aunt, but she didn't want to force Elliot into doing even more for her than he already was.

'Definitely,' Elliot answered before she could say anything. 'I mean … I'd love to … we just uh … haven't discussed our um … schedules yet.' He looked at Daisy with a slight panic in his eyes like he'd somehow just blown their cover. She squeezed his hand, and he blew out a breath.

'We'll figure it out and get back to you,' she told Jeanie before attempting to steer Elliot toward the door again.

'You two are leaving already?' Jacob asked with a little pout. 'You should stay.'

'We didn't read the book,' Elliot told him, as though that would get the book club off their back.

'It's okay,' Jeanie said. 'You're still welcome.'

'Yeah, it's a good one this week,' Jacob went on. *The Duke's Fake Fiancée*. It's a marriage-of-convenience story.'

Daisy swallowed hard. Were they messing with her?

'He has to marry her to save her reputation.'

'That sounds … ridiculous,' Daisy said, gripping tight to Elliot's hand again. The poor man was going to have her fingernail marks all over him by the end of today.

Do not think about where else your fingernail marks could go.

Do. Not.

'Ridiculously sexy!' Isabel added with a laugh. Damn it, could everyone here read her mind?!

'That part where she convinces him to give her *lessons*!' The way Kaori said 'lessons' made it very clear they were not of the horseback-riding variety. And honestly, it was all reminding Daisy a little too much of the offer she made to help Elliot practice dating.

Not that she meant practice *that*.

She was sure Elliot didn't need any practice with … not horseback riding.

He'd been married. She was sure he'd already had plenty of practice.

He was probably very good at it…

'We have to go!' She nearly shouted the words, and the book club looked at her in alarm. 'I mean, we have plans.' She forced another smile. 'So, we should go. Now. Sorry. Maybe next time!'

She dragged Elliot from the bookstore like it was on fire. It may as well have been, with how hot she suddenly felt. Was it unseasonably warm today? It felt unseasonably warm.

'You okay?' Elliot asked with a bemused smile as Daisy stopped in the middle of the sidewalk to tug her sweater over her head.

'Fine,' she answered from inside it. She was all tangled up now, her left arm stuck, and she couldn't get it over her head. She let out a little growl and then felt Elliot's hands on her arms.

'Hold still,' he laughed. 'Let me just…' He pulled the sleeve, and the sweater came free, her hair flying up in a static-y mess around her head. Elliot ran his big hands over her hair in an attempt to calm it and instead set off little electric shocks zipping around her ears.

From the static.

Not from his touch.

It was science.

Shut up, brain.

'There,' he said, still standing too close, his hands resting gently on her shoulders. 'All better.'

'Right. Thank you.'

'You sure you're okay?' he asked, peering down at her with concern. She must look insane dragging him out of there like that and then promptly getting trapped in her own clothing. Had thinking about sex with Elliot really gotten her that twisted? Yes, yes it had.

'We don't have to go up to the farm. I didn't mean to agree without talking to you. It's just me and my history-nerd stuff ... hard to resist.'

'It's fine. I'm actually excited to go.'

'Okay, good.' His brow furrowed between his glasses, giving him a stern-professor vibe. Like, maybe she was in trouble. Maybe she had to stay after class...

What the hell was wrong with her?!

'So, is there another reason you just got in a fight with your sweater and now you're staring at me like I just grew horns?'

She laughed, sounding just as unhinged as she felt. 'Nope! All is good! You do not have horns.' She patted his head like an idiot and tried to turn and walk toward the pub to get their lunch, but Elliot's fingers wrapped gently around her biceps, holding her in place.

'Did I do something wrong in there? Was it too much ... touching? I'm sorry about your hair and I think I got a little carried away and maybe held you too ... close?' His cheeks were flushed red again, and it was too adorable, and she was having a hard time keeping it together.

'That was all totally fine.' She cleared her throat. 'It was really ... good, actually. I mean, it felt nice.' She flicked her gaze up to his and watched the smile bloom across his face.

'Oh. Good.'

'Yeah, good.'

'Really good.'

Her smile matched his, and she didn't realize they were just standing there beaming at each other until she caught the book club staring at them through the window of the bookstore. As soon as she turned and saw, they all lifted their books and pretended to be reading.

Mac's was upside down.

She shook her head with a laugh.

'Should we continue with our date?' she asked, and Elliot grinned.

'I'd love to.'

Daisy refused to acknowledge that the excitement she felt about spending the rest of the day with Elliot was not fake at all.

Chapter Sixteen

'So where did you grow up?' Daisy asked before taking a bite of one of the massive burgers they'd gotten from Mac's pub. They were sitting at a picnic table in the sun at the public beach. Daisy told him there were more private spots along the shore, but they were sticking with their goal of being seen today.

There were more people on the beach and at the surrounding tables than Elliot had expected, considering it was only April, but it was unseasonably warm today, and there were plenty of townsfolk out soaking in the sun.

Elliot finished his mouthful of fries before answering. 'Not too far from here, really. I grew up in North Bedingfield.'

'Just a few towns over! Does your mom still live there?'

'No, she moved south a few years ago. Said she couldn't stand another winter.'

'I get that,' Daisy said, tipping her face up to the sun. 'I feel like I'm finally defrosting.'

Elliot chuckled.

'I went to school at Cornell, though, so I lived in New York for a while.'

'That's where you lived with your wife?'

'Yep.'

'And your dog?'

Elliot sighed. 'Yep.'

And his brother, but he didn't feel like bringing that up.

'Dream Harbor is a big change from New York.'

'I needed a change, I think. I kept running into Leigh in our old neighborhood. It wasn't … healthy for me to stay there.'

That and Caleb was driving him crazy.

'That makes sense. That's how I ended up back here. I needed to not be in all our old places. Well, and I had nowhere else to go.' She gave him a rueful smile as she popped another fry in her mouth.

'On the plus side, these burgers are delicious.'

Daisy smiled. 'That's true.'

'And you can't beat this view.'

They were sitting on the same side of the table so they could look out over the water and it really was a beautiful view. Deep blue sea met rocky coastline met pale blue sky. Even the seagulls swooping overhead looked idyllic.

'Yeah, it's pretty good,' Daisy agreed with a sigh. 'I'm not sure anyone is paying much attention to us over here, though.'

Elliot looked around the beach. There were a few families with small kids set up in the sand, a game of beach volleyball happening down by the nets, a couple of very brave young women in bathing suits, sunbathing, despite the fact that it wasn't *that* warm, and a few sleek black seals swimming out in the water. No one seemed the slightest bit interested in them.

'Should I stand on the table and start shouting a love poem or something?'

Daisy giggled. 'Would you?'

'Uh…'

She laughed harder. 'I'm just kidding.'

'Okay, good. I'm not much of a poet.'

She turned on the bench, so she was facing him. 'What were you like as a kid?'

'More things you think we should know about each other in case it comes up around other people?'

'No,' she took a sip of her Coke, the straw tucked between her lips. 'I genuinely want to know.'

Elliot turned, too, so their knees were touching. 'I was painfully shy, actually.'

'*Painfully*?'

He nodded. 'There was an entire year in elementary school when I just didn't speak. Refused. That got me sent to therapy.'

'Did therapy help?'

'A little. I just never liked the feeling of being the center of attention. Even if the attention was just the teacher calling on me in class. It made me feel all hot and panicked.'

'Oh, God, Elliot!' Daisy's eyes had gone wide in horror making Elliot feel like a seagull was about to land on him or something.

'What?!' He waved a hand over his head to protect himself.

'No, nothing's there.' She grabbed his hand and sandwiched it between hers. 'I just feel horrible.'

'About what?' he asked, still not able to figure out what she was so upset about.

'I've been making you *perform* and be the center of attention all over town! You stood up at a town meeting for me!'

'Of course, I did.'

She shook her head, her hair flying wildly around her shoulders. She'd never put it back up, and Elliot realized he was still wearing her hair tie around his wrist. He liked seeing it there—a little piece of her on his body.

'No, Elliot. Not *of course* you did. You were the only person in this damn town that stood up for me, and I didn't know that it was basically your worst fear!'

He tucked her hair behind her ear and she stilled, her eyes going wide.

'Daisy, I'm not eight years old anymore. I can talk in front of people. Is it my favorite thing? No. But I can do it. I present designs to clients all the time. It's really okay. I'm not doing anything I don't want to do.'

At some point, he'd gone from tucking her loose hair back to cupping the side of her face. Her eyes fluttered closed as she leaned into his touch.

'Okay,' her voice was breathy when she finally spoke again. 'But you have to tell me if this goes too far.'

Too far with Daisy … what would that look like? He didn't know anymore. He knew he was falling too hard for this woman who wasn't looking for another relationship. He knew he was repeating old mistakes.

But he also knew he wanted to lean forward and kiss her more than anything.

He ran his thumb over Daisy's cheekbone, and a whimper left her lips.

Was this going too far?

He didn't have a second to think about it before someone called out,

'Heads!'

And he had to shift from nearly kissing Daisy to shielding her from the incoming Frisbee. Luckily, the plastic disc hit his forearm and not Daisy's lovely face.

She blinked up at him from under his arm.

'What the hell was that?'

'Frisbee.'

A young woman came running over to retrieve it.

'Sorry!' she called. 'The wind took it.'

'No problem.' Elliot handed it back while Daisy sat, still dazed beside him. If the stunned look on her face was from their almost kiss or from nearly being decapitated, he wasn't sure.

'Oh, Daisy!' the girl said. 'I was trying to convince my sister to use you for her wedding flowers.'

That snapped Daisy out of it.

'Really? That'd be—'

The Frisbee girl cut her off. 'She didn't go for it, though, which is too bad because I really hate her fiancé and I was hoping you could do some of your magic on him.'

'I don't … it's not … magic.'

She shrugged. 'Whatever it is, I was really hoping to get rid of this guy. I hate to think he'll be my brother-in-law soon.' She shrugged again. 'Oh, well. I'll let you two get back to your date.' With that she ran off and left a deflated Daisy and an imprint of her Frisbee in their lunch.

'You'll figure it out, Daisy.'

She sighed. 'Yeah, maybe. Or maybe I'll let down generations of women who have kept the shop running for decades. You said it yourself, remember? Daisy's flower shop has always been known for weddings, and I can't seem to book a single one anymore.'

'You won't let them down.'

'You have an awful lot of faith in me for someone that barely knows me.'

Elliot shrugged. 'It's my job as your fake boyfriend.'

'Gee, thanks.'

At some point they'd started holding hands again, their fingers intertwined in his lap. He gave her a little squeeze.

'Don't you want to keep quizzing me on my childhood? I have some real interesting sibling rivalry stuff we could get into.'

'Ooh … sounds juicy.' Her smile was slowly returning. 'I always wanted a sibling.'

'It can be nice sometimes.'

'And not nice other times?'

'When you have an older brother, it's not always great,' he said with a rueful smile, remembering all the fights he and Caleb used to get into. Especially the last one, the one they'd had right before he quit the business and left. Suddenly, he was sorry he'd brought up the subject.

'Were you a lot alike?'

Elliot shook his head. 'Complete opposites, actually. Caleb was always … bold. Loud and confident. Still is. People notice him when he walks into a room.'

'I notice *you* when you walk into a room.'

His face heated at her words. He was going to argue that that was a recent phenomenon, but he stopped himself. It was nice to be noticed by Daisy. He didn't need to be noticed by anyone else.

'Thanks. I've been noticing *you* for a while now.'

Daisy ducked her head, letting her hair obscure her face again. 'Oh, yeah?'

'How could I not, when you're always causing a stir at the town meetings.'

She lifted her head and laughed, giving his shoulder a playful shove.

'Not always.'

'I'll just say, things got a lot more interesting when you moved back to town.' He remembered the town meeting, nearly a year ago, when Daisy showed up to weigh in on the new name for the diner-turned-pancake-house. He'd been in town for six months at that point and still wasn't sure why the hell he'd uprooted his life and moved here.

Daisy had caught his eye right away, and right away he knew that was a problem.

He'd tried to avoid her, but then he saw her at Jeanie and Logan's wedding, laughing with her friends, dancing in that slinky black dress, arms above her head like she could dance away whatever it was that always made her look so sad.

She looked gorgeous that night.

Maybe *that* was the day his libido woke up.

'Oh, really?' Daisy asked, and he decided not to tell her just how much he'd noticed.

'Yep. It was a total snooze fest my first few months here.'

Daisy giggled.

'I was ready to pack up and head back to New York until you showed up and started yelling at elderly people.'

Daisy laughed harder. 'I don't yell at elderly people!'

'It's fine with me. They totally deserve it!'

She rolled her eyes at him, but she was still grinning. 'They do sometimes, don't they?'

Elliot nodded. 'Totally.'

'I'm sure you staying had nothing to do with that big fancy job you got redesigning the inn.'

He shrugged. 'That may have played a small role.' It certainly made him feel like he hadn't made a big mistake moving here, after all.

'So did you and your brother fight a lot?' she asked, pivoting back to their earlier topic.

'When we were small, yeah. All the time.' Being a year apart, they really gave their mother a run for her money. Thinking about it now reminded him that he should probably be nicer to his mom. 'But at some point, Caleb decided he needed to protect me, like at school. He did a lot of my talking for me.'

'That's kinda sweet in a way.'

'I guess so, yeah. Problem was, he didn't notice when I started speaking for myself again, when I actually grew up.' His brother still thought of him as that scared kid. Still thought he needed protecting, even all these years later. And the way Elliot fell apart after the divorce only seemed to prove Caleb right.

'He worries about you?'

'Yeah.' All the unanswered texts from his brother ran through his mind. 'He and my mom. They've been …

well ... they've been hounding me since the divorce. I don't think they believe that I ever leave my room.' He attempted a laugh, not wanting Daisy to know how close to the truth that had been for him in the beginning, how many days he *hadn't* left his room in those early weeks after the break-up.

He'd moved to prove to himself and his family that he didn't need protecting, that he could do this on his own.

Daisy's face lit up with an idea. 'Let's call him.'

'What? Right now?'

'Yeah! Let's do a video chat. He can see that you're out and about on this beautiful day with your cute new girlfriend,' she said, fluttering her eyelashes. 'Might as well take advantage of our arrangement.'

Arrangement, right.

'Okay.' He cleared his throat. 'I guess we could do that.'

'Great!' Daisy clapped her hands. 'Let me get into character. What kind of girlfriend do you want me to be?'

'Just be you, Daisy.'

'Just be me?' She sounded like she wanted to tease him about that, like she couldn't believe that he didn't have any special requests for his fake girlfriend.

'I wouldn't change a thing.'

His gaze held hers. 'Oh,' she breathed, a small, pleased smile crossing her face. 'Okay.'

Elliot broke eye contact to grab his phone and make the call. They arranged themselves on the bench with the view of the ocean in the background. Daisy tucked in close to his side, so they would both be on screen. Elliot held his breath while they waited for the call to go through. Maybe Caleb wouldn't answer. Maybe he was out. Maybe...

'Elliot, hey! Where have you been? I've been trying to get in touch.'

Damn it. He really needed to get better about answering those texts, or Caleb would be next to show up on his doorstep.

'Hey. Sorry about that. Just been really busy lately.'

Caleb's attention shifted to Daisy. 'I guess so.'

'This is Daisy, my new … girlfriend.'

His brother's brows rose to his hairline. 'Your new girlfriend? Wow. Hi, Daisy. So nice to meet you.'

'Hi! It's nice to finally meet you, too! I've heard so much about you.'

Elliot nearly laughed. Everything she'd heard about him had been in the last five minutes.

'Wish I could say the same. My brother's been MIA lately, so I haven't heard much of anything.'

'Just busy with work,' Elliot repeated. He really didn't need to be scolded by Caleb right now. Not in front of Daisy.

'How is that job going?'

He was sure that to Daisy it seemed like a casual enough question, but to Elliot the subtext was loud and clear. *How's the job you decided to do without me going? How are you managing things alone?*

'Pretty well,' Elliot ground out. 'The owners keep changing their minds. You know how that goes.'

His brother laughed. 'Oh, yeah. I know.'

'Wait,' Daisy cut in. 'Are you an architect, too?' she asked, giving away how little Elliot had actually told her about his brother.

'Oh, no,' Caleb chuckled. 'I leave all that math stuff to El. I'm a contractor. I do the heavy lifting.'

'Yes, you're very big and strong,' Elliot muttered, waiting to see if his brother was about to tell Daisy the whole story. The one where Elliot fell apart and then ran, ditching his brother. The story in which Elliot was actually the worst.

'Looks like a nice day there,' Caleb said, sidestepping the whole conversation. It was embarrassing how relieved Elliot was. He knew his brother had managed to keep the business going without him, doing simpler remodels and less restoration work, but Elliot still felt guilty about the whole mess. Something he didn't really feel like working out during this beach phone call.

'It's beautiful,' Daisy said. 'We were just having a picnic and Elliot said he'd been meaning to call you, so it seemed like the perfect opportunity for us to meet.'

Caleb flashed his obnoxiously charming smile. 'I'm certainly happy to meet you, Daisy. I'm glad you're getting my brother out of the house.'

Elliot clenched his back teeth together so hard he could hear it.

'Oh, that wasn't me,' Daisy said. 'Elliot's always out around town. It's how we met, actually. He came into my flower shop.'

'Oh, really?'

'Yeah, Elliot is really social. Goes out all the time. Tons of friends…'

He nudged her leg with his and gave her a don't-push-it stare. Daisy just grinned. 'He's a lot of fun to be around.'

Caleb's smile was so damn genuine when he said,

'I know that much is true.' It was like a punch to the gut. Even after everything, leaving Caleb in a lurch and ignoring him all the time, his brother was still nice to him.

It was sweet. And annoying.

'Right, well.' Elliot's face was turning red again, an affliction his brother never suffered from. 'We should probably go.'

'Okay, enjoy your date. And answer your damn texts so I don't think you're dead.'

'You know I'm not dead. Mom is here visiting, and I'm sure she would alert you if she found me buried under my bedsheets.'

'Jesus, El. Don't say shit like that.'

'Sorry.'

'And text me back.'

'Okay.'

'Bye, Daisy!' Caleb said with a wave before ending the call.

'He's sweet,' Daisy said. And Elliot waited for the inevitable. Every woman preferred Caleb over him. It just made sense. He was charming and handsome and outgoing…

'But you're cuter,' she said with a grin.

'And you're the best fake girlfriend ever.'

Chapter Seventeen

A few days later, they finally took Logan's grandparents up on their offer to come to the farm and talk Dream Harbor history.

'You sure I can't get you two something to eat?' Estelle asked, bustling around the kitchen. Elliot sat at the kitchen table with Henry poring over the older man's photos, but Daisy had stood up a while ago to stretch her legs.

She was about to accept Estelle's offer of food, when she caught Logan's eye from across the kitchen. He gave a subtle shake of his head as if to warn Daisy away from his grandmother's cooking.

'Oh, that's all right,' Daisy said, smiling at Estelle. 'I had a big lunch.'

Estelle glared at her grandson. 'What did you tell the poor girl? My cooking is just fine,' she said, turning back to Daisy as Logan chuckled on his way out of the kitchen.

'Whatever you say, Nana,' he said as he left to go pick Jeanie up from her shift at the café. Daisy thought it was sweet that he picked up his wife after work. And she was secretly relieved to see her curse hadn't affected them yet.

'I'm sure it's delicious,' Daisy said, eyeing the slop Nana Estelle was stirring in the crock pot. 'But I really am full.'

She was actually starving. They'd been here for hours now, and while the first two hours listening to Henry tell the history of the town had been interesting, here in hour three, as Henry pulled out a literal chest of old pictures his parents had left him, Daisy was getting tired. And hungry. But not hungry enough to eat whatever was in that pot. Was food supposed to liquify like that? Daisy couldn't even guess what it had started out as.

'Suit yourself,' Nana said with a shrug, replacing the lid on the food crime. 'I'm off to aerobics. You all can help yourself if you get hungry.'

The men barely lifted their heads from where they were peering over the pictures.

'Okay, dear,' Henry murmured when Estelle pressed a kiss to the top of his head. 'See you later.'

Daisy plopped back down next to Elliot, leafing through the pictures spread out in front of her while she tried to think of a polite way to suggest they get out of here.

And then she found a familiar face.

Her Great-Aunt Daisy was staring up at her from a black and white photo. She stood with a few other men and women, all looking around the same age like maybe they were all friends. But in this photo, her aunt was smiling. Beaming really. And she wasn't turned toward the camera like everyone else. Her gaze was set on the man beside her. And that was the part of the picture that had Daisy staring in disbelief.

That man also had a familiar face, kind and shy with disheveled hair.

Somehow Elliot's face was staring up at her from the past.

Two immediate and horrifying possibilities sprang to Daisy's mind. One, Elliot, the Elliot sitting beside her, had died years ago and was actually a ghost. Which was certainly unsettling, but not quite as horrifying as option number two, which was that she and Elliot were related because her great-aunt clearly had a thing for this Elliot lookalike, who could very well have been his ancestor. And if they had had children, then, quite possibly, Daisy and Elliot were some kind of cousins, and she certainly hadn't been thinking about him in a cousin-like manner lately.

Ew.

A full-body shiver ran through Daisy, big enough to get Elliot's attention.

'You okay?' he asked. That furrow of concern between his brows, the one that made Daisy think impure thoughts about a naughty professor, deepened.

Oh, no.

'Look at this,' she said, pushing the photo toward Elliot who peered down at it, a lock of hair flopping over his forehead in a way Daisy really did not need right now! *Stop looking at your hot cousin like that!*

'It's your great-aunt,' he said and then stopped as his eyes tracked over to his lookalike. 'Jesus, that looks exactly like—'

'You.'

He cleared his throat. 'That's uncanny!'

'You're not a ghost, right?' Daisy poked him in the arm.

Very solid. Didn't seem like a ghost. And he usually made her feel warm, not cold...

Elliot laughed. 'I'm definitely not a ghost.'

'So, who is that, then?'

'I'm not sure. Henry, do you know who this is?'

Henry peered down at the picture. 'Well, this right here is my father,' he said, pointing at one of the other men in the photo. 'And my Aunt Blanche is there.'

'Okay, but who's the guy who looks exactly like this guy?' Daisy asked, cutting in and jabbing a finger at Elliot. 'And do you happen to know if he procreated with my great-aunt?'

Henry's bushy gray brows rose. 'Well, *that* I wouldn't know. As for who he is, I'm not sure. You got family around here?'

'My mother's family is from nearby.'

Henry shrugged. 'Could be a relative, then, I suppose.'

'Do you mind if I take the picture to show my mom? Maybe she'll recognize him.'

'Of course.'

'Thank you, Henry. We should probably get going,' Daisy said, jumping on the opportunity to wrap up this little history fest.

'Yes, thanks so much. You are a wealth of knowledge.' Elliot shook the older man's hand while Daisy continued to stare at the photo. It was like she and Elliot had gone to one of those old time-y photo booths where you can get your picture taken in vintage costume. It just looked so much like them!

The way *that* Daisy was staring at *that* Elliot...

Daisy wondered if she looked at this Elliot in the same way.

After saying their goodbyes to Henry, they made their way out of the farmhouse and down the dusty drive to where they'd parked. Several fluffy chickens followed them out.

'Are these normal chickens?' Elliot asked.

'I don't know. Who cares?' Daisy snapped, her emotions bubbling over.

'You're upset.'

'Of course I'm upset, Elliot! Our relatives were clearly in love and what if they had a secret baby and what if we're related!' she yelled and the nearest chicken gave a startled cluck.

Elliot blinked. 'I think you're jumping to a lot of conclusions. We don't know if I'm related to that man.'

She scowled at him as the weird chickens circled their feet.

'They seem fluffier than normal chickens.'

'Shut up about the damn chickens!' She continued storming off to his car, ignoring his shocked expression.

'Why are you so mad about us possibly being distantly related?' he asked when he caught up to her. She was leaning against the passenger-side door, and he came to stand in front of her.

'Because.' She crossed her arms petulantly over her chest.

'Because, why?'

'Because, Elliot,' she said with a sigh, 'if we are related then I need to stop having sexual fantasies about you.'

The man turned bright red in an instant.

'I … well … uh…'

Daisy waved him away. 'Never mind.'

'Never mind?! Daisy, you can't say something like that and then expect me to forget it.'

She sighed. This was a strange day.

'What can I say? I have a professor-kink and you've been looking very … professor-y lately; always poring over a book or looking at me all stern-like. And then, when you're not doing that, you're holding my hand or being all sweet. And frankly, Elliot, what is a girl to do?!'

He stared at her, his mouth hanging open.

She may have broken him.

'Say something.' She nudged his foot with the toe of her black boot.

Elliot met her gaze.

'Your grandmother said your great-aunt never had children.'

'That we *know* of.'

'We'll find out. We'll find out for sure.' Suddenly, he was a man on a mission.

Daisy smirked. 'And why are you so eager to find out?'

He stormed around to his side of the car and wrenched open the door. 'Because I have plenty of my own sexual fantasies, Daisy, and they all involve *you*.'

The ten-minute car ride back into town had been incredibly long and deafeningly silent, their confessions lingering in the air between them. But Daisy couldn't let this awkwardness continue, not with Beltane coming next weekend. They needed to look normal and in love in front of everyone. Not weird and terrified of each other.

'So…' she ventured as they pulled in front of the shop. 'That was—'

'I'm sorry,' Elliot blurted out.

'For what?'

'I shouldn't have said that.'

'Was it not true?'

Elliot turned to face her. 'No, it was very true.'

Daisy couldn't help her nervous giggle.

'Why are you laughing?!'

'I'm sorry! I just, this hasn't happened to me before!'

'Well, me, neither!' Elliot gave her an awkward smile. 'You're my first fake girlfriend, I'm not really sure of the protocol here.'

Daisy blew out a long breath. 'I know our arrangement is for show but these … physical feelings I think are … real. I mean … I'm attracted to you … *for real*.' Her face heated. She hadn't put herself out there like this in so long, but Elliot's answer was quick and sure.

'Same,' he said, blowing out his own sigh of relief.

'So, what do we do now?' What *should* they do now? She had a few fun ideas, but would that just confuse everything between them?

The fact that she even found someone else attractive felt like a huge breakthrough, but she didn't want to finally start moving on from David, just to get her heart broken by someone new. Especially by someone who was still hung up on his ex, too.

Ah, there was the red flag.

It was the same as her own. Still not over her ex. Still trying their damnedest not to repeat old mistakes.

But this level of sexual tension was becoming a problem. So maybe they could just … get it out of their systems? Or a friends-with-benefits situation? Or maybe…

'We should probably confirm we're not related first.'

Well, that knocked all the fun ideas out of Daisy's head. Nothing kills the mood like the possibility of being related to the dude you've got the hots for.

She still had the old photo in her hands. 'Right,' she said, studying it again. 'It really is crazy how much this looks like us. It's freaking me out.'

'It is pretty eerie.' Elliot held out his hand and Daisy gave him the photo. 'I've done some ancestry stuff already, and I don't remember my great-grandfather looking all that much like me. Definitely not like this.'

'So, who *is* he then?'

'Maybe a great-grandparent's cousin or something?'

'The more distant the better,' Daisy muttered.

'I really don't think we're related. Your grandmother told you her aunt never had kids, right? That's how she ended up as the next Daisy?'

'Yeah, true.' She *really* wanted that to be true.

'I'll do some digging, okay? We'll figure it out before we…'

'Before we?'

Elliot cleared his throat. 'Uh … do anything more … real.'

'Right. Good. Thanks.' Daisy nodded, trying to keep

everything sounding businesslike when her heart was thumping against her rib cage at the thought of doing more *real* things with Elliot. She thought he was going to kiss her during their beach date, and she wasn't sure how she felt about that until they were thwarted by that Frisbee, and her disappointment had been *big*. Girl-with-Frisbee had robbed her of something she was now positive would have been great. She hadn't stopped thinking about it since.

'Your Great-Aunt Daisy looks so much happier in this picture than the other,' he commented, looking down at the smiling faces in the photo again.

'I know,' Daisy said. 'It's like night and day.'

'And you think it's because of this man?'

'Look at how she's gazing at him. In the other photo, it's like someone took away her favorite toy.'

Elliot chuckled. 'Her favorite toy?'

'Or something like that,' she said with a cheeky grin. 'I just think they had some kind of doomed love affair.'

'It's a lot to assume from two pictures.'

'I have a hunch.' A hunch that her great-aunt and this man who looked exactly like Elliot had some sort of relationship. Until they didn't. And clearly her great-aunt hadn't gotten over it. It seemed clear to Daisy, anyway.

'A hunch is usually a good place to start.'

'I guess we'll just have to pore over more dusty old books and find more evidence.'

'You're really speaking my language now,' he said and Daisy laughed.

'Getting a little too close to those sexual fantasies?' she teased.

Elliot's ears burned pink, but he laughed, too. 'A little bit.'

'How about we go to the library and dig into the *archives*,' she purred, putting on a fake sexy voice, having a little too much fun with this flirting game.

'You think you're joking, but that's really doing it for me.' He waggled his eyebrows suggestively, and Daisy burst into more giggles. She hadn't felt this silly in a long time, like her insides were fizzing and her cheeks hurt from smiling.

It felt *good*.

'Okay, then go talk to your mom and find out who this guy is so we can finally make out!'

Elliot's grin grew. 'Okay.'

Daisy held his gaze. 'Okay.' It was too warm in the car. Unseasonably warm. 'I'm really glad you're not a ghost.'

Elliot let out a laugh. 'That would definitely complicate things even more.'

'Like if I couldn't touch you.'

He cleared his throat.

'Right.'

'Right.'

Elliot leaned closer, his warm breath tickling her cheek. 'That would be a shame.'

She nearly leaned in. Elliot was right there. And it had been so *long* since she'd wanted someone. But then she remembered what they'd literally just been talking about, and she pushed him away. 'Go talk to your mom!'

'Right. Sorry. Right. Go talk to your grandmother. Maybe search for family birth certificates or something.'

Daisy nodded, opening the door and launching herself

out of the car before she did something crazy and possibly incestuous.

'Okay, got it. Bye, Elliot!'

'Bye, Daisy.'

Chapter Eighteen

'Grandma June!' Daisy yelled, bursting into her grandparents' apartment at the senior living facility. Daisy was hoping she wasn't at one of her daily activities. Between her bocce-ball league and her watercolor class, Grandma June had a packed schedule.

Luckily, both her grandparents were parked in their matching recliners watching the evening news when Daisy stumbled into their living room.

'What on earth is going on?' June asked, her eyes wide. Daisy's grandpa Jim didn't bother to take his eyes from the TV.

'Your Aunt Daisy never had kids, right?'

Her grandmother frowned. 'You come charging in here like it's the end of the world to ask me about people that are long dead? Again?'

'May they rest in peace,' Jim muttered. '*Someone* should have peace.'

'Yes! I just … really need to know if she had any children.'

'I already told you she didn't. That's why I'm named Daisy.'

'But like she probably didn't have any secret babies, either … right?'

Her grandmother looked truly scandalized at that. 'Secret babies? Daisy, what is going on with you?'

Daisy shrugged, trying and failing to pretend this wasn't a matter of the utmost importance. 'I'm just curious about our family history. That's all.'

'Sounds fishy to me,' Jim said, his eyes still focused on the news.

'You shouldn't watch that,' Daisy told him. 'It's bad for your mental health.'

Grandpa Jim scoffed. 'My mental health's just fine. You're the one going on about secret babies.'

Daisy stuck her tongue out at him, but he didn't see; his eyes were still on the screen. She turned back to her grandmother. 'I just look so much like her, I'm wondering if somehow … she's actually my … great-grandmother?' Was that even right? Daisy was getting all these distant relationships confused.

'Do you really think someone could keep a baby secret in this town?' her grandmother asked with a laugh. 'It was the same then as it is now. Probably even worse. If your Aunt Daisy had a baby, we all would have known about it and I'm telling you she didn't.'

Daisy blew out a sigh. 'This is amazing news!' She leaned down and kissed her grandmother on the head before wandering into the kitchen. 'Do you have any of those cookies I like? You know the ones in the blue tin?'

'Of course I do. Top cabinet.'

'Thank you!' Daisy found her cookies and joined her grandparents back in the living room. She sat at her grandma's feet and let her run her fingers through her hair like she used to do when Daisy was a little girl. She picked her favorite butter cookie from the tin (the pretzel-shaped one with crystals of sugar coating the top) and munched on it happily. Who knew that finding out you're not related to someone could be so exciting?

'Feeling better now?' Grandma June asked.

'Much. Thank you.'

'Are you going to explain why that was so important to you?'

'It will just sound crazy if I do.'

'Already does,' Grandpa joked, and Daisy smacked him playfully on the knee.

'I just needed to make sure I wasn't getting myself into a situation that I shouldn't be getting into and now I'm sure, so everything is fine.'

'Not crazy at all.' Grandpa leaned down to snag a cookie.

Her grandmother just hummed a little skeptical sound but didn't comment. At least not on that.

'And how are things at the shop?' she asked instead, and Daisy would rather discuss her near brush with incest.

'Fine.'

'Fine?'

'Well, thanks to some new business with the inn, we can pay our bills this month, so, fine.' Daisy had been so relieved when she got the call from Mary. She'd be providing monthly arrangements for the lobby for now, and then once the breakfast room was done, she'd be doing mini arrangements for each table. It wasn't a season filled with weddings, but it was something.

Another skeptical hum.

'I heard you and your new boyfriend were caught in the act at the bookstore.'

Daisy nearly choked on her cookie.

'We were not!'

'Well, according to Marissa who heard it from Gladys who heard it from Iris who heard it from Jeanie, you and that Elliot were looking mighty *disheveled* when they spotted you.'

'We were looking at books! That's it!' Maybe they had been too convincing that day. Now she had the whole town thinking she got plowed between the shelves at the bookstore. Hazel was going to kill her. That was not the kind of publicity she would want for the store.

'The book club seemed to think you were doing more than that. They said you looked flushed and with your hair all a mess...'

Daisy groaned.

Grandpa Jim turned up the volume on the TV. Apparently, he'd heard enough about his granddaughter's bad decisions. Decisions she hadn't even really made!

'I would never...' Daisy started to protest, raising her voice above the din of the news but Grandma June patted her shoulder, giving her an encouraging squeeze.

'Keep it up, dear. The town thinks that boy is in love with you and that's just what we need.'

The town thinks that boy is in love with you.

Now there was a sentence that was sure to keep her up at night.

But the town could think whatever they wanted. In fact, they were thinking exactly what she wanted them to think. So, everything was going as planned. She and Elliot were pulling it off.

And besides, there was no way Elliot was in love with her. He was like her. Neither of them were capable of falling in love again. Neither of them *wanted* to.

But if they wanted to make out a little, now that she was sure they weren't some kind of cousins, then what would the harm be in that?

Daisy took another bite of her cookie and pretended that she totally believed she could kiss Elliot with zero repercussions.

Daisy was getting very good at pretending.

'What do you think the moral implications of sleeping with one's fake boyfriend are?' Daisy asked as she weaved another flower stem through the wire frame of the crown she was working on. She didn't need to lift her head to feel Iris staring at her from her spot across the worktable Daisy had hauled out of the storage room. They'd been working on crowns for so long that Owen had fallen asleep in his baby seat beside them.

Long enough for Daisy to work up the nerve to bring up what had been weighing on her mind since Elliot confessed to having fantasies about her. Which was only yesterday.

But it had been a long (and mentally graphic) twenty-four hours.

'Are you asking me if you should have sex with Elliot?'

'Maybe.'

Iris laughed. 'I'd say if he wants to have sex with you, then you are morally good to go.' She placed her completed crown on top of her head with a flourish. The purples and blues looked lovely against Iris's copper hair.

'I just don't want him to get the wrong idea about the whole thing.'

'And what would the wrong idea be?'

'That I want something more than what we're doing. A real relationship.'

'So just tell him that.'

'Do you think we can do it and get it out of our systems?'

Iris laughed so loud that it startled Owen awake. He looked at her accusingly. 'Oops.' She winced, leaning down to pick him up when he started to fuss.

'That's a no, then?' Daisy asked.

Iris arranged herself in her chair, positioning Owen so he could nurse before she looked back up at Daisy. 'You do realize that this little guy exists because me and Archer were *getting it out of our systems*, right?' She gazed down at her baby as he ate, the flower crown still on her head. And with the golden light of the evening streaming in, they looked beautiful together. It was quite a change from the last time Iris was in here crying. Motherhood, what a ride.

'How are you feeling, by the way?'

Iris raised her head again, a bemused smile on her face. 'Don't think you're off the hook. We are circling back to you and Elliot. But...' She ran a finger down the plump curve of Owen's cheek. 'I'm doing better. I think. Crying less, so that's nice.'

'You know I'm always here to help. And my mom would die to hold the baby for the afternoon.'

Iris smiled. 'I know. Thank you.'

'And Archer's been...?'

'Incredible. He jumps up at the littlest peep from the baby. Gets to him before I'm even half awake.' She smiled as she said it. 'And he makes sure I'm eating and Olive is feeling included, and it's a lot. He's basically holding us all together.'

'That's good.' Daisy liked Archer, but he was new to the whole parenthood thing, too. So much had been thrown at him in such a short amount of time. It was good to hear they were working it out together.

'Now,' Iris said, pointing an accusing finger at Daisy. 'Back to you. What is going on with Elliot?'

Daisy picked up a new wire ring and started on her next crown, trying to think of another change of topic but coming up with nothing.

She sighed. 'I don't know. He's cute, you know? And we're spending a lot of time together. And I think it's just been too long since I've...'

'Made love?' Iris said with a grin.

'Ew. Don't ever say that again.'

Iris laughed and Owen snorted at the disruption to his meal.

'Okay, so it's been a while since you've been *intimate* with a man.'

'I don't love that, either, but yes, it's been a long while

and … I don't know… That combined with being around an attractive guy all the time, it's—'

'Making you super horny?'

Daisy thunked her head down on the table in defeat. 'Yes. It's making me super horny.'

'Well, then it sounds like you should probably do it with your fake boyfriend.'

'What are the odds it doesn't end in disaster?'

'Fifty-fifty, I'd say.'

Daisy lifted her head, and Iris was burping Owen, his small body curled in a ball on her chest. His little footy pajamas were covered in turtles which made Daisy smile.

'And I'd recommend two forms of birth control, unless you really like staying up all night,' Iris added.

'Right.' Owen was adorable and it had worked out for Iris and Archer, but a baby with Elliot was…

Something that made her feel dizzy to think about.

She shook her head.

'I think he'll understand,' she said weakly, trying to convince herself more than Iris.

The town thinks that boy is in love with you.

Her grandmother's words reared their ugly head.

Maybe fooling around with Elliot would be a mistake.

Her mother came bustling in through the door carrying a poster board, glitter and paint before Daisy could think about it further.

'I got sign-making supplies, girls!' she said, cheerfully. 'Now, hand over that baby.' She put the supplies on the table and held her arms out to Iris, who happily gave her a full and sleepy Owen.

'Thanks, May,' Iris said.

Daisy's mom dipped her face and breathed deep, right over Owen's head. 'New-baby smell,' she said. 'Divine.'

Daisy and Iris laughed as they made space for the art materials. Her mom hummed and rocked Owen while they worked on the sign to hang on their Beltane booth. And between the work and the laughter, Daisy managed to put Elliot out of her head until later when she was alone in bed.

Alone and lonely in bed.

And that was when Daisy thought maybe it wouldn't be such a bad idea to work out some of her physical frustration with Elliot.

Maybe it was a great idea.

Chapter Nineteen

'We're not related,' Elliot burst out as soon as Daisy opened her door. An incredibly smooth and charming thing to say when you pick up a woman for a date. *Well done, Elliot.*

'I know,' she said with a smile. 'Come in. I'm almost ready to go.' They were supposed to be headed to karaoke night at the pub, which he'd only agreed to when Daisy assured him that he didn't have to sing.

'You know?'

'Yeah, I talked to my grandmother, and she assured me that Great-Aunt Daisy never had children.'

'Oh. Good.'

'What did you find out?' Daisy asked, grabbing a sweater from the hook by the door.

'After looking through some ancestry stuff and talking to my mom, I think the man in the picture is a cousin of my great-grandfather. So, I wouldn't be a direct descendant of his.'

'So that means…'

'We're definitely not related.'

'Right.'

Daisy was watching him, looking like she wanted to say something but was fighting the urge.

'What is it?' he asked.

She sighed and then launched into it. 'Remember that little sexual fantasy confession?'

'I couldn't forget it if I wanted to.'

'Okay, well, I think it's just been a really long time since I've, well, you know … and I think it's making me a little nutty so maybe we could just like … you know…'

Elliot nearly groaned, struggling to keep his sanity at the idea of what Daisy was suggesting. 'I think I know, but I really don't want to be wrong about this, Daisy, so if you could just spell it out for me.'

She sighed again, twisting her hands into the sleeves of her sweater.

'Look, I know you don't want a relationship and that you're not over Leigh.' He wasn't sure that was true anymore, but he let Daisy keep talking. 'And I'm definitely not interested in anything serious for obvious reasons.'

'Wait, what obvious reasons?'

She looked at him like he was being purposefully obtuse.

'Elliot, I told you, I can't do this again. Relationships are not for me.'

'At all?'

'Right.'

'Ever again?'

'Elliot, I didn't date for two years after my divorce from

Matthew. I didn't get out of bed for a month after David broke up with me. I am barely hanging on here. I have a sinking business to run. I do not have the energy or the strength to try this again.'

He swallowed hard. Well, that settled that.

He just thought…

They'd been having so much fun together.

And sometimes the way Daisy looked at him, it just seemed like…

'Anyway, that's why this is perfect and makes so much sense,' Daisy went on. 'Neither of us wants anything emotionally real so we can just, you know, be fuck buddies.'

Elliot nearly choked on his own tongue.

'I can't do that.'

Daisy's face fell. 'Oh.'

Shit.

'Okay.' She tucked a piece of hair behind her ear and tried to push past him to get to the door. 'That's fine. It was just an idea. Forget I ever said anything.'

She looked so damn hurt.

Shit, shit, shit.

'That's not what I meant.'

'It's really fine, Elliot. Let's just go.' She tried again to get past him, but he grabbed her arm and held her still.

'Daisy, look at me.'

When she looked up, her expression was so devastated, so embarrassed, that Elliot couldn't stand it.

'You are beyond sexy.'

She rolled her eyes. 'Okay, Elliot. I don't need your pity compliments.'

'It's not pity. I want you, Daisy.'

'You just said you didn't. It's fine. Let's just go, please.'

He almost let her go. He should have, for his own good. He knew if things got physical between him and Daisy, he'd be lost. He'd be all-in. And after what Daisy just told him, he knew he'd be the only one.

But he couldn't leave her looking like that. He couldn't leave her thinking she was anything less than the most beautiful woman he'd ever met, that he'd give anything to have her, to touch her, to *fuck* her.

'I mean it.' He turned her so her back was against the door, his hand on her hip. Her eyes widened. 'And if I wasn't afraid of falling in love with you, I'd show you just how much.'

'You can't fall in love with me,' she whispered as he bent his head and kissed her neck.

'I know.' He buried his face in her hair, kissing behind her ear, along her throat. She gasped, pressing against him. 'But I need you to know how badly I want you.' He twined his fingers with hers and brought her hand to where his cock was straining embarrassingly hard at the front of his pants.

'Jesus,' she hissed.

'I need you to know how sexy you are, how your body drives me crazy, how I haven't stopped thinking about it since I saw you dancing at Jeanie's wedding.'

Daisy whimpered, her hand moving on its own now, pressing against him, feeling the shape of him through his pants. He nearly blacked out at the pleasure of it, the not-enough-but-too-much-ness of it.

'Do you believe me now?' he asked, his mouth still working its way down her neck, over her collarbones to the other side. He didn't know what he was doing, didn't know why his mouth was still on her skin, why he was practically thrusting against her hand, when he knew how this ended.

But it had been so damn long since he'd been touched.

And he refused to let Daisy think she wasn't desirable, to think she wasn't wanted.

Even if it killed him later.

She squeezed a little around him and Elliot grabbed her wrist, moving her hand above her head instead of on his dick. He wasn't going to survive another second if she left it there.

He had her pinned against the door now, one hand holding her wrist above her head and the other gripping her hip. She was staring up at him, dazed, her pretty lips hanging open in surprise.

A small smile crept over her face. 'Okay, I believe you.'

He groaned in relief, his mouth back on her neck, her hips pressing against his.

'So, we can do this?' she asked, her voice breathy and tight. 'We can do this without feelings?'

He could *not* do this without feelings.

But he certainly wasn't going to walk away now.

'Don't worry,' he told her instead. 'I know what this is. I get it.'

He moved his hand from her hip, skating across her stomach. He wasn't going to leave Daisy wanting. She needed something from him, and he would give it to her. He'd pick up the pieces later.

He unbuttoned the black jeans she'd put on for their night out with one hand, eliciting a surprised gasp from Daisy. He smiled against the skin on her throat, still not kissing her lips. Kissing would make this something else entirely. Something intimate and real. And Elliot was barely surviving this as it was.

He slid his hand down her pants.

Daisy whimpered.

'I've got you,' he said, pushing into her underwear and she was so … wet… His knees nearly buckled. He squeezed his eyes shut.

'Elliot,' she rasped and that was it. That was all he could take. His fingers found her clit and Daisy rolled her hips toward him. 'God, yes,' she said and he circled his fingers right there, right on the spot that made her gasp those words against him. He still held her hand above their heads, but her other arm was wrapped around his back, her nails digging in as she panted his name.

This was too much, *too much*. He wasn't going to survive it. Daisy's body against his, her mouth on his neck now, her whimpers and moans. But he was determined. He would give her this and then he would back off. He would explain why he couldn't go any further. He would protect himself.

Daisy's breath quickened, coming in short little bursts.

'Elliot, Elliot, Elliot,' she crooned, rocking against his hand until she stilled, her whole body tense and shaking. She met his gaze, her eyes wild. And then she fell apart, her orgasm breaking over her until she was trembling and Elliot lowered her hand, holding her up instead as she shook against him.

They stayed like that for a while, too long probably, Elliot wrapping both arms around her.

'That was really, really good,' she said, talking into his shoulder instead of to his face.

'I'm glad.'

'What about you?'

'I'm ... okay.' He was *not* okay. He was completely wrecked but doing anything else with Daisy would only make that worse.

'Still afraid of falling in love with me?' she asked, not lifting her head.

'Something like that, yeah. I'm not good at doing this without feelings.'

'You're a rare breed.'

'I've been told.'

She pulled away and looked up at him. 'So, we probably shouldn't...'

'Right. I don't think I can be your...'

'Fuck buddy?' she asked, the teasing smile working its way back onto her lips. At least she wasn't upset with him.

'Sorry.'

She gave a little shrug. 'It's probably for the best.'

'Agreed.'

'And I don't think you have feelings for me, anyway, Elliot.'

'Oh, really?'

'I mean, besides the obvious pants feelings.'

He adjusted himself. The pants feelings hadn't exactly gone away yet.

'Why do you say that?'

'You're just repeating what happened with your ex-wife. I was the first woman who asked you out. Even if it was for pretend.'

He stood there, slightly stunned by that observation. She was right. It was what he'd been afraid of since he met her, but to have Daisy call him out on it … it was like being splashed with cold water.

Leigh was the first girl who'd asked him out in college, and he'd hung on to her for dear life. And now here he was, developing feelings for the first woman who he'd spent any time with since the divorce.

And the worst part was Daisy knew. She knew what was happening even if he wanted to ignore it.

'As your friend,' Daisy went on. 'I can't let you repeat your mistakes. Just like I'm not going to repeat mine.'

She rebuttoned her pants and smoothed down her shirt, all business again.

'Now, should we go listen to our friends and neighbors butcher our favorite songs?' She grabbed her purse from the bed while Elliot struggled to process everything she'd just said.

Was she right? Maybe a few weeks ago he would have agreed, but now he refused to think of Daisy as a mistake. Nothing that happened with Daisy felt anything like it had with Leigh.

Elliot's feelings for Daisy felt brand new.

But Daisy wasn't ready to hear that. Not yet.

'Sure,' he said, taking her hand. They were still fake-dating after all. He still got to hold her hand. For now, anyway. 'Let's go.'

Chapter Twenty

It was very hard to sit next to someone who'd had his hand down your pants making you come harder than you had in a long time and just pretend like everything was normal. But thanks to the final Beltane planning meeting, that was exactly what Daisy was being forced to do.

She had been trying to be cool since The Great Orgasm Incident, which was what she was calling it in her head, but for the past forty-eight hours, she hadn't stopped thinking about it.

About how good it had been.

About how sexy Elliot was, how competent and confident he was.

About whether or not it could happen again. Or if it should happen again.

About Elliot saying he was afraid of falling in love with her.

About how she was becoming more and more afraid of that herself.

The Great Orgasm Incident had unlocked a lot of shit for her, and now she had to sit here at this town meeting and pretend to care about whether the food trucks would set up outside of the town hall or on Main Street.

And she did not care.

'Well, *we* care, Daisy,' Nancy, head of the Beltane committee, said, eyeing her over her meeting notes.

Oops, apparently, she'd said that out loud.

'Right, sorry.'

'I think we're all agreed that the food trucks should line up along Main Street,' Nancy said, moving on. 'That clears up space for the stage in front of the town hall.'

'What's the stage for?' Elliot leaned over, whispering in her ear.

Daisy suppressed a full-body shiver at his nearness. 'The crowning of the May Queen.'

'What does that entail?' he asked, but Daisy didn't have time to explain before Tammy and Marissa, the other members of the Beltane committee were chiming in with tasks left to be completed.

'As you all know, folks have been casting their ballots all week for this year's queen, and we are looking for help tallying the votes,' Tammy started.

Annie nudged Daisy from her other side. 'I've got my money on Andy,' she whispered. 'Do you want in on the pool?'

'We don't even know who the finalists are yet.'

Annie looked at her like she was being ridiculous. 'Yeah, you're right,' Daisy conceded. 'Andy is a shoo-in. I'll put my money on him.'

Annie grinned.

Bennett turned around from his seat in front of them. 'You're betting on the wrong horse, ladies. This girl right here is going to win.'

Kira rolled her eyes. 'Please don't refer to me as a horse.'

'Sorry, babe. But you are totally going to win.'

Kira just shook her head with a laugh. 'I never should have let you nominate me.'

'Did you vote, Elliot?' Bennett asked.

'Uh ... yeah. Of course.'

'For Kira, right?'

Elliot's gaze flicked from Bennett's to Daisy, but she couldn't save him from Bennett's *Kira for May Queen* campaign. He'd been going on about it all month. He even made posters and buttons. She just shrugged.

'Well, I voted for Gladys, actually,' Elliot confessed.

Bennett groaned so loud that Nancy cleared her throat and glared at him.

'Sorry,' he mouthed and gave Daisy and Elliot an apologetic smile before turning around.

'I liked the changes to the pancake house. Seemed like a good reason to vote for the owner. What should I have been looking for in a May Queen?' he whispered, sounding suddenly concerned, like his vote for May Queen could have actual consequences.

Daisy patted his knee. 'I wouldn't worry about it. The May Queen doesn't exactly have a lot of political sway. It's more of a figurehead position.'

He huffed a laugh.

'We also need a volunteer to add up the money we took in from the sale of the voting ballots,' Marissa added.

'And what exactly does the Beltane committee do?'

Daisy asked, eliciting a laugh from Annie and a glare from Tammy.

'We've been planning the logistics for months,' Marissa said, not deterred by Daisy's comment.

Daisy was being unnecessarily rude. She knew that. She normally saved her town meeting arguments for important things, like the fight to put a cap on town bake sales (an insane idea) or the petition to move the farmer's market inside of the town hall for the winter (very smart and something she argued in favor of for months). Hassling the Beltane committee about their work wasn't exactly a hot button issue for her. But Elliot's leg was pressed against hers and his steady presence was making her feel…

Like she may burst.

'And you've done a wonderful job.' Mayor Kelly stepped back up to the podium. 'Anything else we haven't covered?'

Nancy looked back at her notes. 'Let's see … the fire department is going to handle the raising of the maypole. Miss Janet's Little Tots dance class have been rehearsing the maypole dance for months.'

'Since Christmas!' Janet called from her seat in the crowd. 'And they've really got it down. They rarely get tangled in each other's ribbons anymore.'

Nancy looked at her skeptically. 'Let's try to make sure they don't get tangled at all.'

'Of course.' But even Janet looked skeptical now. Daisy didn't envy her the job of getting twenty five-year-olds to weave in and out and back and forth around a giant pole holding a forty-foot-long ribbon and somehow not crash into each other.

'Cliff's Midnight Dreamers are set to perform.'

Noah hooted from the back and Daisy caught sight of Cliff shaking his head with a begrudging smile.

'And Logan and Bennett have offered to keep our bonfire going all night.'

'Ben sure keeps *me* going all night,' Kira said to plenty of whistles and laughs from the crowd.

Nancy just pursed her lips like she was still dealing with kindergarteners and continued down her list. 'Daisy, how are the flower crowns coming?'

'Nearly done.' She and Iris had worked their fingers to the bone to get them finished in time. Daisy braced herself for someone to argue about her providing the flowers again, but no one did. Elliot gave her knee a squeeze. Daisy didn't dare look at him. If he was smiling at her with that damn blush on his cheeks, she might implode.

'Great,' Nancy tucked away her list into her back pocket. 'Then I think we are all set to welcome summer!'

'Everyone knows it's only the first of May, and still far too cold out to be summer, right?' Kira whispered.

Annie leaned forward. 'It's an ancient tradition, *babe*. Plus, it's fun. Just go with it.'

'You can hang out by the fire with me,' Bennett said, slinging his arm around Kira's shoulders, and she immediately leaned into him.

Daisy sat up straighter to avoid pressing her arm against Elliot's even as he leaned to whisper in her ear again.

'I'm excited to go with you,' he said, his words tickling her skin. 'Sounds like a fun night.'

A fun night.

A fun night of simultaneously wanting to let Elliot do

magic with his hands again and wanting to run far away from this thing that was definitely going to break her heart.

A fun night for sure.

Five days later, on the morning of the Beltane festival, Daisy had decided to get back on track with this fake relationship. *Fake* being the key word.

Yes, The Orgasm Incident had been fun, but Daisy had a heart to protect and business to save. She didn't have time for fooling around.

With that decided, she was spending the morning loading up Logan's truck with her table and tent and several hundred flower crowns. She was heading back out to the truck with a cooler filled with crowns, when she nearly ran straight into her grandmother.

'Hey, Grandma. What are you doing here?' she asked, handing the cooler off to Logan.

'I have something for you.' Her grandmother had a cardboard box in her arms. She walked into the shop with Daisy right behind her. She unceremoniously dropped the box onto the counter, brushing the dust off her hands.

'What is it?'

'Some things I thought you might be interested in since you keep asking about dead relatives all the time.'

'Grandma, it was like twice.'

'Still, thought you might want them.'

Daisy peered into the box. It was filled with old notebooks and photos and shop ledgers, the pages yellowed and worn.

'Wow, this is actually amazing.'

Grandma June shrugged like she wasn't interested in looking at the past and couldn't quite understand why Daisy wanted to.

'I hope it's useful.'

'Where did you find all of this?' Daisy asked, riffling through the pictures. Some were newer, glossy and in color. She found a few of herself as a baby, her parents on their wedding day. Others were old and brittle and in black and white, with names and dates scrawled on the backs. *Arthur 1943, Emilie 1956, John and Lyddie 1933.* Decades passed through her fingertips.

'Remember when we had the shop renovated a few years back?'

Daisy looked up from her digging. 'When I was five?'

Grandma chuckled. 'I guess it was more than a few years! I had to clean out the back apartment, and I found a bunch of my parents' old things. Some of it felt worth keeping. Or I just felt guilty throwing it all away. I've added to it over the years. Anyway, I'm sure my father's sister, Daisy, whom you're so interested in, makes an appearance in some of those old photos.'

Daisy gave her grandmother a big hug. 'Thank you! I'm sure it will be useful.'

Grandma June patted her back. 'You're an odd duck, Daisy-girl. But I love you.'

'Love you, too. Can't wait until I have time to go through all this.' Great-Aunt Daisy was never far from her mind as she worked in the shop, probably standing in the exact spot her aunt had. Did her aunt like working in the shop, did she take pleasure in arranging flowers into something new and beautiful like Daisy did? Did she like going home smelling like roses and lavender?

What did that Daisy think about as the sun moved throughout the day, throwing different colors through the stained glass and onto the wood floor? What did *she* want with her life?

'So, are you all set for the festival today?' Grandma asked, looking around the shop at the mess of supplies that still needed to be loaded into the truck.

'Yep.'

'And Elliot will be escorting you?'

'*Escorting* me? What year is it, Grandma?' Daisy asked with a laugh.

'Don't be fresh.'

'Sorry. Yes, he will.'

Her grandma nodded in approval. 'I think seeing you two together at Beltane will do some major damage control for your image. I overheard several people at the diner this morning comment on how happy and in love you two seem.'

Happy and in love.

If I wasn't afraid of falling in love with you…

The whole town thinks that boy is in love with you.

No, no, no.

Nope.

Love was not happening. Hadn't she just decided that?

She and Elliot were just really good actors. Actors who were physically attracted to each other. That was it. That was all she would allow.

Was it warm in here?

Daisy started pulling off her sweater, yanking it over her head and leaving her hair a staticky mess in its wake.

When she emerged, her grandmother looked alarmed. 'Are you okay, dear?'

'Fine. Why?'

'You look … terrified.'

Daisy scoffed. *Terrified*. Terrified? Terrified of falling in love again. With the wrong person *again*. Getting her feelings destroyed and her heart broken *again*. No, not her. Of course not. Why would she be?

'I'm fine. Totally fine. Now if you'll excuse me, I need to finish loading these things into the truck so I can go set up our booth and make lots and lots of money.' She tried and failed to smooth her hair down.

Grandma June gave her a worried smile. 'Okay, but you know where to find me if you need me.'

'Thanks, Grandma.'

Grandma patted the old cardboard box. 'And don't spend too much time in the past, Daisy. Sometimes you need to focus on moving forward.'

Moving forward. Right. Easier said than done.

When Daisy emerged from the shop again with her next armload of supplies, Jeanie was out front on Main Street, as well, giving Logan instructions for his return trip.

'I'm going to need at least two folding tables, tablecloths, cups, napkins, at least three of the coffee carafes…' She listed things off on her fingers.

Logan nodded after each item. 'We can fit it all.' He patted the side of the truck. 'Let me get Daisy's stuff dropped off and I'll come down to the café.'

Jeanie planted a kiss on his cheek. 'Perfect.' She smiled at Daisy. 'Excited about today?'

'Excited to sell a lot of flower crowns.'

Jeanie laughed. 'I'm sure you will.'

Daisy sure hoped so. She needed these sales for next month's rent.

'You want to come down for a cup of coffee? Hazel's meeting me.' Jeanie gestured down the street. It was still quiet. The festivities didn't start until late afternoon, but the food trucks were already rolling in.

'No, thanks. I should get over to the town square and set up.'

'Okay, see you later.' Jeanie waved and headed back to the café. Daisy locked up the shop and hopped into the passenger side of Logan's truck.

He closed the truck bed and climbed in beside her. It would be a short drive, but it was much easier than trying to haul all this stuff in multiple trips in her car.

'Thanks for the ride.'

'No problem.'

Daisy knew Logan wasn't much for small talk, so she was surprised when he cleared his throat and said, 'I really respect what you're doing.'

'Uh...'

'I mean, coming back to town and not letting everyone rattle you with this curse bullshit.'

'Is that how I'm coming across? As not rattled?' Daisy gave a disbelieving laugh.

Logan chuckled. 'Just hang in there. They'll move on to something else soon enough.'

'Thanks, that means a lot.'

He pulled into the parking lot near the town hall. Everyone was setting up in the area surrounding the fountain.

He nodded.

Apparently, that was the end of the conversation.

'Right. Well, thanks again,' Daisy said, hopping down from the truck. Logan helped her unload and then headed back to pick up the supplies for Jeanie's café booth.

All around her, other vendors were setting up, getting ready for the hustle and bustle of the crowds later today. Daisy spotted George hanging The Gingerbread Bakery sign over at Annie's table. Bennett and Mac were dumping out a load of firewood in the grassy area beyond the square for the night's bonfires, and Kira was helping the committee decorate the stage.

Daisy set up her tables and her tent to protect her from the sun. She covered the tables in dark purple tablecloths and hung the homemade sign she had made with Iris.

The Daisy Chain Flower Shop it proudly read. Iris had added vines and flowers around the letters, and at her mother's insistence, Daisy had been liberal with the glitter.

It looked good.

She was going to do this.

She was going to save this damn shop and make her ancestors proud.

For now, she kept the crowns in her coolers to keep them from wilting. Her mother would be by soon to help her lay them out. Kira may have been worried about the lack of warmth in May in New England, but it was shaping up to be a beautifully sunny day.

A day filled with possibilities.

Maybe Daisy was excited about more than selling crowns.

Maybe she was excited to celebrate a new season.

Maybe she was ready for one.

Chapter Twenty-One

It was the afternoon of the Beltane festival and Elliot was standing inside Daisy's tiny apartment, waiting for her to be ready to leave. And while he and Daisy had been hanging out together for a few weeks now, today still felt like a big deal. The entire town would be there, and Daisy needed to show off her beautiful flower crowns as well as her totally real, and not at all cursed, relationship.

And that was why Elliot was already sweating.

That and the fact that he hadn't been able to stop thinking about *touching* Daisy.

About how she'd gasped his name.

About how he wanted to do it again.

About how he'd never been harder in his entire life.

About how he nearly confessed his very real feelings for her.

About how he was absolutely going to get hurt if they continued down this path.

Not to mention how Daisy had totally called him on his

bullshit, and now he couldn't stop wondering if he really was just repeating his old pattern. Was it possible he'd gotten attached to Daisy just because she'd talked to him first? Was he really that pathetic?

A woman talks to him and he's ready to marry her.

Could it have been anyone?

He was a mess, and he was characteristically nervous about this date.

It was one thing to talk to the book club or be spotted together at the beach, but a Dream Harbor festival was no joke. He'd briefly popped into last year's Midsummer festival, and he hadn't lasted more than a half hour. It had been packed, and he'd been completely out of his depth.

After today, Daisy would probably be wishing she'd picked a better fake partner, one who was more adept at being charming and chatty. One who would sell her story better and help her save her shop.

'Okay, all set.' Daisy emerged from her bathroom, dressed and ready to go. As soon as he saw her, his earlier question was immediately answered.

No, it could not have been anyone.

Daisy was different.

'You're not wearing black.' A brilliant thing to say. He was nailing this already.

Daisy glanced down at her dress like she'd forgotten what she'd put on. She ran a hand over the velvety material. The dress was long with billowy sleeves, and her black boots peeked out from the bottom.

'I thought dark purple was more … festive.' There was a hesitation in her answer, a touch of nerves. It made him feel better to know he wasn't the only one feeling that way.

'I like it.'

She smiled, tucking a piece of hair behind her ear. 'It's a pagan festival, might as well go with a witchy vibe.'

'It suits you.'

Daisy laughed.

'I mean…' He winced. Shit. Was it bad to say she looked like a witch? He meant she looked like a sexy witch. 'I just meant you look really … beautiful.'

Daisy's laughter faded and as she held his gaze, he felt his cheeks pinken. 'Thank you.'

'You're welcome.'

'Should we go?' Daisy asked, and he realized he was just staring at her stupidly and completely blocking the door.

The door he had pinned her against only a few days earlier.

Elliot swallowed hard.

'Yes. Definitely.'

He followed Daisy out of the apartment and through the shop to Main Street, cursing himself the whole way for being so damn awkward. Daisy had wanted to change after setting up this morning, and he offered to walk with her back to the festival. He would be by Daisy's side while she sold her flowers, and then later, they'd get to enjoy the festival together.

It all sounded very simple, but the whole plan hinged on him surviving that long and not making a fool of himself sooner rather than later. This day was reminding him of every reason he avoided dating. The main one being he was bad at it.

'So, what should I expect at this festival?' he asked, grasping at something to say to fill the silence, even though he'd been at nearly every town meeting and knew perfectly well what was planned for the day.

The street was already busy with townsfolk heading toward the square. After another long winter and a rather dreary spring, it was the perfect day for a festival celebrating the coming of summer. It was warm and sunny, the air scented with flowers and the sea. The effervescent mood of the crowd was contagious and Elliot felt himself getting caught up in the excitement. Neighbors waved and greeted each other as they came out of the café with iced teas and lemonades complete with edible flowers floating on top of the ice. Even the drinks were festive. A few people waved and smiled at Elliot, and he couldn't help his flush of surprise and pleasure. They probably only said hello because he was with Daisy, but it was nice to finally feel like he belonged here. At least a little bit.

A little girl ran past them chased by another. They were each holding balloons that flapped wildly behind them, squealing with delight as they ran.

'Cece, Ivy! Slow down!' Noah called, appearing beside Daisy and Elliot, flushed and out of breath.

'Hey, guys,' he said.

Hazel hurried to his side. 'We're losing them again.'

'Nah,' Noah assured her, scanning the crowd. 'That's why I strapped those balloons to their wrists. See, there they go.' He pointed to the two pink balloons floating ahead of them.

'Your nieces are back in town?' Daisy asked with a laugh and Noah smiled.

'They are back. And I told my sisters that Hazel and I

would take them to the festival while they take the night off.'

'You're a good brother,' Elliot said.

Noah shrugged. 'Making up for lost time.'

'We should probably catch up to them,' Hazel said, pulling him along. 'See you two later!' They disappeared into the rest of the commotion.

'So, Beltane...' Elliot said when the silence had dragged on for too long. Or what felt like too long anyway.

'Just your typical pagan festival,' Daisy said as though every town hosted an annual Beltane festival. 'Bonfires and maypoles and all that.'

'A bit syncretic,' Elliot said as they made their way down Main toward the town square and the green space beside it where most of today's activities would take place.

'Syncretic?'

'Uh ... melding practices from different cultures. The maypole has Germanic roots while the bonfire tradition has Celtic origins.'

Daisy stopped and looked up at him with a curious smile. 'You should have brought that up at a town meeting.'

'I wouldn't dare.'

Daisy laughed, some of their earlier awkwardness fading.

'I never met anyone who uses words like syncretic before. Or knew about the origins of maypoles,' she said as they continued their walk, the crowd thickening as they got closer.

'The symbolism of the maypole is still debated, you know,' Elliot said, rambling on as though Daisy cared about maypoles. Rambling about history happened to be a nervous habit. One he'd bored several blind dates with. But he couldn't seem to stop himself. It was either talking about the historical significance of the maypole or rehashing their fuck-buddy conversation. History was much safer. 'Some scholars think the shape represents the Earth's axis, while others think it's more likely a representation of a sacred tree.' They were approaching the town square now, where the maypole rose from the lawn in front of the town hall decorated with ribbons and greenery. 'Of course, some people think it's just a big phallic symbol.'

Daisy stopped in her tracks and stared up at the maypole, while Elliot wished for the power to go back in time and shut the hell up.

And then she started giggling, beautiful, fizzy, delighted giggles.

'That's a really big phallic symbol,' she said, laughter still bubbling out of her and Elliot had to join her, his own laughter easing the sting of embarrassment in his gut. If Daisy found his rambling funny, then he'd happily keep talking.

'Yep.'

'You are just full of interesting facts,' she said, turning away from the pole and heading toward her booth.

'Sorry. I tend to spew facts when I'm nervous.'

'You're nervous?'

'A bit, yeah.'

She stopped, having arrived at her designated spot.

'Why are you nervous?'

'I don't want to let you down.'

'You won't.'

Elliot scoffed. 'Don't be so sure. There's a reason I've only ever dated one woman. I'm not very good at this.'

'You've been good all along. Today won't be any different. Unless you'd rather leave … that's totally fine…'

'No!' The word was too loud, too abrupt, but Daisy smiled.

'Okay.'

'I want to stay. I want to help sell these…' He gestured to the table where Daisy's crowns were laid out, looking at them for the first time. 'These are … incredible,' he said, letting the awe for her work fill his voice. Delicate crowns with flowers in every color and shape were laid out in tidy rows. Some had ribbons trailing off the back, others were clearly designed for kids: smaller and covered in glitter; Elliot could imagine them making some little people very happy. Daisy had created magic.

'Thanks. I missed a few nights of sleep to finish them.'

'They're beautiful.'

'Thank you.' She was gazing at him, her cheeks pink and her smile warm and soft, and his determination not to let her down was renewed. If this town needed to see her in a loving relationship before they could trust her with their weddings again, then that was what they were going to see. He could put all his own confusion and feelings aside. Because Daisy was *talented*. She was so damn good at what she did, and this town should appreciate her for that. They should be lined up around the block for the chance to buy a little piece of the joy that Daisy made with flowers.

Fools.

He stepped closer, wishing he could touch her. She'd worked a few small braids into her hair, and he couldn't resist running one through his fingers. Daisy's breath hitched.

'We can do this,' he whispered, leaning toward her and she nodded, her eyes still locked on his.

'Daisy?' A familiar voice broke through the moment. 'Hey, is that you?'

Daisy's eyes widened. 'You have got to be kidding me,' she mumbled.

'David?' Elliot asked, not pulling away, not looking away. Maybe if they stayed very still David would just disappear.

'Yes. What is he doing here?' she asked, and her eyes were so full of pain at this reminder of her past that Elliot couldn't help it when he leaned forward and brushed his lips against hers. It was instinct. To protect her. To make that pain go away. To tell David that Daisy didn't need him anymore. Didn't want him.

Was it a bit territorial? Maybe. But he liked Daisy too much to care.

She stilled and then softened, pressing her mouth to his in a sweet kiss that stole his breath. And David did disappear. Everything did. It was only them. It was only Daisy's lips, soft and warm, and her hands gripping at the front of his shirt, and her hair slipping through his fingers. Nothing else mattered. Nothing else existed.

Until of course, it did.

She pulled away after only a moment, her gaze flicking to his, a small smile on her lips before she turned to face David and Hailey.

'Oh, you're back in town,' she said, her smile

transforming into a fake one. However she had felt about the kiss that was still vibrating through Elliot's body, she reached out now and grabbed his hand like she needed the support.

'Yeah, Hailey saw the signs for Beltane last time we were here and was just dying to come back,' David said, his gaze shifting from Daisy to Elliot. Something about the way he looked at them, like he couldn't quite fathom how Daisy had managed to move on from him, made Elliot want to punch him in the face.

'How nice,' Daisy said through clenched teeth.

'I'd love to buy a crown,' Hailey said, ignoring the tension.

'Of course.' Daisy snapped into business mode, dropping his hand and moving around the table to help Hailey with her purchase. Other people were starting to notice the stand and were milling around discussing which color combination they liked best. Elliot realized he should probably make himself useful and came around the table to help.

A man and a woman stepped up to browse, and Elliot was about to ask if he could get them something, but the man ignored him completely.

'Crazy Daisy!' he said with a laugh. 'I was wondering if you'd be here.'

Daisy looked up in horror from where she was helping Hailey try on crowns. 'I cannot believe this,' she muttered before saying, 'Matty, hey.'

Matty? This man who smelled like patchouli and was sporting a messy man bun could not possibly be who Elliot thought he was...

'Hey, babe,' Matty said, nudging the woman beside him. 'This is my ex-wife!'

Oh, dear God.

'The one you married in high school? How sweet!' the woman cooed, picking up a crown and trying it on. Her long hair hung nearly to her waist and her flowy skirts reached to her ankles. A perfect match for Matty, if you asked Elliot. Now if they could just...

Matty laughed. 'We weren't *in* high school.'

'Yeah, it was a full week after graduation,' Daisy added dryly while Hailey looked on in amusement.

'So, how've you been, Daze?' Matthew asked, all smiles and good cheer. Elliot wondered how often they ran into each other. Daisy seemed surprised to see him but not like it was out of the realm of possibilities. 'You still engaged to that banker guy?'

David cleared his throat. 'I'm the banker guy, actually, and Daisy and I aren't together anymore.'

'Oh, shit! Sorry to hear that, man.'

Daisy, for her part, looked like she wanted to crawl under the table, so of course that was when Elliot's mother appeared on the scene.

'Elliot, there you are!' his mom called, hustling over to the table. 'It's so crowded,' she went on, completely disregarding the conversation that was already in progress. 'Is this Daisy? It's so nice to finally meet you!' She reached out and grabbed Daisy's hand as Daisy stood in shocked silence.

'Wait,' Matthew said, far too invested in everything going on at the booth. Couldn't he just get his damn flower crown and leave? 'Who's this?'

'That's Elliot, Daisy's new boyfriend,' Hailey contributed helpfully as she switched crowns, taking selfies of herself with each one, apparently to help her make a final decision.

'And who are you?' Elliot's mom asked.

'I'm Matthew, Daisy's ex-husband. And this is David, Daisy's ex-fiancé.'

Sweet lord. What had Elliot done in his life to deserve this? Certainly, Daisy didn't deserve it.

'Really?' His mother's eyes had gone wide.

Daisy groaned quietly beside him.

And Elliot couldn't stand for that.

'Right. Hi, Mom. This is Daisy, she's lovely and perfect. These two men are her past and have come to buy flowers, which I think they were just finishing up.'

He looked pointedly between Matthew and David. He'd had enough of this bizarre episode of *This is Your Life*. These two had to go.

'Yeah, we were just leaving,' Matthew said, giving Elliot a big smile. 'I like him,' he whispered to Daisy before taking his crown and his girl and leaving.

David didn't bother addressing Elliot, but told Daisy he would see her around, which Elliot found somewhat ominous, before taking Hailey and her multiple crowns (she apparently planned on changing 'vibes' throughout the day) and leaving. Thank the pagan gods of exes for that.

'Ugh, thank you,' Daisy whispered hastily before turning back to his mom. 'Hi, Mrs. Parker, it's so nice to meet you.'

His mom smiled, some of her earlier hesitation slowly leaving, although Elliot could still see the worry around her eyes. He hadn't exactly mentioned Daisy's past relationships. It hadn't seemed relevant at the time, but he knew how his mother's mind worked. If Daisy had so many failed attempts, what were the odds this one wouldn't end badly, too? As though Elliot didn't have an entire failed marriage of his own. As though he wasn't perfectly capable of ruining this relationship on his own.

Probably not something he'd be pointing out anytime soon, though.

'It's nice to meet you, too, Daisy.' His mother glanced down at the flower crowns spread across the table. 'These are just beautiful.'

Daisy beamed. 'Thank you.' The gratitude at the change in topics from her exes was clear in her voice.

'Hey, Mom, why don't you get us a table by the food trucks, and we can grab something to eat. I'll be over in a second and then Daisy can join us when she's done here.'

His mother's knowing gaze flicked between the two of them; he was obviously trying to get rid of her. But she agreed and strode over to the cluster of picnic tables, her mission to secure one now clear.

Daisy turned to face him as soon as she was out of earshot. 'I'm so sorry. That was horrible timing!'

'It's fine.'

'It's not fine!' she groaned. 'Fake-dating me was supposed to help get your mom off your back; now she's just going to worry about what kind of woman you're dating.'

'Daisy, you're the perfect woman.' That was probably too much to confess, but Daisy was too busy spiraling to notice.

'Nothing like seeing all your past mistakes lined up in front of you to really solidify what a hot mess your love life is.'

'Hey.' The word was sharp and maybe a little too scolding, but Daisy's gaze snapped to his, a pink flush working its way up her cheeks. 'You are *not* a hot mess. There is nothing wrong with having a past, Daisy. So you made a few bad choices. So what? So does everybody. This town has you believing that there is something wrong with you but there isn't. You are fucking amazing. And anyone that doesn't see that can fuck right the hell off.'

Her eyes widened in shock.

Maybe he'd gone too far, but he couldn't stand it, couldn't stand the way she carried these mistakes with her, like it didn't take two people to end a relationship. Like she needed to be punished for having her heart broken.

'You just said fuck,' she whispered. 'Twice.'

He huffed a laugh. 'It felt necessary.'

Daisy's lips twitched. 'Is that why you kissed me before? Because David was watching?'

'I don't care if David was watching. Look, I know what I said the other night, but I kissed you because I wanted to.'

'Oh.' The smile that broke across her face was enough to convince him that kissing her was the right decision. Even if he still didn't know if he could trust his feelings for her, even if he still wondered if she was right about him replacing Leigh with the first woman who paid him any attention.

But that kiss didn't feel like Daisy was just a placeholder.

It had been a very long time since Elliot had had a first

kiss but nothing in his memories could compare to the feeling of Daisy's lips on his.

'Now, I'd like to buy two flower crowns, please,' he said and Daisy raised a brow. 'One of those purple and yellow ones, and that one with the daisies.' He pointed to the ones he wanted, and Daisy handed them over, an amused expression on her face.

He placed the purple one on her head. 'Goes with your dress,' he said, letting his fingers brush her cheek after he put the crown in place. He put the other on his own head. 'Daisies are my favorite flower,' he said, defiantly, ready to fight anyone who dared argue with him about the superiority of the bloom.

Daisy reached up and adjusted the crown, her body grazing his. Elliot bit back a groan.

'Since when?'

'Since now.'

She held his gaze a breath longer and maybe if she hadn't told him she only wanted him for sex, and if he hadn't told her he couldn't do this without feelings, and if there wasn't a line of people waiting for their own crowns, maybe then he would have kissed her again.

But the moment passed.

And Daisy got back to work.

Chapter Twenty-Two

'I always heard baking soda is best.'

Daisy smiled at his mom. The two had been swapping tips for the past half hour. His mother had already passed along her recipe for banana bread and her secret for getting grass stains out of denim. 'Baking soda is fine but diluting vinegar in water with a tablespoon or two of sugar really works great for keeping cut flowers fresh longer.'

'Well, that is good to know!'

'Getting a lot of flowers from your boyfriends, Mom?' Elliot had meant it as a joke, but the way his mother's face turned pink, told him he might have hit on some truth.

'That is none of your business,' she said, smoothing down her long skirt. Funny how *his* love life was everyone's business, but his mother's was a secret. Daisy tossed him an amused smile.

She had sold out of flower crowns in the first hour of the festival, and she hadn't stopped beaming since. Everyone wanted one to wear for the rest of the festivities so now the sea of people around them were adorned by Daisy's creations.

Then she joined him and his mother, and after their initial awkward meeting, the two had gotten along great. So well, actually, that Elliot had the pleasure of just quietly listening to them talk without having to contribute much, which was one of his favorite ways to spend an afternoon. And his mom provided the perfect buffer to any lingering sexual tension.

They had just finished watching a group of small children attempt to do the maypole dance. Despite Miss Janet's assurances at the last town planning meeting, it did *not* go well. She ended up having to cut one of the little boys free from the ribbons twisted around him, while he giggled manically, and the crowd held its breath. It was very dramatic.

At the moment, Elliot and Daisy and his mom were eating funnel cake and waiting for the crowning of the May Queen. It seemed most of the town was crowded together in front of the makeshift stage in front of the town hall. The sun was setting, and strings of white lights around the stage had just flickered to life.

The finalists were a middle-aged man named Andy, Gladys, from the diner and Kira. Bennett cheered wildly from the front row as all three contestants smiled and waved to the crowd. Anyone in town was allowed to enter, and these three had made it to the final round.

Daisy nudged him with her elbow. 'Did you place any bets?'

Elliot chuckled. 'Not after I got called out for voting for Gladys.'

The mayor stepped onto the stage.

'This is so exciting,' Elliot's mom whispered.

Daisy giggled as she pulled off another piece of funnel cake and popped it in her mouth. Elliot's attention snagged on the powdered sugar that dusted her bottom lip. He wanted to kiss her again. And again and again ... possibly forever. But he would settle for tonight. He knew Daisy didn't want forever.

No more relationships.

But she had offered ... other things.

She ran her tongue over her lip, cleaning off the sugar and leaving behind her glistening pink mouth. God, he wanted her. Again, the intensity of that feeling threw him off-guard. Had he ever wanted anyone the way he wanted Daisy?

'And the winner is...' Mayor Kelly paused dramatically while the school band played an actual drumroll. Elliot tried desperately to pull his mind out of the gutter. But what was it that Jack said about Beltane? It was when everyone *hooked up*.

Could Elliot survive hooking up with Daisy? The other night had nearly killed him. What did he think would happen this time? He would walk away unscathed? Impossible.

'Andy Sinclair! Congrats, Andy!'

Andy beamed as the mayor put the May Queen sash over his head and replaced his flower crown with a bejeweled plastic tiara.

'Yes!' Daisy cheered beside him. 'I just won fifty bucks!'

'That's wonderful!' Elliot's mother said. 'Doesn't he look lovely?' She smiled up at the stage where Andy was doing a victory lap, and Kira and Gladys were hugging and congratulating him.

'I told you,' Daisy said, turning to Elliot. 'You enter enough of these things and you're bound to win eventually.'

'I'll keep that in mind for next year,' he said, just so he could hear Daisy laugh again. She didn't disappoint.

'I want to thank our contestants. The runners up will receive gift cards to Mac's pub to drown their sorrows,' Mayor Kelly said over the din of the crowd and Kira cheered. 'Thanks to everyone who voted and donated, we were able to raise almost two and a half thousand dollars for the children's hospital.'

After everyone was done congratulating themselves, the crowd began to disperse, heading to the food trucks to refuel or to Mac's booth for drinks.

'Well, this has been fun,' Elliot's mom said. 'But I'm beat. I'll leave the nighttime festivities to you two.'

When everyone hooks up.

Elliot's face flushed hot, and he was thankful the sun had gone down.

'It was so nice to meet you,' Daisy said, giving his mom a big hug, who looked at him over Daisy's shoulder.

I like her, she mouthed.

He liked her, too, and that was the whole problem.

He'd nearly forgotten that half of his motivation in fake-dating Daisy was to get his mother to stop worrying about him. Mission accomplished. His mother could officially return to Florida believing Elliot was happily paired up.

She could imagine him out on the town with Daisy instead of home alone. At the very least, he'd given his mom some peace and, hopefully, bought himself some time between her visits.

'It was such a fun afternoon. Thank you for letting me crash your date,' his mom said, giving Daisy one last squeeze.

'I'm just glad we got to do it,' Daisy said.

'Me, too. I'm heading home next week so I'm glad we got this time.'

'I'll call you tomorrow, Mom,' Elliot said, giving her a hug before she walked back to her rental car with one last wave over her shoulder.

'She's sweet,' Daisy said.

'Yes, she is.'

'I think we convinced her.'

Convinced her that this fake thing was real. But Elliot didn't need to pretend. He hadn't been pretending for a long time. Maybe ever.

Maybe Daisy didn't believe that he could fall in love with her. Maybe she thought he was following old patterns, but every second spent with her proved Daisy's theory wrong. And what was he supposed to do? Go date a bunch of other women just so he could come back to Daisy and tell her he wanted her for real, that he didn't like her just because she grabbed him that day in the flower shop?

'Should we head to the bonfires?' Daisy asked.

'Sure.'

She took his hand, and they weaved through the throngs of people, and Elliot wished he could relax. He wished he could hook up or make out or whatever the hell other people did just for the fun of it. He'd replayed their fuck-buddy conversation a million times in his head since that night. He was sure he should have handled it differently, should have given Daisy what she wanted, settled for just sex. But just *kissing* Daisy this afternoon had made him want to drop to his knees and promise to be by her side forever. He wished he could detach from his feelings, but he couldn't.

He *liked* Daisy.

More than he should. More than he planned on. And in true Elliot fashion he was blowing this whole thing up way bigger than it needed to be.

And now that they'd made it to the night when everyone hooked up, he didn't know if he could go through with it. At least not without accidentally proclaiming his feelings for Daisy and scaring her away for good.

Chapter Twenty-Three

Elliot's flower crown was askew. It sat crooked on his head as he stared into the Beltane bonfire. His dark hair contrasted sharply with the white petals of the daisies, and his cheeks were pink from the warmth of the fire. When he turned to look at her, his eyes were bright with excitement behind his glasses, their lenses reflecting the flames.

Daisy was going to reach up and fix the crown, but she liked it this way, a little crooked, a little messy. Elliot looked playful and undone. He looked like maybe she'd found him dancing in the forest, celebrating the coming of summer, lush and full of life.

'This is fun,' he said, gesturing to where townsfolk were walking and skipping and dancing between the two fires, some with their pets in tow, to protect them in the coming year. 'I mean, historically speaking it's not exactly accurate. I don't think the ancient Celts cared much about blessing their pet iguanas, and I'm pretty sure this "May wine" is just sangria...' He lifted his plastic cup and some of the wine sloshed over the rim. Daisy wondered just how many refills he'd had. 'But it's really *fun*.'

Daisy smiled at him in agreement. They were set up on an old blanket she'd thrown in her bag this afternoon. Plenty of other groups and couples were seated on the grass as well, with the two fires in the center. It was fully dark now, the sky above them dotted with stars, and the fingernail crescent moon hung just above the treetops.

She leaned against Elliot's side, and he put his arm around her, surrounding her with his warmth and she didn't know anymore what she was doing but she knew she liked Elliot's arm around her. She liked how he looked at her and how he kissed her. She liked how he made her feel safe and wanted.

Daisy liked a lot of things about Elliot, but she didn't want to add him to her list of mistakes. She didn't want to run into him a year from now and have to call him an ex (would she call him that if this whole thing stayed *fake*?). Running into David and Matthew simultaneously had been a timely reminder of how much she'd screwed up her love life in the past.

And she'd meant what she told Elliot when she'd proposed a friends-with-benefits situation. She was too tired to try again. She was just coming back to life after a year of mourning her last failed relationship.

Falling into another one was a mistake.

Right?

She sighed and Elliot held her closer.

She leaned against him and tried not to think about the future. Things never seemed to work out for her there.

Maybe she wouldn't think about how this thing ended. Because all things *did* end. Daisy had been sure she'd found this before, this feeling, this connection with another person, and she'd been wrong every time. That was what she'd tried to tell Elliot the night he made her come harder than either of her exes ever had. But orgasms alone didn't make for lasting relationships.

She couldn't put her heart on the line again.

But as she sat snuggled close to Elliot, she couldn't help but wonder: had being with David ever felt like this? Had Matthew ever made her feel safe? She didn't know anymore.

Beyond the fires, on the stage, Cliff's Midnight Dreamers started up, playing Celtic music on fiddles and drums, and was that Norm on the accordion?

'They're pretty good,' Elliot said, his mouth close to her ear, his breath warm on her skin.

'They really are!'

Alex from the bookstore was wailing on the fiddle and soon Cliff joined in with a surprisingly deep and soothing singing voice. The crowd was up and dancing, abandoning their blankets and gleefully grabbing partners to swing wildly around in a dance that no one really knew, but everyone pretended to.

'Should we dance?' Elliot whispered against her ear.

'Only if you want to.'

'Do *you* want to dance, Daisy?' he asked and he sounded looser than usual, sillier. She could hear the laughter in his voice. Maybe that May wine was working its magic.

Maybe she should give in. Just for the night.

After all, Elliot wasn't asking for marriage. He was just asking for a dance.

'Yes,' she said, and Elliot stood and reached down for her hand. She took it and he pulled her up, laughing when she ended up crushed tight to his chest. They stood like that for a moment, with her pressed against him and his grin lighting up the night, and then he grabbed her hand and twirled her round.

Her giggles joined the rising tide of laughter and cheering around them. She spotted Noah nearby, spinning a niece with each hand. The girls giggled as they spun. Hazel and Jeanie skipped together between the fire with a disgruntled Casper between them. As soon as they were through, the cat jumped down from Jeanie's arms and sprinted into the darkness.

'At least you're protected from evil spirits now!' Jeanie called after him.

'He is the evil spirit,' Hazel said with a laugh, circling back to Noah's side.

'More wood, boys!' Jeanie called, and Logan and Bennett brought over a few more armloads to add to the fires. As soon as Bennett was done, Kira tugged him away into the shadows, a cheeky grin on her face.

Iris waved to Daisy as she and Archer made their way through the dancers. Olive was perched on Archer's shoulder with her flower crown still on her head, even if it was a little more squished than it had been when she picked it out. Daisy knew Owen was safe at home with a babysitter.

'Bye, Daisy!' Olive called. 'Thank you for my flowers!'

'You're very welcome,' Daisy said, waving to the little

girl. Archer grinned, grabbing Iris's hand as they wandered off into the darkness beyond the fire and toward home.

A home filled with love and babies…

Something Daisy always thought she'd have.

She shook her head, spinning and dancing with Elliot until his crown was even more crooked, and Daisy was out of breath. He pulled her close again.

'Is that the mailman and the lady who sold me my house making out over there?' he asked, nodding his chin in the direction of the couple in question.

'It sure is.'

'And is that Crystal who makes me my coffee every morning riding away on the back of a very large man?'

Daisy giggled. 'That's her fiancé. Football player.'

'Wow.'

'And, oh, my God,' he whisper-shouted. 'There goes Jack and Gabe, sneaking off together!'

'We told you! It's Beltane. It makes everyone … frisky.' She tried to say it like she was joking but his gaze snagged on hers and she was sure if it was light enough, she would see the red creeping to the tips of his ears.

I want you, Daisy.

He'd said that, hadn't he?

'Right,' he said, his voice hoarse from laughing and dancing. 'You mentioned that.'

'It doesn't mean we have to … you've made your feelings about a casual hook-up very clear. You've done plenty just by coming with me. If dancing at Beltane doesn't break the curse, then I don't know what will.'

'You're not cursed, Daisy,' he whispered, tucking her hair behind her ear. 'You're perfect. Just in case I haven't been clear about that.' He cupped her face in his hands so that when he leaned down to kiss her, she was held captive, trapped in his grasp, *safe* in his hands.

His lips were soft and sweet, and he tasted like wine and fruit. Daisy wrapped her arms around his neck and let her fingers toy with the longer hair at the nape of his neck. She let herself melt into him and sway to the music. She let herself surrender to the magic of the night.

Everything was warm and glowing. The music vibrated through her, keeping her blood humming and her body calling out for more.

Elliot groaned against her lips when she pressed her body to his, and she sighed in return when his arms wrapped around her, holding her tight.

'Maybe I was wrong about what I said the other day,' he said, his eyes dark when he pulled away to look at her. 'Maybe we should…'

She was about to say they absolutely *should*, lust once again winning out over rationality, when they were interrupted by a teasing voice.

'Don't you two look cozy,' Annie said, carrying a tray of drinks. 'More May wine?' Mac's pub was providing the libations for the evening and, apparently, after selling out of her baked goods, Annie was helping as a server.

'I'll take another,' Elliot said, grabbing a cup and pulling out his phone to Venmo the pub.

'I'm good.' Daisy figured one of them should keep their senses about them, or she really would end up knocked up by the end of the night.

Annie smiled at her, her blonde brows rising just slightly, just enough to make Daisy's cheeks heat.

'You guys having fun?' she asked.

'I'm having a great time,' Elliot said, slinging an arm over Daisy's shoulder and Annie's smile grew.

'Great. Glad to hear it.'

'Hey, Annabelle, you selling drinks or chatting?' Mac called from the drink tent.

'Hey, Macaulay, call me that one more time and see what happens,' Annie yelled back and Mac laughed.

'Just get your cute butt back here,' he called again, eliciting some hoots and hollers from the crowd.

Annie flipped him off and the crowd cheered.

'So, it's going well between you two?' Daisy asked with a laugh.

'Very well. I remind Mac every day how lucky he is to be with me,' Annie grinned. 'I should continue my rounds. Enjoy!' She walked off, quickly selling off her wares and then heading back to Mac. He scooped her up and kissed her in front of the whole waiting line and Annie didn't look mad at all.

Beltane magic.

Maybe it could work for Daisy, too.

Elliot was drunk. That much had become increasingly clear over the last hour of the festival, and now as he and Daisy meandered back to the flower shop, it was obvious. Main Street was empty save for a few stragglers heading back to their cars or walking the few blocks home, which was for the best considering drunk Elliot apparently liked to sing. Loudly.

'*Daisy, Daisy, give me your answer do,*' he crooned as they walked. '*I'm half-crazy all for the love of you…*'

Daisy hadn't heard this song since her grandpa used to sing it to her when she was little. Despite the curious stares from a few people walking across the street from them, Daisy smiled.

'*It won't be a stylish marriage. I can't afford a carriage. But you'll look sweet upon the seat of my bicycle built for two.*' Elliot threw his arms out on that last note, really going for it, and he got a smattering of applause from the others on the street and one call for an encore.

'Do you know that one?' he asked, ignoring his new fans.

'I do, actually.'

'It's a good one.'

'Very good.'

'It's about you.'

'Is it?'

'It should be.'

'Okay, Elliot,' she said with a laugh, steering him toward the shop with one arm around his waist. He slung his arm over her shoulder.

'You're so pretty,' he said.

'Thank you.'

'No, I mean it. You're the prettiest girl in the entire town.'

Daisy bit down on a smile. Sure, he was drunk, but it was still nice to hear.

'Thank you, Elliot.'

'Probably in the entire world.'

'I think you're getting carried away.'

She could feel him shrug.

'I don't think so. I think you're the prettiest girl in the entire world.' He started humming 'Bicycle Built For Two' again, and she realized there was no way he was driving home. Or walking for that matter. He was barely putting one foot in front of the other as it was.

'Hey, Elliot, where do you live?'

'Here.'

'I know, but like what's your address?'

This seemed to stump him. He told her several addresses, none of which were in Dream Harbor. He was very insistent on a particular one in New York that she was sure must have been his house with his ex, and she wasn't about to point that out. Not right now. Not when Elliot's version of being sloppy drunk involved serenades and compliments.

'I think you need to spend the night.'

His brows rose comically high above his glasses. 'A sleepover?'

'Yep.'

He groaned a little bit. 'I'm sorry I drank too much fairy wine,' he said, leaning into her as she unlocked the door and she tried not to laugh at his new name for the wine he'd been drinking all night.

'That's okay. That stuff packs a punch.' They walked through the darkened shop, Elliot's arm still draped over her shoulder. He wasn't putting his weight on her, but he was definitely letting her guide him past the flowers and the mess she'd left behind in her hurry to get to the festival.

'I was nervous about tonight. About *hooking up*,' he whispered, his breath tickling her ear, confessing.

'I was, too.'

'You were?' He sounded shocked, which almost made Daisy laugh.

'Of course. I didn't know … I mean, I wasn't sure what you would … want. After you said you didn't want to be fuck buddies.'

'Me, neither,' he said with a groan as he plopped onto the end of her bed which, luckily, she had pulled down from the wall before she left. Elliot looked suddenly lost as he took the crown from his head. Daisy moved closer to brush the petals from his hair. He opened his legs, and she stepped between them. His hands found her hips.

'We're not going to hook up tonight,' she said.

'I know.'

'And maybe we should stop calling it that. It sounds ridiculous.'

'Definitely,' he said with a laugh. 'I *am* sorry, Daisy.'

'Don't be. This is for the best. It's … safer this way.'

Elliot let out a sad little moan and rested his head against her clavicle. His fingers gripped her hips tighter, like maybe he didn't think this was for the best at all. Like, maybe he wished they were having an entirely different type of sleepover.

'You're probably right,' he said as she ran her fingers through his hair. It was thick and dark, and she resisted the urge to tug on it. He smelled like wine and fruit and bonfire smoke. She probably did, too. Like summer and desire.

She nearly changed her mind. She nearly pushed him back on her bed and climbed on top of him—consequences, be damned.

But then what?

'I'm definitely right.' She pressed a chaste kiss to his head, forcing herself to do the right thing, the responsible thing. Sleeping with Elliot while he was drunk was morally questionable at best, and definitely not going to lead to a good time. She hadn't been able to convince him that they could sleep together casually while he was sober, she certainly shouldn't try while he was drunk.

She extracted herself from between his legs, his hands lingering on her hips but finally letting go as she pulled away, backing up toward the kitchen.

'You should have some water.' She poured him a glass, needing to put some space between them, which was nearly impossible in this tiny apartment.

'Thanks.' His eyes were dark, his lips wine-stained, and his hair a mess from her fingers as she handed him the glass. She needed to get out of here.

'I'm going to get ready for bed. I'll be right back.' She left him on the bed singing quietly to himself as she went into the bathroom, closing the door behind her, shutting Elliot and his tempting mouth and strong hands out. She gulped a deep breath, repeating to herself that this was for the best. Sex would only make things worse, more complicated, harder to recover from.

But then she thought about the way Elliot's fingers dug into her hip bones, and the way his hair felt in her hands, and the way he kissed her like he meant it—like he had put his whole self into that kiss—and she thought she needed to give Mac a piece of her mind tomorrow about the strength of those damn drinks. Because this did not feel like it was for the best at all. It felt like they'd gotten so close only to have the moment ruined.

She went round and round like that as she did her nightly routine, wanting Elliot while not wanting to get hurt by him. Or to hurt him. Round and round until she had no idea where she'd landed.

By the time her face was washed and moisturized, and her teeth flossed and brushed, and she returned to the bedroom, Elliot was fast asleep. The decision was made for her.

Daisy gently took off his glasses. He sighed a little when she did and she couldn't help but push his hair away from his forehead. Why did he have to look so damn pretty?

She put the glasses on the table and then curled up on her own side of the bed, determined not to touch him anymore, not to make this feeling in her chest worse.

The first night they slept together was turning out just as fake as the rest of their relationship.

But the frustration of not having him for real was building.

Chapter Twenty-Four

Elliot was somewhere between asleep and awake, drunk and sober, when Daisy inched her way to his side of the bed. He draped his arm over her waist and she snuggled in closer, the haze of sleep making it safe. She was a dream in his arms. There was nothing to overthink when she sighed, her breath skimming over his neck. Conscious thought was not an issue when she pressed her lips to his throat. She whimpered when he ran his hands over the curve of her hip, daring to run his fingers under the hem of her sleep shirt, over the soft, warm skin of her belly, over her ribs. She pressed tighter against him, and he was so hard, he ached even in his sleep. If it hadn't been for the jeans he'd fallen asleep in, he was sure he would have come, just from the feel of her next to him, just from the sound of her sleepily whispering his name.

'I'm here,' he murmured back and Daisy settled again, her head tucked right below his chin, her breathing levelling out as she fell deeper asleep.

He kept her close for the rest of the night, his hands on her skin, his lips on hers when she wanted him there, when her needy voice broke through the fog of sleep.

She was the most realistic dream he'd ever had.

He didn't want to wake up.

Someone was humming a familiar song. Elliot cracked open one eye and confirmed what he already knew. This was not his bed. This was not his house. And the person humming was the beautiful and perfect Daisy as she made tea in her tiny kitchen. The woman he'd made a complete ass of himself in front of last night.

It hadn't been a dream. *Shit*.

Elliot really had had too much to drink (like the lightweight that he was) and then *sang* on the streets of Dream Harbor (dear God, kill him now) and then passed out in Daisy's bed (like an absolute loser). He wouldn't be surprised if she never wanted to see him again. At this point, he wasn't really wild about having to see himself.

While he was horrified by the memories of last night, a small part of him was vindicated. *See, he really was bad at dating*! He was right to stay in his home and never leave it and to die alone someday. All perfectly reasonable after last night's antics. His therapist would say these were not productive thoughts, but Dr. Bill wasn't here, now was he?

'*And you'll look sweet upon the seat…*' Daisy sang quietly before fading back to humming. She was singing the song he had last night, the one that always sprang to mind whenever he said her name. She sounded ... happy? Maybe all was not lost.

Time to bite the bullet and face his mistakes.

He opened his eyes and stretched a little before sitting up and facing Daisy, who was now sipping her tea at the kitchen table. The one that was only about a foot from the bed.

'Good morning,' she said with a shy smile. 'Sorry if I woke you.'

'You should have shoved me out of your bed first thing this morning.'

Daisy laughed, and the sound, while usually his favorite, split through his head. He must have winced.

'Hungover?' she asked.

'Very.'

'Whatever Mac was serving, it was definitely stronger than wine.'

Elliot shook his head and then immediately stopped when the room spun. 'Regardless,' he said, squeezing his eyes shut again. 'I'm a grown man. This whole thing is on me. Passing out in your bed? Ranks in my top five most embarrassing moments.'

'Ooh ... now I really want to know the other four.'

He opened his eyes, and Daisy was smiling at him again, teasing like she was willing to forget the whole drunken night. But Elliot wasn't ready to. Not yet, anyway. Not before clearing the air.

'Well, serenading you also ranks pretty high.'

'I feel so honored to take up two spots.'

'You're being far too nice about this.' He found his

glasses on the table and put them on, running his fingers through his hair to put it back in some sort of order.

'It's not that big of a deal, Elliot,' Daisy said, taking another sip of her tea. 'I'm sure half the town is hungover this morning.'

'But how many of them woke up in someone else's bed?'

'I would bet a pretty high percentage, actually. Beltane, remember?'

'Right. Beltane.' Elliot felt his cheeks flush hot at the reminder of why he'd had so much to drink in the first place. He was nervous. He'd wanted the evening to go well for Daisy. He'd wanted to be fun and charming and to give Daisy the boyfriend she deserved. After running into her exes, he'd wanted to prove he was different from them, *better* than them, because at some point he'd started trying to convince Daisy this could be real between them, without even realizing it. Without even meaning to. Probably right around the time he'd had his hand down her pants and his lips on her neck.

Damn it. He was screwing this all up. His feelings had become too much, and he didn't know what to do so he'd gone hard on fairy wine.

Like an idiot.

'Do you want some tea? You'll have to pop down to the café if you want coffee.'

'Tea is fine, thank you.'

Daisy prepared him a mug and handed it to him where he was still perched on the edge of the bed. He just needed to make this right…

'I'm sorry, Daisy.'

'For what?'

Elliot sighed. 'For ruining your night.'

'You didn't ruin it.'

'I drank far too much, inflicted my singing voice on you and then took up three quarters of your bed.'

Daisy rolled her eyes like he was being overdramatic.

'We had a great time at the festival. We ate and drank and danced. It was a perfect evening. Tell me you remember that much.'

'I remember it all.'

'Good.' Daisy crossed her arms over her chest, like she was angry with him now for ruining her memories of their night. 'And then you sang a song that is near and dear to my heart as we walked home together under the stars, and while we didn't end the night in quite the way I had imagined, you kept me warm all night long.'

At her mention of it, more memories flooded in. Memories of him holding Daisy in the night, her soft little body tucked against his, of her sweet sighs brushing across his neck, of the way his hands had roamed over the delicious curves of her—

'You're pink again,' she teased.

'I know.'

'You don't have to be sorry about anything.'

'Okay.' He nodded and she came to stand between his thighs, the way she had last night. But now his mind wasn't hazy from the wine and his hands were sure. He gripped her hips and tugged her closer. 'How did you imagine the night would end?' he asked and Daisy smirked.

'In the traditional Beltane way.'

Elliot swallowed hard, his hands tracing from her hips

to her waist and back again. Time for honesty. Time to tell her what he should have told her yesterday.

'But I'm glad it didn't,' she added, beating him to it.

Elliot's heart dropped with a devastating splash into his still wine-filled stomach.

'You are?'

'Yeah, I mean, better to not confuse things between us. Better to keep this … platonic.'

'Platonic?' Elliot echoed, his newly patched heart breaking all over again. Even though it shouldn't be. Even though none of this should be a surprise.

'Yes, platonic. We're friends, right?'

She looked down at him, studying his face, her fingers raking through his hair again like she'd done last night, and Elliot could cry at the feel of it, of Daisy touching him, of Daisy telling him this was all they would ever be.

He swallowed hard. He couldn't sleep with Daisy and pretend it didn't mean anything, not when he knew it would. He'd told her that and she clearly didn't want it, didn't want him to fall in love with her.

So, friends it was.

Daisy didn't need to know that it was already far too late for him.

'Yeah, of course, friends.'

'We can stop fake-dating if you want,' she said. 'If it would be too weird now.'

'Have you booked any weddings yet?'

She shook her head.

'And what happens if we break up now?' he asked, already knowing the answer. Their break-up would just be more evidence of Daisy's bad luck in love, and all of this would have been for nothing.

Daisy shrugged like it didn't matter to her, when he knew it did. It meant everything to her.

'Okay, so we keep going,' he said, signing himself up for more pain. 'At least until you book a wedding for next year. How about that?'

She bit her bottom lip, thinking, like she wasn't sure this was a good idea.

'And we still have research to do on these lookalike ancestors of ours. So, we might as well let the town think we're together while we do it.'

'True...' She still didn't sound convinced.

'Afraid you won't be able to keep your hands off of me?' he joked.

'I think I can manage,' she said with a smirk, even as her hands moved from his hair to his shoulders. He hadn't let go of her hips. She was still *right* there.

Wouldn't it be easy to tug her forward? To tip back onto the bed and give in?

As easy as running his hand over the tip of a knife and wondering why it hurt.

Daisy shook her head, finally letting her hands fall from his body. 'Okay, so still fake-dating, but maybe with less ... touching.'

Elliot gave her hips one last squeeze before dropping his hands to the bed.

'Sure.'

'Thanks, Elliot.'

'Of course, yeah. I should get going, though. I'm supposed to be at the inn in half an hour.' He glanced down at his rumpled clothes. 'And I clearly need to shower and change.'

'You definitely shouldn't go to work looking like that.'

'I'll text you later?'

'I'd like that.'

The urge to kiss her goodbye was strong enough that he knew he'd just signed on for something that would amount to torture, but he wouldn't change any of it.

Chapter Twenty-Five

'Well, would you look who it is,' Jack greeted him with a smug smile. 'Elliot Parker...'

Elliot stopped at the check-in desk at the inn like he did every morning and grabbed a muffin from the basket. Banana chocolate-chip today. 'Why are you being weird?'

Jack waggled his eyebrows suggestively. 'I heard that you were spotted doing the walk of shame down Main Street this morning.'

Elliot groaned. How was it possible that he had left Daisy's apartment twenty-seven minutes ago and his short walk home in the same clothes he'd worn yesterday had already made its way to Jack.

'Not that there's anything to be shamed about!' Jack went on, fully grinning now like he couldn't wait to get all the details. By lunch, Elliot's night with Daisy would be front-page news. 'How was your night?' Jack asked eagerly, leaning his elbows on the desk. Elliot did not have time for this. He'd barely had time to process everything that had happened in the past twenty-four hours, and he definitely didn't have the brainpower to break it down for Jack right now.

'It was fine. I'm meeting with the contractor in like two minutes, though...' He attempted to keep right on walking past Jack's post, but Jack's words stopped him in his tracks.

'No, you're not.'

'What do you mean? Yes, I am. He's starting the demo next week and we need to discuss—'

'The meeting was canceled.'

'What? Why?' He'd rushed all the way over here and no one bothered to tell him the meeting was canceled? He could have actually used soap in the shower instead of just splashing still-cold water on his body and hopping back out.

Although, after a night spent pressed against Daisy, the cold shower was a must.

'The contractor quit.' Jack winced when he said it, his earlier glee wiped out for the moment.

'He what?!'

'He quit. He called this morning. Apparently, his pregnant wife needs to go on bedrest for the next six weeks and someone needs to take care of his twin toddlers. And that *someone* is him.'

'Shit.'

'I know.'

'How are Mary and Joseph taking it?'

Jack scrunched up his nose. 'They are not pleased. To say the least.'

'Say more.' Elliot ground out. This was not good. They'd already encountered so many delays on this project. Issues with the town board, issues with permits, issues with design changes. Finally, next week they were supposed to demolish the motel-style rooms, and now this.

'They've already stopped booking people in those rooms, and that's a lot of lost business with the summer months coming. To lose out on the revenue *and* not have work being done is not a good thing. They really want this project to move forward. Like now.' All this Elliot already knew and unsurprisingly hearing it from Jack didn't change anything.

'Did they try getting someone else?'

'They called a few other contractors, but none were comfortable with the historic nature of the project. They're all used to tearing things down and starting new. No one has the expertise to preserve the character of the buildings like you planned.' The entire reason that Joseph and Mary hired him, and the Dream Harbor planning board even approved the renovations, was because Elliot had sworn he would maintain the historic charm of the inn. And if the contractor wasn't totally comfortable with that, then the whole thing went down the toilet.

'Shit.'

'You said that already.'

Elliot pinched the bridge of his nose. Unfortunately, the painkiller he took this morning hadn't kicked in yet, and he had a raging headache. And if he wasn't totally desperate, he would never say what he was about to say next. But he was desperate.

'I know someone we can call.' He nearly choked on the words.

'You do?! That's fantastic.'

Elliot groaned. 'I'm not sure it's *fantastic*.'

'Joseph and Mary will just be thrilled to get the project moving. Who is it?'

'My brother.' The last thing Elliot wanted to do was to call Caleb and beg for help. It felt like admitting that his brother was right to worry about him all along. Unfortunately, he also knew his brother was the perfect person for the job. They'd restored plenty of old houses when they worked together. It was their whole thing.

'You have a brother?! Elliot, how do I not know about a brother?'

Elliot shrugged. 'He never came up.' After living in his brother's shadow for years, it was nice to live in a place where no one knew who Caleb Parker was.

Jack narrowed his eyes. 'I have a lot of follow-up questions but obviously you are in no state to answer them. Honestly, what happened last night?'

'Other than drinking too much of that damn May Day wine and passing out in Daisy's bed, nothing really.'

'Oh, no.'

'Made a complete ass of myself.' And he agreed to keep everything *fake* even though his feelings for her were very much not fake.

'Yikes.'

'How did it go with Gabe?' Elliot asked, eager to change the subject.

Jack bit into his bottom lip. 'I'm not sure.'

'Why are you not sure?'

'Well … there was some making out…'

'So that's…' Elliot trailed off, waiting for his friend to fill in the blanks.

'Good? I guess? But now I don't know if it was real or just you know...'

'Beltane?'

'Right.' Jack looked about as miserable as Elliot felt. Apparently, he wasn't the only one swept up in the bizarre pagan rituals of Dream Harbor and left confused the next day.

'Anyone helping you at the desk today?'

'Mabel should be in soon.'

'Good. Let's grab coffee after I get things sorted out with Joseph and Mary. We can drown our sorrows in the caffeinated drink of your choice.'

'Perfect.'

Elliot pulled out his phone as he walked back outside to make his least favorite type of phone call. The one in which he asked his brother for help.

Caleb answered on the first ring. 'You okay?'

Elliot sighed. 'Yes, I'm fine. Why do you assume I'm not?'

'Nobody calls unless it's an emergency.'

'Fair.'

'So, what's going on?'

Elliot steeled himself. 'Are you in the middle of a job?'

'Just finishing one up, actually.'

He could hear the questions in his brother's voice. Elliot hadn't spoken to him since his video chat with Daisy. It was weird for him to be calling. It was weird that he was asking about jobs. None of this was how their relationship worked. At least, not anymore, not since Elliot had abandoned their business and run off to this town to lick his wounds alone.

He sat down heavily on a bench on the front porch of the

inn. The paint was peeling off the railings. A ceiling fan spun lazily overhead. He could see the ocean from their perch on the hill. It could be beautiful here. He was going to make it beautiful here … he just needed…

His damn brother.

'Any chance you want to come down and work on this inn job with me?'

Silence.

It stretched out so long Elliot moved the phone away from his ear, thinking maybe the call had dropped, but then Caleb spoke.

'You want to work together again?'

'Well, the contractor had a family emergency.'

Caleb chuckled, but Elliot could hear the hurt in his voice. 'Oh, got it. You're out of options.'

'That's not it.'

'That is it, and you know it, El. At least be straight with me.'

This conversation was going about as well as the one they had before Elliot left when he'd tried to explain to his brother that he needed to do things on his own for a while, that he needed to prove to himself he could survive without his wife, without his family. Or he'd just wanted to be alone to wallow. He didn't know anymore what his reasons were or if any of them were valid.

And as he sat on the sunny front porch, thinking about what to say, about how to be honest, he couldn't find any good reason to keep his brother at arm's length anymore. Why would he want to? Who wants to survive *alone*? Hadn't his life gotten a thousand times better when he let Daisy in, even if she only wanted friendship. Hadn't he been happier in the last few weeks than in the last few years?

Why then was he still being a dick to his brother?

'Okay, yes,' he started. 'I am out of options, but the real reason I'm asking is that you're the best man for the job and I ... I need your help. I *want* your help with this.'

More silence.

Elliot went on. 'I'm sorry I ditched you and the business we built. It was a shitty thing to do. I was hurting and I ... I just...'

'It's okay, El—'

'It's really not okay,' Elliot cut him off. Now that he'd started, he needed to get this off his chest. 'All you've ever done is look out for me and I've been acting like a giant baby about it lately.'

Caleb laughed. 'Agreed.'

Elliot shook his head with a laugh of his own. 'Sorry.'

'Lucky for you, I'm a very forgiving man.'

'Gee, thanks.'

'The divorce messed you up. I get it.'

'Says the man who never bothers with a second date.'

'Hey! I'm trying to be all understanding and shit.'

'Sorry. That was a low blow.'

'And I will have you know, my dating style works very well for me.'

'I'm so happy for you,' Elliot said dryly, watching the seagulls swoop over the water. It was nice to hassle his brother again. He'd missed it.

'Anyway, I'm finishing this job at the end of the week,' Caleb said, getting back to the task at hand. 'I can be in Dream Harbor the week after.'

Elliot blew out a sigh of relief. 'Thank you. I owe you.'

'I'll be sure to hold this over you forever,' Caleb said with another chuckle.

'I would expect nothing less.'

'See you in a week.'

His brother would be here in a week to save his ass, something that just an hour ago would have made Elliot want to crawl into a hole, but now he felt nothing but relief.

Chapter Twenty-Six

It was well past midnight, and Daisy was still up.

The contents of the box her grandmother brought her were spilled out on her bed, like they had been most nights in the week since Beltane. She'd given up trying to be organized and had just been riffling through things, making piles based on her own chaotic categories. She'd found more pictures of Great-Aunt Daisy—Aunt D, as she'd started to think of her—some with the Elliot lookalike and some without. Thanks to the dates scrawled on the backs, Daisy narrowed down their relationship to a two-year period in the mid-twenties. She still didn't know what happened between them, but her great-aunt just didn't glow the same way in the later pictures as she did in the earlier ones. Something haunted lingered behind her eyes, even late into her life.

Daisy had not taken her grandmother's advice about not getting lost in the past. She was all-in.

She probably should have listened. She probably should have put that old box aside and focused on her work. She should have made beautiful things with her hands. She should have had coffee with her mom and visited Iris and held baby Owen. She should have lived her own life, but instead she'd spent an awful lot of time sorting through that cardboard box, falling deeper and deeper into the past. She couldn't help herself. She needed to *know* about Aunt D, about why she felt so connected to her. The woman had taken up permanent residence inside Daisy's head. She visited her in her dreams, always sad, always searching, driving Daisy to dig deeper, to look for more answers.

Her great-aunt needed her.

It didn't matter that she was long dead.

Daisy needed to help her.

Her phone buzzed from somewhere under the piles of papers on her bed. She tossed a few photos aside until she found it.

A text from Elliot.

Oh, right, digging through this box had also given her something to obsess about other than her own life.

> Are you still awake?

She couldn't help but smile at his complete sentence with proper punctuation and everything. Elliot never sent a '*u up*' text.

> Yeah. Probably shouldn't be. What are you doing up?

> There was a three-part American Revolution doc on.

> Nerd.

> If loving history is wrong, then I don't wanna be right.

Daisy laughed out loud.

> Are you still looking through that old box? That's history, you know.

> I'm aware.

Daisy picked up a photo of her grandmother perched on her great-aunt's lap. Aunt D's mouth was turned up in a smile, like she was happy to be holding her new little niece, but her eyes told a different story. Daisy turned it between her fingers, wondering again what had been going through the woman's mind. And she just might be able to find out, because the real big find had been the diary buried at the bottom of the box. She hadn't seen it at first because the small diary had been wedged between the pages of an old flower-shop ledger.

Daisy picked it up and flipped to the page she'd left off on. All the entries were written in the same slanting script as if her aunt had been rushing to get her thoughts down. Daisy wondered if she rushed in other parts of her life, too. Or was she slow and careful when she made flower arrangements for the shop? How did this relative of hers move through her day? What did she eat for breakfast? Who did she talk to?

What did she love?

This diary might be history, but to Daisy it was personal, and she wanted to know everything.

The first few pages were rather uneventful, spanning several months and detailing the ins and outs of opening the flower shop with her brother, John. But Daisy had a feeling things were about to get interesting. The last entry that she read involved a handsome stranger appearing on the scene…

May 16, 1925

He came in again today. Nathan, he says his name is. I've never seen him around town before and now he's come in for flowers, twice in two days. I find this suspicious. John says he must have taken a fancy to me. Which I find absurd. He must have a sweetheart. Who else is he buying all these flowers for? Besides, I have no need for men to fancy me. Not anymore. Not ever again.

Ooh … okay, now things were getting good. Nathan had to be the guy in the photos, right? She kept going.

May 20, 1925

Nathan bought a dozen roses today. And he had the nerve to try and hang around the store after he was done picking them out. I went to the back and left John to make small talk.

May 27, 1925

Today he came for lilies. His home must look like a funeral parlor. He told me I looked nice in blue. I told him to have a good day.

Ha! Aunt D was sassy. Daisy liked that.
Her phone buzzed again.

> I'm going to tuck in. Don't stay up too late.

She sighed. She'd wanted to show Elliot the diary as soon as she found it, but she'd been kind of avoiding him since Beltane. Or avoiding him in real life, anyway. They texted nearly every night.

But Beltane had really freaked her out. The kissing, the middle of the night ... cuddling, the way Elliot *looked* at her, it was all getting a little too close to real. And even though Elliot had agreed to just being friends, Daisy wasn't sure that was possible anymore. Maybe they'd already gone too far.

But she missed him.

She missed his crooked smile and his glasses and the way he turned pink when he was embarrassed.

She missed him, and that terrified her, so she was staying away for now. Elliot had been joking when he asked if she was afraid she wouldn't be able to keep her hands off him, but he wasn't wrong. She didn't know if she could.

Her fingers itched to type:
Come over.
Fall in love with me.
Hold me.
Keep me safe.

She shook her head. Instead, she texted:

> Okay, goodnight, Elliot.

> Goodnight, Daisy.

She flopped back on her bed, diary still in hand. Maybe her aunt was handling things better.

May 31, 1925

I got the nerve up to ask him what on earth he was doing with all the flowers he buys. I said your girl must have run out of vases. He just smiled and said he didn't have a girl. And that I looked nice in pink.

June 10, 1925

I had thought he was finally done with his flower shopping excesses, but Nathan was back today. He bought two bouquets of daisies. Said they were his favorite flower. Told me I looked nice in yellow and left before I could argue.

Well, that didn't help. It only made her think of Elliot proclaiming daisies as his favorite and wearing a crown of them all night.

The man refused to leave her thoughts.

She started to clean up, stacking everything back into piles and placing them in the box. She couldn't keep her eyes open much longer and, apparently, her stupid brain wanted to keep circling back to Elliot.

And she couldn't think about him anymore right now. The rest of her waking hours had been enough.

Anyway, before she went on with the diary, she had to know who Nathan was. Unfortunately, the pictures with the man she figured was him only had dates and no names. It seemed there was one good way to find out. Maybe Elliot had learned more about this relative of his and had discovered his name…

She should probably call him.

For their shared love of history.

And because they were still friends.

She told herself it was for research purposes, that she needed to get to the bottom of her great-aunt's story, but she couldn't even fool herself.

The idea of seeing Elliot again was too tempting, even though she was the one putting space between them. She didn't know what she wanted. She was a mess.

She glanced down at her phone. Elliot had gone to bed half an hour ago. She couldn't call him now. Okay, so she would text Elliot in the morning. Maybe he would want to meet up. She imagined how excited he would be to get his hands on some primary sources. History nerds liked that sort of thing, right?

She could keep her hands to herself, couldn't she?

June 12, 1925

Looking back on my last few entries I feel utterly embarrassed to have wasted so much paper and ink on a man, but it looks like I'm not done. I can only hope no one ever finds this little book. Perhaps I'll burn it when I'm done, but I find I need to get these thoughts out or I can't sleep!

Nathan came into the shop again today while I was working alone. John had gone out with the deliveries. I decided I needed to put an end to this ... this ... whatever it is. I said, why do you keep coming in here? And he said to buy flowers, of course. Just like that. Like he wasn't doing anything out of the ordinary. So, I said he needed to stop complimenting my appearance and, do you know, he had the nerve to blush! Like I was the one being inappropriate when it had clearly been him who started the whole thing.

He apologized. Which, I will admit, surprised me. He said if it made me uncomfortable, he would stop coming in.

And here's where I am embarrassed again, because I couldn't bring myself to say it. I couldn't bring myself to tell him to stop. I had the insane thought that I would miss him if he did. So I straightened my shoulders and tried to act very businesslike and I told him that wouldn't be necessary.

His answering smile made my heart hurt.

Daisy knew exactly what her aunt meant about a hurting heart. Daisy's heart ached. She missed Elliot even more than she thought possible.

But she'd chickened out again and hadn't asked him to meet up. It had been another week of friendly texting, and Daisy was going out of her mind. She'd made up so many bad excuses not to see him that Elliot had stopped asking her out. He still checked in on her, but he hadn't suggested grabbing coffee in days. Pretty soon, he'd probably stop texting all together. She'd successfully pushed him away. And she felt like shit about it.

Her phone buzzed.

> U up?

Despite her current mood, Daisy smiled. It was 2 a.m. but she was getting a text from Iris.

> Yep.

Her phone started ringing.

'Hey.' Iris's voice was thick with sleep.

'Hey, everything okay?'

'Yeah,' Iris sighed. 'Owen just thought it'd be fun to be wide awake for a few hours. Archer took the first hour, but I told him he should sleep. So, it's my turn.'

'Oof, that's rough. I assume it'll get better?'

'So people claim. What are you doing up?'

'More diary-reading.'

'Ooh … what's the auntie up to now?'

Daisy smiled. She'd been keeping Iris posted on Aunt D's adventures. 'Still trying to push Nathan away.'

'Sounds familiar.'

'What's that supposed to mean?'

Iris snorted. 'Nothing at all.'

'You know I have my reasons.'

'We all do, but at some point you have to wonder if it's worth it. You're torturing yourself, Daze.'

Daisy was laying back on her pillows, looking up at the ceiling. There was a crack up there making the shape of a bunny.

'It'll be worse if I give in. It'll be worse when it ends.'

'It doesn't always end.'

'You got lucky, Iris. Archer is amazing and a great dad and a good cook, blah, blah, blah. I'm thrilled for you, I just don't think that's in the cards for me. Historically speaking, I have not lucked out in this department.'

Iris was making shushing noises, Daisy assumed at Owen and not at her. She waited, tracing the bunny's ears with her eyes.

'Sorry, I'm back,' Iris said. 'I think you have to ask yourself, is Elliot anything like David? Or Matthew?' Iris laughed to herself. 'Actually, I know Matthew, and Elliot is definitely nothing like him. And you're not the person you were at eighteen when you married him.'

'True.' Daisy thought about that girl, so carried away with the romance of it all, not thinking about if she really wanted to build a life with Matthew. She'd grown up since then.

But what about David?

She didn't even really have to think about it. She knew the way she felt about Elliot wasn't the same as how she felt about her ex. And more importantly, the way Elliot treated her was different, the way he talked to her and cared about her was different. He'd looked out for her since the beginning. She'd never felt like she had to chase him down or vie for his attention like she had with David.

Elliot was different.

'How are you so wise at two in the morning?'

Iris laughed softly. 'This is when I do my best thinking.'

'How's the little man? Any sleepier?'

'Actually, he just filled his diaper, rather aggressively.'

'You should probably go.'

'Definitely.'
'Thanks, Iris. I hope you get some sleep.'
'No problem. And you should sleep, too.'
'I will. Love you.'
'Love you, Daisy.'

After her late-night conversation with Iris, Daisy woke up a little braver.

> Can we meet at the library? I want to show you something.

Elliot's response was almost immediate.

> I'm intrigued.

Daisy smiled, her heart fluttering in her chest.

> So that's a yes?

> Of course.

Of course. Of course, like she could ask for anything, and he'd be there.

> How about today? I can meet you during my lunch break.

> Perfect. Thanks, Elliot.

> Any time.

Any time. Even after she'd hid from him for two weeks. Even after she'd propositioned him for sex and then told him she couldn't ever be in a relationship with him. Even after Beltane, after sleeping next to each other, even after she backed off again and said they should just be friends.

Of course, any time.

Elliot had been showing her all along that he was different.

Maybe it was time she started paying attention.

Chapter Twenty-Seven

'Good book?' Elliot asked, startling her out of her reading.

She looked up at him and her heart stuttered back to life. 'Hi,' she whispered.

'You're smiling while you read,' he said, still standing over her like he wasn't sure if he should join her. 'Must be a good one.' His hair was wet from the rain, and a dark curl dripped over his forehead. Daisy yearned to push it back, but she was afraid she'd given up that privilege.

She put the diary down on the library table and stood up to meet him, feeling suddenly awkward and nervous. 'It's my aunt's diary. It's part of what I wanted to show you. Can you stay?'

'For a bit, sure.' He shucked off his wet coat and draped it over the back of a chair.

She blew out a sigh of relief.

'Thanks.'

Elliot gave her another small smile and then silence

settled between them as they made themselves comfortable at the table. She'd picked one in the back corner so they wouldn't disturb anyone, not that there were many people here. Finals were over for most schools, so it was mainly toddlers running around after story time and some older folks browsing the shelves. Elliot picked up a few photos and flipped through the old flower-shop ledger. She hadn't brought the whole box. Just a few of her best finds. And certainly, no photos of her as a little girl in frilly dresses.

But she didn't feel like they could get down to business until she apologized.

'I'm sorry I've been avoiding you,' she blurted and Elliot looked up in surprise.

'Is that what you've been doing? We text every day.'

'In person, I mean.'

'Right. I did think it was odd that you had three hair appointments in one week.'

'It's worse than that.' Daisy took a deep breath before confessing. 'You get coffee at eight so I don't go into the café until nine. Tuesday when you came into the shop, I ran out the back door and hid in the alley until you left. I skipped the town meeting on Thursday even though the book club was presenting their summer reading list, which I never miss.'

Hurt flickered in his eyes. 'It's nice to know I wasn't imagining it, I guess.'

'I'm sorry.'

'It's okay.'

'It's really not.'

Color rose in his cheeks, and he looked like he wanted to say one thing and instead said another. 'We weren't really together,' he said and why did hearing that hurt so damn much? 'You don't owe me an explanation.'

'But we're friends.' Weren't they? Had she ruined it all? 'I mean, I want to be friends and that was a really shitty thing to do to a friend.'

'I agree.'

Daisy winced. 'I'm sorry.'

Elliot blew out a long sigh. 'You could have just told me.'

'I know.'

'I was trying to give you space. I was trying to be respectful.'

'I appreciate that, I just—'

'You just what, Daisy?' The question was clipped, his voice verging on anger. She'd never heard him like that before. 'You just what? I'd love to know because it was really damn hard not seeing you for two weeks.'

'It was?'

He scoffed. 'Of course it was.'

Daisy bit down on a smile. 'Oh.'

He looked up and caught her smiling. 'That makes you happy?'

'A little.'

He shook his head, his lips tipping into a rueful smile of his own. 'I hated not seeing you. A few texts a day was not enough, Daisy. I hated it but I was trying not to…'

'Not to what?'

'Scare you away.'

'Everything about this scares me,' she confessed, her voice barely a whisper in the quiet library.

Elliot's gaze was gentle when it met hers again. 'I know.

So, what happened? Why were you diving behind trash cans to avoid seeing me?'

'I didn't say that.'

He laughed. 'Practically.'

'I don't know. After Beltane, I panicked...'

He pushed the wet hair back from his face. 'I did some of my own panicking.'

'You did?'

'Yes. Ever since I realized you were wrong.'

'Wrong about what?'

He put down the photo he was holding, giving her his full attention.

'I'm not repeating old patterns.'

Daisy swallowed hard. 'You're not?'

'Nope.'

'Are you going to elaborate?' she asked, exasperated, and Elliot smirked. *The gall!*

'I don't think so.'

'You don't think so?! You're just going to tell me I'm wrong and that's it?'

His smile grew. 'I don't think you're ready for me to elaborate, Daisy. Just know this, my feelings for you are nothing like my feelings were for Leigh. *This* is nothing like that.'

Daisy's throat went dry. 'And what is this, exactly?' she rasped.

'Whatever you want it to be. I just like spending time with you.'

'You just like spending time with me?'

'Yes, I want to spend time with you, Daisy November. If that's all right with you.' He stared at her from across the table, his eyes dark behind his glasses, waiting for her answer. As if there was anything else she could say besides yes. But he waited anyway.

'Yes,' She cleared her throat. 'It's all right with me.'

He smirked, *again*. 'Good.'

She stared at him, but he turned his attention back to the spread of documents in front of them.

Elliot turned the diary over in his hands with reverent awe. 'This is very cool. It's in such good condition. Where did you find it?'

She was torn between her desire to tell him all about it and her desire to kick him in the shins under the table for teasing her like this. But maybe he was right. Maybe she wasn't ready for him to elaborate.

'My grandmother had a box of things she'd cleared out of the shop a while ago, and this diary was in there. It's like it was fate for me to find it.' That's how she'd been feeling, like fate or … or … something had been reaching out to her, like she was meant to learn about her great-aunt, to fix things for her. But all of that was a bit too crazy to admit out loud.

'It's certainly incredible that it ended up with you.'

'She cannot shut up about this guy named Nathan, and I think it must be your lookalike from the photos, but I don't have any proof of that, really. So, do you know any more about him? The guy that looks like you?'

Elliot winced. 'I started looking through some ancestry stuff I had worked on years ago, but things got kinda chaotic at work, so I haven't had a ton of time. He's definitely my great-grandfather's cousin. His name is Nathan. That's about all I know.'

'Nathan! So, it *is* him!'

He smiled at her, and she had to look away.

'What's going on at work? I don't want to keep you.'

'I needed a break. And I wanted to see you.'

Daisy couldn't help her smile. 'So, what's going on?'

'My brother's here.'

'Caleb?'

'Yeah. The original contractor bailed and so I had to call in my brother. The whole project is late because of it, and he just arrived last week so I've been catching him up on everything.'

Had their texts been that superficial? She didn't even know his brother was in town. She'd almost lost him as a friend, as everything. That thought had her feeling far more panicked than anything that had happened after Beltane.

She needed to get him back.

She wanted to keep him.

'And how do you feel about your brother being here?'

'I'd kinda rather talk about dead relatives than live ones,' Elliot said wryly, taking off his glasses and rubbing the lenses with the bottom of his shirt to clear the drops of water left by his hair.

Daisy laughed a bit too loud and got a censoring look from an old man with a newspaper. She mouthed a quick *sorry*, even though that same old man had been nearly yelling across the library just a few minutes ago, wondering where the most recent edition of the paper was.

'Dead relatives it is,' she whispered, leaning closer as Elliot pulled out his phone to show her the ancestry app he'd been using. 'My great-aunt has been talking a lot about Nathan in her diary.' Their heads tipped together, and his thigh pressed against hers and every nerve ending in Daisy's body woke up.

Hiding from him hadn't stopped her from *wanting* him. Elliot had somehow managed to wake up the part of herself she had shut down after David left. And that part, the part that wanted to push his hair back and run her fingers through it, the part that wanted to kiss him, to taste him again, the part that wanted to feel his skin pressed against hers, to hear the sound of his pleasure and want and need taking over, *that* part was wide awake now.

He looked up from his phone and caught her staring. His cheeks flushed pink like he knew exactly what she was thinking about.

'That's very interesting,' she said, her voice unnecessarily breathy considering Elliot had been talking about Ellis Island records.

The corner of his mouth quirked up. 'Oh, yeah?'

Daisy gave a slight nod. Their faces were so close now she could see the fan of his eyelashes behind his glasses and the stubble growing in on his jawline.

'I'm glad you think so,' he said.

'I'm glad you came,' she said, and his smile grew.

It would be so easy to lean forward and kiss him in this dim corner of the library with the rain streaming down the window, to press her lips to his and stop pretending she didn't have feelings for this man who'd done nothing but help her since they met. But her emotions were still a jumbled mess, and her thoughts were even worse. She didn't know if she could give Elliot what he deserved, and she certainly didn't want to hurt him again.

Elliot held her gaze a moment longer like he was waiting for her to decide.

'You were saying?' she said, letting her gaze return to the family tree on Elliot's phone.

He cleared his throat. 'Right so here's where my great-grandfather's family arrived but they stayed with a cousin named Nathan, who was already living here. I think that might be our guy.'

'Incredible!'

They spent the rest of Elliot's lunch break attempting to decode old census records and birth certificates. They didn't kiss, but Elliot's leg stayed firmly pressed to hers, his foot occasionally tapping against hers when he found something exciting, their elbows knocked together as he tapped on his phone, and more than once their heads dipped close enough to touch, Elliot's damp hair against hers. She couldn't help how she leaned into him, the way she craved every accidental brush of their bodies.

By the time they packed up their little corner of the library, Daisy was not thinking about the past at all. She was obsessively thinking about the present and how to have more of Elliot in it.

Daisy was falling and she didn't know if she wanted to catch herself this time.

Chapter Twenty-Eight

It was a beautiful sunny day in June, and Daisy was wearing a navy-blue T-shirt dress and a pair of bright white sneakers. Elliot wanted to comment on the color change, but he decided against it. Maybe she didn't want to explain why she'd re-incorporated color back into her wardrobe. Maybe he wanted to pretend it was because of him. She'd certainly made the color come back into his life.

They were walking down Main Street after a quick stop at the café. Daisy had an alarmingly large iced coffee in one hand and her great-aunt's diary in the other. She was filling Elliot in on the latest events from the diary. Her excited voice floated on the warm, early summer air.

'So, Aunt D has finally stopped refusing Nathan, who she now calls Nate, did I tell you that?'

Elliot shook his head as he sipped his smoothie. She hadn't told him that yet, but she'd told him lots of other things. They were back to hanging out together, and he'd seen her nearly every day over the past two weeks.

And it was absurd how glad he was. How much he had missed her.

How much he *liked* her.

Neither of them had mentioned fake-dating again, and they certainly hadn't mentioned real dating. Apparently, they were just going to spend a lot of time together and let the townsfolk call it what they wanted.

Last he heard, the book club had declared them this summer's *couple to watch*. Ominous, to say the least.

'Okay, well, she calls him Nate now, which I think is really cute. And they're going to a town dance together on the weekend!' She said it as though it were all happening right now as she read it, and not a hundred years ago. He'd be lying if he said her newfound interest in history didn't delight him. 'We should bring back town dances,' she concluded, taking a big sip of coffee. She looked so damn cute when she was excited that Elliot had to remind himself to stop staring and respond.

'If any place could bring back town dances, it would be Dream Harbor.'

Daisy laughed. 'You're probably right. I shouldn't say it too close to a town meeting or it will end up happening.'

'And you'll get roped in to the planning committee.'

'That's true… Oh, my goodness, puppies—' Daisy stopped abruptly in front of The Second Chance pet shop. Elliot stopped, too, and couldn't help but agree with Daisy's squealed delight. Those were some darn cute puppies, all golden and soft, with black noses and pink tongues lolling out of their mouths.

'Look at those little balls of fluff! They are adorable!' Daisy went on, her hands pressed to the glass as they watched the wriggling pile of puppies stumble over each other to get to the window. 'We have to go in!' She was tugging Elliot by the hand into the pet shop before he could protest, but why would he? He was always down to pet some puppies. And frankly, at this point, he would pet an alligator if Daisy was the one asking him to.

Once inside, the barking and yipping of the puppies nearly drowned out Daisy's cooing and laughing. She leaned right over the gated area and was petting each puppy as they fell all over themselves to get to her. Elliot knew the feeling well.

There was one little puppy that couldn't seem to get into the mix. Too tiny to keep up with its siblings, the runt of the litter kept getting pushed aside. Elliot decided to give this puppy some love. He scooped her up and held her in his arms, scratching right between the ears. The puppy immediately fell asleep.

He looked up from petting his new little friend and found Daisy staring at him. Not just staring. Daisy looked like she may jump him. Even more than she had when he was talking about census forms at the library or when he'd suggested they spend an afternoon at the bookstore—or any number of other times during the past two weeks when their gazes had snagged or their hands had touched. They may have not been talking about the parameters of their relationship, but their bodies certainly seemed to have some ideas.

Maybe he needed to hold cute things more often. First Owen, and now this puppy. Did other men know this? That if they hold babies, women melt on the spot?

'She loves you,' she whispered, her eyes tearing up. 'That little puppy loves you!'

'I just ... she couldn't ... keep up with the others...' Her reaction had him completely flustered.

Daisy's tears were threatening to spill over, and Elliot was at a loss as to what his next move should be when one of the owners of the shop, Shawn, emerged from the back. He and his husband Greg were two older gentlemen who had initially struck Elliot as more urban and sophisticated than you would expect for a small town, like they should be running a boutique in New York and not a pet-rescue shop in Dream Harbor. But then he met them and realized they fit right in. 'Hi, Daisy. Hi, Elliot. I see you've met our latest guests.' *Guests* like the puppies had checked into a luxury hotel. Elliot smiled.

'Where did they come from?' Daisy asked, her eyes still on Elliot. His cheeks heated under her stare.

'They were found abandoned under a car, actually.'

'No!' Daisy gasped, turning back to Shawn. 'That's terrible. Who would just leave these babies like that?'

He patted her gently on the shoulder. 'They're safe with us now and it won't be long until they're all adopted. In fact, a few of these guys are already on hold for several families that saw them on our socials.'

Daisy pressed a hand to her chest in relief. 'I love that you do pet rescues here.'

'Me, too,' Shawn said with a smile. 'And I see you've bonded with the littlest member of the family,' he said to Elliot. 'Isn't she sweet?'

'The *sweetest*,' Daisy sighed.

'Are you looking to adopt?'

'I'm not sure if I can...' Elliot looked down at the little ball of fur in his arms, and he wanted to cry. Sam had been even smaller when he and Leigh got him and used to sleep just like this, curled up in Elliot's arms. God, he missed that dog.

Was he ready to have a new one?

Could he find the space to love a new furry friend?

'What about you, Daisy?' Shawn asked and now Daisy looked like she might cry again.

'I would love to, I just don't have the room at the moment.' Her brow furrowed like she was thinking about whether she could fit a dog larger than a teacup poodle in that apartment of hers. She definitely couldn't. 'They're going to get big, aren't they?'

Shawn nodded. 'We think they're at least part golden retriever, so yeah, pretty big.'

He smiled at the two of them, clearly not wanting to pressure them into anything. 'If you change your mind, you know where to find us.'

Daisy looked at Elliot. Elliot looked at Daisy. The puppy sighed in her sleep.

'I'll take her,' he said.

Daisy clapped her hands in delight.

Shawn smiled wider. 'Okay, let's get that paperwork done.'

And just like that, Elliot was a dog-dad again.

'How about Buttercup?' Daisy suggested.

Elliot shook his head. 'Maybe Mustard?'

Daisy wrinkled her nose. 'Mustard is not a name.'

'And Buttercup is?' he asked with a laugh, rubbing the puppy's belly as she rolled over. The three of them were sitting on the floor of the flower shop four days after Elliot signed the adoption papers. He had just picked her up and obviously Daisy's was the first stop they made.

He was already so in love with the little dog.

Daisy gasped. 'Have you not seen *The Princess Bride*? Of course, Buttercup is a name.'

'Sure, a name for a princess. Not for a dog.'

'Are you saying this sweet girl is not a princess?' Daisy laughed. The puppy had crawled into her lap and was already dozing off. 'Sleeping beauty, maybe.'

'Shawn says it's normal for puppies to be sleepy at first, just like human babies.'

'Makes sense. How about Sunny?'

They were sitting with their backs against the counter. Their arms pressed together when he reached over to pet the puppy. Like every other time they touched, Elliot wanted more. He was glad he and Daisy were back to being friends, but his body was having a hard time remembering the just friends part.

'That could work.' He ran his fingers through the puppy's soft fur, and Daisy rested her head on his shoulder. It was the best moment of his week, and he soaked it in. Work had been nothing but chaos and sitting here in the quiet sunshine of Daisy's shop with a snoring puppy was the perfect break.

'What about Marigold,' he murmured.

'I like that. You could call her Goldie.'

'Perfect,' Elliot agreed as they settled back into silence.

The shop was bursting with color, summer bouquets filling the racks. Yellows, pinks and oranges, tied together by Daisy's expert hands. In the window hung green vines and ferns and spider plants. When his mom went back home, he kept the philodendron he'd bought on that first visit to the shop. He thought of Daisy every time he looked at it. Although that wasn't saying much, because he thought of Daisy all the time.

Sunshine filtered in through the windows between the leaves, and Elliot knew it was this perfect golden moment he would think of when he called Goldie's name, not the color of her fur.

'Oh!' Daisy said after a few more minutes of quiet. 'I thought we could read some diary pages. Before you have to go.'

'Sure.' Daisy passed him Goldie, who barely opened an eye at the disruption, and got up to grab the book.

They still didn't know what had happened between Nathan and Aunt D, but Elliot noticed that Daisy had slowed down her reading, like she didn't want to get to the part where it all went wrong. It was as though, if she didn't read it, she could protect her great-aunt from heartbreak.

Her curiosity generally got the better of her, though, and she usually ended up reading Elliot little snippets when they were together.

'Okay,' she said, joining him on the floor again. 'Here we go.'

July 18, 1925

The town has begun to talk, of course. Nate is in the shop nearly every day and after attending the dance together, the word is out about us. They act as though we should have a chaperone! You should have seen their scandalized faces when Nate showed up in his car to pick me up. It was the talk of the town meeting, I'm sure. But I don't care about all that. I want to be happy. I should be giddy to have a man like Nate take an interest in me, but I can't help but feel like I'm betraying William.

'William again!' Daisy said, looking up from the book. 'She's mentioned him before, but no explanation! I wish I had more than this one diary. I feel like we're missing out on so much information.'

Elliot chuckled at her exasperation. 'It is too bad we don't have the whole series.'

'It's like my great-aunt didn't even consider that we'd be reading this diary in the future,' Daisy teased before getting back to the diary.

July 23, 1925

I will certainly have to burn these pages now because Nate kissed me, and I simply can't leave that detail from this book.

'Ooh' Daisy squealed. 'It's getting juicy!'

Maybe my mother is right in calling his car a Devil's Wagon, because I couldn't resist him as we sat in the back seat after our night out. Maybe I should have but I didn't want to, and I can't feel sorry for it! This kiss wasn't anything like the chaste kisses my William gave me before he left for good. This kiss ... this kiss burned. It sparked. It made me want things, so help me for saying it but I would have done more. I would have given Nate everything, if he wasn't such a gentleman.

His lips, his mouth, his hands, they set me on fire, and I'm afraid I don't want to put it out.

When Daisy looked up her cheeks were pink and her eyes bright. At some point, she had drifted closer to him again, her knee pressed against his. Unable to resist touching her anymore, he reached up and traced her cheek, letting the back of his hand caress her jaw and down her neck. She shivered beneath his touch despite the warmth of the shop.

'If that journal gets any more explicit, you're going to have to stop reading it out loud,' he teased and Daisy laughed softly, her face tipping toward his, like maybe she didn't want to resist any more, either.

'What's this?' she asked, her gaze flicking to his wrist. 'Is this a hair tie?'

'It's um...'

'Elliot,' she said, running a finger between the elastic band and his skin. Her touch sent his pulse skittering. 'Are you wearing my hair tie on your wrist?'

'Maybe.'

Her grin was delicious.

'For how long?'

'Since our bookstore date.' He was surprised she'd never noticed before.

'The one where we pretended to make out?'

Just the memory of it, of Daisy pressed against him was enough to make him groan.

'Yes.'

'Why?' her voice was barely a whisper now, her face so close to his, her finger still trapped under the hair tie.

'It's a little piece of you. I wanted it near me.'

'Elliot,' she breathed his name, tugging him closer with just her finger.

'Daisy?'

'Yeah?'

'Can I kiss you?'

Her smile was positively edible. 'Yes. *Please.*'

His heart thundered in his chest as he cupped her face in his hands. Her breath caught. It turned out *this* was actually the best moment of his week. Month. Year.

He leaned forward and his lips met hers. The sweet sigh that escaped her when he did was almost too much to bear.

'Daisy,' he whispered and she whimpered. He felt the sound down to his bones. 'I want you so bad.' Honesty. It was all he had to give her. His raw, honest words.

Her hands were in his hair, tugging. 'Same.'

Same.

What a gift to have his feelings reciprocated.

He groaned and kissed her again, deeper, his tongue sliding against hers, his fingers slipping into her hair. She was lips and breath and she tasted like honey, sweet and earthy at once. He wanted to lap her up.

He was about to haul her onto him when he suddenly remembered where they were, the hardwood floor beneath them, the counter at their back, the smell of flowers surrounding them. He pulled away, panting and

Daisy was doing the same. She leaned her forehead against his.

'Woah,' she breathed.

'Yeah…We probably shouldn't do this here,' he managed to say. Even though he wanted to go right back to kissing her and possibly never stop.

'I guess you're right. We are kinda in the middle of the store.'

'While it's open.'

'And you have a puppy in your lap.'

'We shouldn't subject her to this.'

Daisy laughed and the sound lit him up. And he was so damn relieved that her reasons for stopping were puppy-related and not something deeper.

Neither of them said they shouldn't do this anymore.

No one said this was a bad idea.

Daisy wasn't putting the brakes on this for any reason other than location, and he was so far past his ability to stop this moving train that he was willing to lay down in front of it and let it destroy him.

He wanted her too much.

'Looks like we stopped just in time,' Daisy said, gesturing to where Kira and Bennett stood outside the door. She waved at them through the glass.

'I guess so.' Elliot stood and reached a hand to Daisy to help her up. They both dusted the dirt from their pants as Kira and Bennett walked in.

'What are you guys up to… Oh, my goodness, *a puppy*!!' Elliot had a feeling a lot of his conversations from now on were going to go like this. Goldie was, after all, the cutest puppy ever.

'This is Goldie,' Daisy said, beaming like it was her puppy too. Like they were a little family. Elliot loved that a bit too much.

'She is so precious! Where did you get her?' Kira cooed, reaching over to scratch Goldie's head. Elliot could swear the dog smiled in her sleep.

'Second Chance, of course. Shawn said she was left under a car with her siblings.'

Kira's face transformed into something so outraged and so sad at the same time, Elliot was afraid of what would happen next. Apparently, so was Bennett.

'Babe, we can't.'

'But they were *abandoned*!'

'We can't take in any more animals! You just brought home three baby goats.'

'They were *also* abandoned.'

Bennett sighed like a man resigned to his fate when Elliot decided he should probably chime in.

'Actually, Goldie was the last one. The whole litter has been adopted.'

'See, Peaches. All the puppies are safe.'

Kira glared at him even as her mouth tipped up in the corner. 'You're off the hook for now, but you know it won't be for long.'

Bennett slung an arm over her shoulder and pressed a kiss to the top of her head. 'I know what I signed on for.' He grinned and Kira laughed and Elliot thought they looked so damn happy and he wanted that, too. He wanted to put his arm around Daisy and adopt pets with her and kiss the top of her head and not have to worry that this thing between them was impermanent.

But he had to go back to work, and despite their most recent make-out session and their previous status of fake-dating, Elliot was at a loss for how to say goodbye to Daisy and not make it weird.

Luckily, Daisy planted a kiss on his cheek before petting Goldie's head and saying goodbye to them both.

It was almost normal.

It was almost real.

It was almost perfect.

Chapter Twenty-Nine

'What brings you guys in?' Daisy asked, happy for the distraction from her swirling feelings. *Damn, Elliot was a good kisser.*

She'd somehow managed to put that out of her mind when she'd been doing the should-I-date-Elliot-for-real math, and now it would be all she could think about.

If Elliot's distant cousin was half as good of a kisser as he was then she totally understood why Aunt D was about to give it all up in the back of that car. Or, in her and Elliot's case, up against a door. Or on the floor of her shop. Or at this point, literally, anywhere.

'Oh, yeah, I got so distracted by the puppy I nearly forgot why we came in!' Kira said with a laugh.

Listen to Kira and get out of your head!

'I wanted to check in with you about something.'

'Okay, sure.' Daisy tried not to get her hopes up that whatever Kira wanted to say had to do with a wedding she was hosting at the barn and maybe they needed a florist and maybe this person hadn't heard about the curse and maybe…

'David wants to book the barn for his wedding.'

And just like that, Daisy's hopes plummeted.

'My ex, David?'

'Yep. I totally understand if you want me to say we're not available for their date.'

'You really don't have to do that.'

'But I can.'

'Kira, I'm not having you turn down a wedding just because the groom is my ex. That's a lot of money.'

Kira waved a hand at the thought of the money. 'But why does he need to get married here? It's weird.'

'You need that money to feed all the baby goats,' Daisy teased and Bennett nodded in agreement.

'She's not wrong, babe. Running an animal sanctuary is not cheap.'

Kira rolled her eyes at him. 'We're not running an animal sanctuary. We just have a few pets.'

Bennett scoffed. 'A few pets?'

'It's really fine,' Daisy insisted, interrupting their little argument. 'If David wants to get married in your gorgeous barn, I totally get it. Your events are amazing.'

Kira furrowed her brow like she wanted to argue more. 'I appreciate that, but I still think it's weird. And kind of aggressive. Like, go find your own small town. This one is taken.'

Daisy shrugged. Maybe it was weird. Maybe she should care, but she found that she really … didn't. David could get married wherever the hell he wanted, and that was just fine with her.

She smiled. How freeing was that?

She didn't care about David. Or his wedding. Or his new fiancée. And if she was being honest, she hadn't for a while now. She hadn't bothered to think about the man since he'd ambushed her at Beltane. And even then, she'd felt nothing but annoyed to see him. The old feelings were gone, even the hurt.

'Book the event.'

'You're sure?'

'Yep. I wish him nothing but happiness.'

'See,' Bennett said, bringing an armful of bouquets up to the register. 'I told you she wouldn't mind. She's with Elliot now, who cares about this David guy.'

Had it really only been a few months ago that Daisy had grabbed a stranger who'd wandered into her shop to be her fake boyfriend, just to spare herself the horror of being alone in front of David? It seemed like a lifetime ago.

And it had brought her to Elliot.

Maybe she actually owed David a thank you.

'I guess you were right,' Kira said to Bennett before turning back to Daisy with a smile. 'I'm glad you and Elliot are so happy together.'

Daisy cleared her throat. 'Right. Thanks.' Were they *together*? They really needed to straighten this out. She needed to talk to him.

'Unfortunately, I don't think they're going to book you for the flowers.'

'I get it.'

'It probably wouldn't be a great look if your ex ends up divorced after you do the flowers at his wedding.' Kira winced. 'Not that I believe that bullshit about the curse.'

'Thanks. Curse or not, it would be awkward.'

'But I always talk you up to everyone who comes to look at the venue.'

'I appreciate it.'

'What are you going to do with all these flowers?' Kira asked Bennett as Daisy rang them up.

He shrugged. 'Put them around the house.'

Kira beamed up at him, and Daisy wanted *that*.

A shared life. Flowers around the house. A puppy on the end of the bed.

She'd thought she'd lost the chance to have it. Multiple times. But maybe she hadn't. Maybe if she could manage to let David go, she could also be brave enough to let Elliot in.

She wondered what her great-aunt had done.

Had she let Nate in?

Had he broken her heart?

Had she ever gotten over it?

Chapter Thirty

Daisy was up late again, tucked beneath her covers, her great-aunt's voice filling her head despite the fact that she'd never heard it before.

August 1, 1925

Nate took me to the new gin joint in town. What a laugh that it's in the basement of the town hall, right beneath the mayor's nose. Nate says he's in on it, but I'm not so sure. We drank and danced and kissed, and even as I laughed and smiled, I couldn't let myself be free. Hadn't I done this before? Hadn't I given my heart to a man only to be left behind?

Nate wants more from me. I know he does. But can I give it?

Same, girl, same, Daisy thought. It seemed she and her great-aunt were not just alike in looks. She'd been wondering the same thing all day after kissing Elliot this morning. Could she give him more?

She grabbed her phone.

> U up?

Iris replied immediately.

> U know I am

Iris picked up on the first ring.

'Hey.'

'What's the little man doing tonight?'

'Well, he started with a bit of projectile vomiting and now he doesn't want to be put down.'

'Iris, are you okay?'

Her friend sighed.

'Yeah. Just very tired.'

'You're doing amazing.'

Iris sniffled. 'I don't know why I'm crying.'

'Probably because you grew and birthed and are now feeding an entire human. And you haven't had a full night's sleep in three months.'

'Oh, yeah, that.'

'You're incredible.'

'Thank you. I don't feel incredible, but it's nice to hear.'

'How's the new-mom's group?'

'It's really good, actually. It's nice to know I'm not the only one going through this.'

'And you're talking to your doctor?'

Daisy could practically hear the eyeroll in Iris's answer,

and she smiled to herself. 'Yes, Daisy. I promise. I'm taking care of myself. Now, what is happening with Aunt D and Nate? Fill me in.'

'Okay, well, they've been kissing a lot and drinking in speakeasies.'

'Scandalous!'

'Very.'

'And what about in modern day? What's going on with Elliot?'

'Um…'

'Daisy November, you know about *everything* in my life. Don't be stingy.'

'Okay fine, also kissing. Not so much with the speakeasies.'

Iris gasped far too dramatically for the moment.

'Kissing?! You've been holding out on me.'

'It just happened!' Although, she was totally holding out on her friend. Iris knew nothing about The Orgasm Incident or the kissing at Beltane, but Daisy figured there was no point in backtracking now. She'd never hear the end of it.

'And how was it?'

Daisy had to bite back the dreamy sigh that nearly left her lips.

'Good.'

'Liar!'

'Incredible.'

'That's better. I'm happy for you, Daisy.'

'I don't know what it means.'

'Maybe just be thankful for incredible kisses.'

'More middle-of-the-night wisdom.'

'You're welcome. Now read me the next entry.'

Daisy cleared her throat, happy to divert Iris's attention to her aunt. She read,

August 12, 1925

Nate says he's going to marry me someday.
I said, we'll see.

'She's sassy. I love that,' Iris said.
'Me, too.'
'Keep going.'

September 3, 1925

If I were a respectable girl, I would have said yes to Nate's marriage proposal and no to everything else, but I did it all backwards. I gave it all up for free, as my mother would say, and now Nate could leave me ruined if he wanted to. Maybe it's a test. Maybe I wanted to see if he would.

As for the act itself, I can't regret it. Nate was as tender and gentle as any man could be.

'Tender and gentle!' Iris practically squealed. 'I think I have a crush on a dead guy.'

Daisy laughed. 'Me, too.'

'Aunt D is really into self-sabotage, though. I mean, Nate is obviously sweet and kind and good in the sack. What more did she want?'

'She's clearly scared.'

Mercifully, Iris did not call Daisy out for being just as

scared as her great-aunt. She was too busy whispering to someone on her end.

'Daisy? Archer is here to relieve me of baby-holding duty.'

'Good man.'

'He is,' Iris said, the smile clear in her voice. 'Goodnight, Daisy.'

'Night, Iris.'

As Daisy ended the call, she knew she should get some sleep, too, but she couldn't seem to put the little book down. One more entry wouldn't hurt.

September 18, 1925

> *John says I can't keep running around town with Nate and not make an honest man out of him. Lucky for me, John is not in charge. He says he wants me to be happy. He says he hasn't seen me like this since before William ran off.*
>
> *He says Nate is nothing like William.*
>
> *But aren't all men the same?*

What happened to you, girl?! Daisy wanted to shake the book until Aunt D came to her senses. Instead, she threw it across the room.

The irony of her feelings was not lost on her, but sometimes it was just easier to be frustrated with someone else than to turn that feeling on yourself. Why berate herself for not sealing the deal with Elliot when she could be angry with a long-dead relative? She pulled the covers over her head and pretended to sleep. Of course, men were not all the same, but she and her great-aunt sure were. And at the moment, she didn't want to know how it ended. For either of them.

Chapter Thirty-One

It was eight-thirty on a Monday morning and Elliot's new puppy had just peed in the corner of the lobby, right next to the foot of one of the few guests still staying here. Said guest was not amused.

His brother was arguing, quite loudly, with the dry-wall guy who apparently had mis-measured and not delivered enough.

Jack was too busy flirting with Gabe to be of any help. (Gabe was flirting right back, which was lovely and all for Elliot's friend, but not really his top priority at the moment.)

They'd found asbestos in the walls of the motel-style rooms.

Mary and Joseph didn't like his designer's choice of wallpaper for the new luxury suites in the main building, and Elliot had to be the one to tell her that. His designer did not take notes well.

The electrician was supposed to come yesterday, and he hadn't shown up or called.

But the mayor did call to tell Elliot he'd had a dream that the inn should lean into a strong nautical theme, which was definitely not happening.

Today's muffins were orange cranberry.

Elliot hated orange cranberry.

But Daisy had just walked in with her flowers for the lobby so the roof could fall on his head, and Elliot would still call it a good morning.

He was a besotted idiot.

'Hey,' he said from his crouch on the floor where he was sopping up dog pee with a towel as Goldie ran around Daisy's ankles, yipping like a deranged … well … puppy. She had certainly woken up over the past few days, and his sleepy baby had turned into a high-strung nightmare. He shouldn't have brought her here, but she cried every time he left (and all night long for that matter), and she should be in her crate behind the desk, but she cried there, too, so he let her out for just a few minutes, and this was how she repaid him.

'Uh-oh,' Daisy said, putting the flowers down on the nearest table. 'What did you do, baby girl?' She kneeled down to pet Goldie, who responded by spinning in delighted circles before trying to climb Daisy's body to aggressively lick her face. This dog had no chill. But Elliot kinda felt the same way around Daisy, so he understood. 'You can't do that on the carpet! That's bad, bad…' Daisy couldn't finish her admonishment because she was giggling too hard at Goldie's attempt for a kiss.

Daisy gave up and sat on the floor and let Goldie get her fill before she ran off to cause more trouble.

'Dog-dad life not going great?' she asked with a wince.

'We're still working out some of the kinks.'
'Like house training?'
'And sleeping through the night.'
'Yikes.'
'Good thing she's cute.'

Daisy agreed with a laugh as they both got up off the floor. Elliot went to toss the towel in the laundry and wash his hands, and by the time he got back, Daisy was happily chatting with Jack and Gabe at the front desk.

'It seems kind of silly to keep bringing in flowers,' Daisy said, gesturing to the plastic sheeting draped up behind Jack to keep the dust from the construction from drifting into the lobby.

'We still have guests staying in the main building and they deserve your beautiful blooms,' Jack said. 'And besides, Mary and Joseph are so busy paying for all this, they'll barely notice a monthly flower budget, so take the win.' He winked and Daisy laughed.

'Thanks, Jack.'

'That reminds me,' Gabe said, running a hand through his artfully messy hair. 'Can you come and look at something ... uh ... outside. I wanted to get your opinion on ... it.'

Jack's face flushed red and he was out from behind the desk in a second. 'Sure, yeah, of course.'

Gabe grinned.

Daisy raised her eyebrows at Elliot as the two walked away, their shoulders brushing together and Jack's laughter echoing in their wake.

'What's going on there?'

Elliot rolled his eyes. 'They sneak away at least several

times a day to make out and I'm sure other things I don't need to know the details of.'

'Wow, scandal at the inn.'

'Jack's had a crush on him for months, so it's kinda sweet.'

'That is sweet.' Daisy took a quick glance around the empty lobby before pinning Elliot against the desk and wrapping her arms around his neck.

'You're sweet, too, Elliot.'

'Am I?'

'Yes, and I can't stop thinking about you.'

'Oh?' The one-syllable sound was the only thing he could make come out of his mouth after his brain stuttered to a stop at the feel of Daisy's body in his arms.

'A lot.' She brushed her lips against his.

'Mmm.'

'I can't sleep.'

Elliot breathed her in. Roses and sunshine.

His fingers flexed against her hips, and she whimpered.

'Actually,' she whispered, her lips brushing the shell of his ear. 'I thought about you last night while I'—her voice dropped even lower like she was confessing to him—'while I touched myself.'

'Fuck, Daisy,' he groaned and she giggled, breathy and sweet.

'I can't believe I just said that.'

'Me, neither, but I...' He squeezed his eyes closed before confessing, 'I do the same. I think about you, Daisy.'

Far too often. Being near Daisy had become his new favorite type of torture. He wanted nothing more than to be with her but being with her only made him want her more.

His hand and his imagination had seen more action in the last few weeks than they had in years.

She hissed out a needy little sigh and Elliot thought he might die. Or come on the spot. Or possibly both.

'I think I'm losing my mind. I've never—'

'Wanted someone like this?' he finished for her.

'Yeah,' she said, her lips tracing his jaw, his neck. 'So, I think we should … I think we *need* to—'

'Elliot! You can't let this dog wander around a job site…' The sound of his brother's voice broke them apart like they were teenagers caught making out behind the school. Caleb stomped out from behind the plastic shield carrying a squirming Goldie in his arms. His disapproving face and obnoxiously huge frame was a very effective mood killer.

'Oh, is this the famous Daisy?' Caleb asked, switching from aggravated to charming as soon as he spotted a beautiful woman.

Elliot cleared his throat, trying desperately not to look as wrecked as he felt. 'Yes, this is Daisy. And I'm sorry about the dog. I'll crate her.'

Caleb handed over the puppy and held a hand out to Daisy, who was half hidden behind Elliot like she was still recovering from their confessions. He knew he sure was.

'It's nice to finally meet you. In person, I mean,' Caleb said.

Daisy took his hand. 'Nice to meet you, too.'

Caleb flashed the smile that had no doubt gotten him into bed with every woman he'd ever chosen but Daisy's gaze flickered to Elliot's. She gave him a secret smile before turning back to his brother. She really was perfect.

'How's the work going?' she asked.

'Oh, you know, a new disaster everyday but that's pretty standard, right, El?' he said, smiling at Elliot now.

Elliot had to admit that despite all the usual hiccups that came with major renovations, things between him and his brother were going quite smoothly. He'd almost forgotten how well they worked together. Their opposite personalities helped them fill in where the other one was lacking.

They were a good team.

'Yep. Always something.' Elliot was about to put Goldie back in her crate, but something was odd. 'Is she breathing funny?' He put his head closer to Goldie's little body, and she licked his cheek.

Daisy leaned in close, too, her forehead creased in concern. 'She does sound a little wheezy.'

'Do you think she swallowed something?' Caleb asked. 'Or maybe she just breathed in too much dust. It's a real mess back there.' To his credit, Caleb did not say he told him so, which Elliot appreciated. He felt bad enough as it was.

'Shit, I don't know. I took my eyes off her just for a minute…'

Daisy looked immediately guilty. She'd make a terrible criminal.

'Maybe we should call the vet?' she suggested.

'Good idea.' He was the worst dog-dad ever. Daisy snuggled Goldie, humming a little song to her, while he made the call. Lucky for him, Dr. Vivienne was in the area and said she would stop by.

'The vet is on the way.'

'I'm sure it'll be fine,' Caleb said, giving him a hearty pat on the back.

The three of them went into the back office to wait for the vet and Goldie was delighted by the extra human attention. They all ended up sitting on the floor, letting her run between them, soaking in all the head scratches and tummy rubs.

'It's possible we overreacted,' Elliot said as Goldie growled and attacked Caleb's work boot. The puppy did not seem to be in any distress.

Caleb shrugged. 'I needed a break anyway.'

'How are you liking Dream Harbor?' Daisy asked.

His brother had decided to stay at the inn while they worked. He'd rented out his house in New York and moved to town. Mary and Joseph wanted to keep at least part of the inn open for guests, so they were working in sections. At the moment, Caleb had a room in the main building. Elliot had offered him the guest room at his house, but ultimately, they decided working together was enough. They were just starting to mend their relationship. Living together would have been too much. Elliot was glad they were getting along, but he still needed time alone at the end of the day.

'It's … quirky. I like it.' Caleb laughed. 'I feel a little like I'm being interrogated every time I go for coffee, but yeah, it's nice.'

Daisy rolled her eyes. 'Yeah, they'll get tired of you eventually, but this town loves to vet its new inhabitants. Unless you're lucky enough to fly under the radar,' she added, winking at Elliot, and he liked the way she made his quietness sound like a superpower.

Caleb's gaze flicked between the two of them. 'So … how are things going between you two?'

'Things are going great,' Elliot was quick to answer, not wanting Daisy to have to deal with his brother's questions. The way Caleb was studying her, Elliot was afraid he sensed something was odd about this whole thing. He'd always seemed to have an extra sense when it came to Elliot, like he knew when something was off about his brother.

Daisy sat up straighter. 'Are you going to give me a lecture about not breaking your little brother's heart?'

Caleb grinned. 'Maybe.'

Daisy leaned into Elliot's side. 'I won't.' She said it to Caleb, but Elliot felt like she was promising it to him.

'Good,' Caleb said. 'Because Elliot deserves to be happy.'

'I agree.'

Elliot could feel his damn face heating. 'Can we stop talking like I'm not sitting right here?'

'Of course,' Daisy said, nudging his shoulder again. 'Anything to add?'

His brother was studying him, his brow furrowed like he really was trying to figure out if Elliot was happy, like he wanted him to be. Caleb could be a giant pain in the ass, but it was always out of love, so unfortunately, Elliot couldn't be too mad about it.

'No. Just that I won't hurt you, either,' he said, turning to face her, not caring that his brother was still studying them like he was trying to crack some secret code.

Daisy smiled at him. 'I know.'

'Good, glad to hear it,' Caleb said, standing and brushing the dirt from his jeans. Apparently, he was satisfied for the moment that Elliot wasn't ready to retreat from humanity again anytime soon. 'I guess I should get back to work. Let me know what the vet says.'

Elliot and Daisy stood, too, right as there was a knock on the door. Goldie immediately started barking in excitement.

'I'm happy she's not scared of the vet yet,' Dr. Vivienne said as she stepped into the office and was greeted by an exuberant puppy.

'Thanks for coming,' Elliot said. 'We may have overreacted, but she got into the work site for a minute, and she was wheezing a little.'

'Okay, no worries. Let's check you out, sweet girl.' Vivienne scooped up the puppy and put her on the table they usually used for lunch breaks.

Caleb was still frozen by the door.

'I thought you were going back to work?' Elliot said, startling Caleb out of his blatant perusal of the vet. He ran a hand through his hair like he was trying to neaten it after it had been under a hard hat all morning, and Elliot nearly laughed out loud.

'No, I thought maybe I should fill the doctor in. Since I found the dog and all…'

'Right. Of course.' Elliot looked back to where Daisy and Vivienne were chatting over the squirming puppy. The vet was cute, small and curvy with dirty-blonde hair pulled back from her face as she worked. He'd just met her a few days ago when he brought Goldie in for her first round of shots. Elliot wasn't sure he would have noticed she was attractive, especially not with Daisy standing right next to her, but with his brother staring at her like a man starved, Elliot could admit she was pretty.

'So … are you going to talk to her?' Elliot prodded and Caleb fixed his hair again.

'Yeah … yep…'

Elliot had never seen his brother nervous to talk to a woman before. Or nervous for any reason really and it was quite entertaining.

He walked over to the table and Caleb followed.

'Vivienne, this is my brother, Caleb. He found Goldie wandering around where she shouldn't have been.'

'Nice to meet you,' Caleb barked, far too loud for the small space.

Vivenne's eyes widened. 'Hi, nice to meet you, too.'

'Vivenne the vet,' he said, emphasizing the 'v's. 'I'm Caleb the contractor.' Emphasis on the 'c' sound that time. Second-hand embarrassment coursed through Elliot's body. Was this why Caleb was always so worried about him? Was it this painful to watch him interact with other people?

'Ha. Yeah,' Vivenne said, politely humoring him and Caleb winced.

'What's wrong with your brother?' Daisy whispered to Elliot.

'I don't know. I think he's malfunctioning,' Elliot whispered back and Daisy giggled.

'So did you notice the puppy ingesting anything?' Vivienne asked, getting back to business.

'Uh … no. I just saw her wriggling around under a paint tarp.'

Vivienne nodded as she examined Goldie, bringing her stethoscope to the dog's chest. 'Do you want to hold her for me?' she asked Caleb, who took the squirming puppy in his hands. 'Thanks,' Vivienne said. Their fingers tangled in the dog's fur as they wrestled her into submission and their gazes locked. The sparks were practically visible. Even Goldie stilled.

Daisy smiled at Elliot, her eyebrows rising as though she was saying, *are you seeing this?*

He definitely was seeing this. His brother was staring at the small-town vet like he'd never seen anyone like her.

Interesting.

Elliot cleared his throat and Vivienne snapped out of it, quickly returning her focus to the examination. 'I … uh … don't hear anything too serious. You're probably right about the dust, but if she still sounds like this in a day or two, you should bring her in for an X-ray. Just to be safe.'

'Of course,' Elliot said. 'I really appreciate you making a house … er … inn call.'

Vivienne shrugged, dutifully avoiding Caleb's eye now. 'It was no trouble. I was in the area.'

'Are you in the area a lot?' Caleb asked, his brain apparently coming back online. 'I'm here for the next few months, at least.' He flashed her his charming smile. 'Maybe we'll see more of each other.' Oh, dear God, did he just wink?

There must have been something about his shift in demeanor, the too-practiced nature of that smile, that *wink*, that Vivienne didn't like, because the moment they'd shared seemed to evaporate.

'I'm pretty busy,' she said, packing up her bag.

'Right,' Caleb said, his smile dimming. 'Of course. Me, too.'

'I bet you are,' she said, slipping past him and out the door. Daisy followed her out.

'What the hell just happened?' Caleb asked and Elliot couldn't help his chuckle.

'I think she just saw right through you.'

'What do you mean?'

Elliot shrugged. 'She didn't like that charming bullshit thing you do.'

'What charming bullshit? Women love that charming bullshit!'

Elliot laughed as he walked out of the office, leaving Caleb behind. 'Not that woman, apparently,' he said over his shoulder and left Caleb stewing over the rejection. He didn't have time to worry about his brother right now.

His dog was fine and now he needed to find Daisy and continue that very interesting conversation they were having earlier.

Chapter Thirty-Two

Daisy was too hot to sleep. The humidity had been building all day, storm clouds gathering out the shop window, but the rain hadn't come. Warm, sticky air blew in through the only window in her apartment. The sweaty sheets were twisted around her bare legs.

She was starfished on the bed, but the air was still, thick with anticipation.

The fact that she kept thinking about Elliot and their unfinished conversation from this morning was not helping. Every time she thought about her confession, she felt like she would combust from embarrassment but then she remembered his pained *fuck, Daisy* and she thought maybe it wasn't the worst thing she could have said.

And then he confessed that he'd done the same…

And she'd never been hornier in her life. What was happening to her? Elliot had taken over her every thought. After Beltane, she'd try to deny it, to pretend it wasn't happening, but she didn't think she could resist the pull much longer.

Unfortunately, after the vet left, they both had to get back to work, and their words were left hanging between them.

He thought about her when he...

Her eyes fluttered closed and her imagination provided a vivid scene of Elliot, his hand wrapped around the cock she'd only felt through the thick denim of his jeans, but Daisy's brain was happy to fill in the details. His eyes squeezed shut, his cheeks flushed red, hair flopped over his forehead. Maybe his teeth dug into his bottom lip. Maybe he groaned her name.

Maybe—

Daisy forced her eyes open.

Stop that.

Ugh, and now she was warm for an entirely different reason.

How many times could she touch herself to thoughts of Elliot before she was just a pervert? She'd probably already hit her max.

She reached for her great-aunt's diary, instead, hoping for a distraction.

October 10, 1925

Nate kissed me between my thighs, and please don't judge, but I almost agreed to marriage, then and there. I never knew it could be like this.

Oh, damn Aunt D, not helping! Daisy nearly threw the book again but decided to forge on.

October 22, 1925

Nate says his parents want to meet me. He wants to introduce me as his fiancée. He's growing impatient. I don't know if I can do it. I feel paralyzed, afraid. I want to believe Nate is forever, but I thought that before and look how it turned out.

October 23, 1925

I've ruined everything.

Daisy groaned. 'What did you do?' she said out loud. The only response was a rumble of thunder. The wind blew her curtains in. Maybe it was going to storm after all.

We got into an argument. A fight. Our first. And probably our last. Nate said he wants a wife, and I said I wasn't sure I could be that for him. I said I was afraid. I confessed he wasn't the first man I've loved. It hurt him when I said it, I know that. He said he'd find someone who would marry him. Someone who really loved him. It was like he ripped my heart out.

He kissed me, then, tears on our faces. He begged me to change my mind.

But how can I ever forget how quickly he said he would find someone else?

How can I trust he's mine?

It was a good thing Daisy didn't have neighbors, because the way she shrieked in frustration would have surely raised some alarms. She flipped to the next page; she was nearly done with the little book. The next entry had skipped all the way to the following year.

Angry with the lack of information, Daisy kept reading. The rain started to pour.

January 8, 1926

> *Nate is engaged.*
> *Not to me, of course.*
> *I want to wish them well, but ... I don't.*

Damn it, Nathan!

February 21, 1926

> *According to the town gossip, Nate married his lovely bride today at the town hall. John had the audacity to provide the bouquet.*
> *I spent the day sick in my room.*
> *Perhaps I'm cursed.*

Cursed?! Oh, hell, no! Not you, too, Aunt D.

Daisy tore off the sheets and threw them aside. She was fired up now.

May 1, 1926

> *Did I curse Nate's marriage? Certainly not on purpose.*

Has it already ended? Yes. His lovely bride is gone, ran off to New Mexico with the neighbor.

So now we are both cursed.

He left town. I'll probably never see him again.

It's my own fault, of course. I let my fear stop me from being happy.

I cursed myself.

I cursed myself.
I cursed myself.
The words ran through Daisy's head like a chant.

She had to get out of here. She knew exactly what she had to do. She knew how to end this curse once and for all. For herself and for Aunt Daisy, too.

She would have to be brave enough for both of them.

Chapter Thirty-Three

Finding a soaking wet Daisy on his front step in the middle of the night was definitely not how Elliot saw his day ending. She'd dropped him off at his house a few times over the past few weeks, but she'd certainly never shown up in the middle of the night.

He'd just taken Goldie out to pee again, for the fourth time tonight, when he heard the knock.

'Hi,' she breathed when he opened the door, a crack of thunder and a flash of lightning lighting up her face in the darkness. Her eyes were huge, her wet hair sticking to her cheeks, but he couldn't read her expression.

'What's wrong? What happened?' Alarm bells were going off in Elliot's body. Why was she here? Was she hurt, sad, scared? A million insane scenarios raced through his head. Luckily, Goldie had fallen back to sleep or she would have been barking like crazy, only adding to his fear.

'Nothing's wrong. I just ... I need your help.'

'Anything.' He didn't hesitate. He'd do anything she asked.

Her face split into a grin.

'I know how to break the curse.'

'Daisy, you're not—'

'Just shut up and kiss me,' she said, flinging herself at him, her arms coming around his neck. He hoisted her up, and she wrapped her legs around his waist as he backed them both into the house. He leaned against the closed door and her mouth found his, frantic and hungry. She kissed him like she might never get another chance. He let her, meeting her with his own breathless need, until she slowed down, her kisses becoming deep and languid. He pulled away just enough to ask again,

'What's going on?'

She kissed him again, a few small pecks on his lips, jaw, cheek, before unwinding herself from him.

'I was reading the diary.'

He waited for her to go on, realizing she was still dripping wet and now she was shivering. Well, he couldn't have that. Whatever she had to tell him could wait until she was dry and warm. He took her hand and led her to the bathroom, wrapping her in a towel. He hugged her close, rubbing his hands up and down her arms until she stopped shaking. She let her forehead fall against his.

She didn't elaborate on what she'd read.

'I don't want to be afraid of this anymore. I want you, Elliot. For real. In all the ways.'

Her gaze when it met his was so open and hopeful. It matched every way he felt inside. *They* were a match.

He kissed her, savoring her this time. The feel of her lips, the slide of her tongue, the taste of her—like the peppermint tea he knew she drank before bed. He catalogued it all.

'I want it all with you, too, Daisy.'

She smiled, sweet and soft, until something else flickered in her eyes, something like *want*. And then the full meaning of what they'd just confessed crashed into him.

'So ... like now?' Daisy teased. 'We could have it all right now...'

'God, yes.'

'Good.' Daisy dropped the towel, and it was then that he really got a good look at what she was wearing: her tiny sleep shorts with what was now a nearly see-through white T-shirt that had been soaked by the rain. The *one* time she wore white...

'Jesus, Daisy,' he choked. 'You were outside like that?' The shirt clung to every delectable curve, every peak and valley. He could see *everything*. His cock was already so hard, he didn't know how he was going to survive the night.

She glanced down at herself, her cheeks turning a delicious pink. 'No one saw me.' She looked up at him again. 'Except you.'

His breath came out in a shuddering exhale.

She was shivering again.

'Are you cold?'

She shook her head. 'No.' Her hands trembled as she peeled the shirt from her body. 'I just need you.'

And there she was, Daisy, *his* Daisy, topless in his bathroom, shaking and telling him she needed him. And fuck, did he need her. Every bit of nervousness he'd had about this moment was burnt up by that need. He stepped closer, cupping her face in his hands.

'I'm here. Tell me what you need. *Anything.*'

She whimpered as his hands trailed from her face down the sides of her body, tracing her. Goosebumps pebbled in the wake of his fingers.

'Yes,' she whispered. 'Touch me.'

Her words made him bold, brave. He let his hand splay across her bare stomach, her ribs, the underside of her breast. Her breath hitched.

'Do you want me to touch you here, Daisy?' His voice was low, raspy. Desperate.

'*Yes.*' Hers was the same.

He wrapped an arm around her, keeping her close, trying to stop her trembling while his other hand cupped her breast, lightly at first, a barely-there touch, his thumb grazing her nipple. They were both trembling now as he touched her, listening for every gasp, every sigh.

He dipped his head and kissed her as he explored, letting his hands rove freely over her body, the dip in her waist, her gorgeous ass. Everywhere he hadn't dared to touch her the last time they did this. This time he wasn't holding anything back.

He wanted more. He needed more of her.

'Come with me.' He grabbed her hand and she didn't hesitate, followed him down the hall to his bedroom. 'Take off the rest,' he said and her eyes widened.

He felt hot all over like he was burning from the inside out.

'Please, Daisy. Take off the rest.'

Thunder rumbled in the distance; rain pelted against the

window. Elliot held his breath as Daisy peeled off her shorts and underwear.

'Daisy,' he groaned. 'You are…'

'The prettiest girl in town?' she said with a smirk, teasing him even as she stood in front of him naked and gorgeous.

He laughed and scooped her into his arms. 'In the entire fucking world,' he said, his lips pressed against her hair.

She sighed and he held her until they were kissing again, his hands full of *her*. The soft skin of her back, the curve of her ass, those perfect breasts pressed against him. He felt so … honored to be allowed to see her like this, to touch her, to taste her.

He pulled away, panting. 'Daisy,' he rasped, struggling for control. It had been so long. So long since he held someone like this, since he'd had someone's skin pressed against his and now that it was Daisy he held in his arms, he could barely keep himself from falling apart completely.

'You okay?' she whispered, her eyebrows knit together.

'It's been a really long time,' he confessed with a wince. 'And I'm trying really hard not to embarrass myself.'

She ran her hands down his arms. He was still dressed, wearing the Cornell T-shirt and sweats he'd worn to bed. Her fingers trailing down his forearms set off sparks in their wake. Christ, he was going to come from Daisy touching the inside of his wrist. The hair tie was still there, and she traced it with her finger.

'Don't be embarrassed,' she said. 'It's been a long time for me, too. Well, since before you made me come on your fingers … it was a long time.'

'Daisy,' he ground out, grabbing her wrist and stopping

the tracing of her fingers, needing her to understand. 'I've only ever been with one other woman.'

She stopped and stared. 'Total?'

'Yes.'

'But what about—'

'One woman, Daisy. You are the second woman I've seen naked. Ever.'

'Jesus,' she breathed.

'I only know what she liked … I don't know…' He didn't know what he wanted to do first, he didn't know if he could please her again. He didn't know…

'I have an idea.' Daisy dropped to her knees in front of him and Elliot nearly dropped dead.

'What are you doing?' he choked.

'Taking the edge off.' She looked up at him, her amber eyes sparking in the dim light of his bedroom. She tugged gently at the waistband of his pants. 'This okay?'

Was it okay? Was it okay that the woman he'd accidentally fallen in love with, the woman he dreamed about every damn night, was on her knees in front of him? Her cheeks flushed pink and her lips swollen from kissing him. It was more okay than anything in his life had ever been. Ever.

'Yes,' he managed to get out of his quickly closing throat.

'I'll be gentle.' Daisy winked at him before pulling his sweats down. He kicked them aside. He was about to tell her she really didn't have to do this, but the way she was looking at him, pupils blown wide, her nipples tight, her thighs pressed together, he thought maybe she wanted to do this. In fact, she looked eager to do this. 'Wait,' he said, and she paused in her efforts to get his underwear off. 'Your knees.' He grabbed a pillow from the bed and laid it on the floor.

She stared up at him, a mildly shocked expression on her face. 'I'm going to make you come so hard.'

He let out a surprised laugh. 'That's a given. God, Daisy, I've never been this hard before. It's *never* been like this before.'

She leaned forward and kissed his stomach before pulling his boxer briefs down over his thighs. Elliot groaned in anticipation. His legs trembled beneath Daisy's hands.

'Damn, Elliot,' she said, giving him a little grin.

'What?'

She shook her head. 'It's just always the ones you least expect to be so…'

'So what?'

'Well endowed,' she said with a smirk before taking him in her mouth and frying any remaining brain cells he had to consider that comment.

Daisy's mouth.

Warm.

Wet.

Tight.

It was all he could think. His entire world came down to the feel of Daisy's mouth wrapped around him, her hand tight around the base of his cock until she could take him further, deeper.

His hands went to her head, fingers threading through the still damp strands. She hummed a little and Elliot nearly blacked out.

'So good, so good,' he murmured, unable to express any

other thought. This wouldn't take long at all. He was wound so damn tight and Daisy's mouth was so good, too good. And all her little hums and moans and whimpers while she sucked and licked, Christ, never in his life had he experienced something this incredible.

He couldn't wait to return the favor.

Daisy was right. They'd get the edge off, and then he'd lay her down and find out every way to make her feel exactly like this, like she was melting, burning. Igniting.

A flash of lightning lit up the room, thunder rumbled through him.

'Daisy,' he groaned. 'Sweet Daisy, you're so good, so good…' He was rambling, words tumbling out of him. 'So perfect, you look so beautiful like that, so … fuck … I need to…'

Her gaze met his and he came so hard his body shook, his hands trembled in Daisy's hair. He may have left his body for a minute, but when he returned to it, Daisy was smiling at him as she stood.

'Feel better?' she asked.

Elliot shook his head, panting and wrung out. A frown crossed Daisy's face.

'That was incredible,' he said, picking her up and laying her on the bed. 'But I won't feel better until you feel the same way.' He was determined now, a man possessed by the need to pleasure this woman. 'You're going to tell me anything you need me to do to make that happen, okay?'

'Okay,' Daisy whispered, looking at him in disbelief.

He crawled up her body and planted a kiss on her swollen lips. 'That was the hottest thing that has ever happened to me,' he assured her.

Her mouth curved into a smile. 'Good.'

He kissed her again. He couldn't seem to stop. 'Spread your legs for me, Daisy,' he whispered against her ear. 'Let me lick you. Let me help *you* take the edge off.'

She let her knees fall open, cradling him between her thighs. He was propped up on his forearms, surrounding her, holding her while they kissed, breathless, needy kisses. He was already getting hard again, but this time he could last, this time he would make Daisy feel how much he wanted her, how much he loved her.

He tore himself away from her mouth, mapping a path down her body with his lips and tongue and teeth. He nipped and licked at her nipple and she gasped, squirming beneath him. He did it again, savoring her reaction, but when he moved to continue his journey, she tugged him gently by his hair.

He looked up.

'More of that,' she said, cheeks flushed and Elliot grinned.

'Gladly.' He sucked at Daisy's breast, teasing the nipple with his tongue and teeth, until her back bowed off the bed.

'Elliot,' she gasped. Her fingers tugged at his hair, digging into his scalp.

'What? Tell me.'

'I need to come. Please.'

He needed that, too. More than anything. He repositioned himself between her legs.

'Like this?'

'Yes.' She gasped as he bent his head and licked, firm, flat strokes until her thighs were quivering in his hands, and she was moaning his name.

'Like that,' she gasped. 'Like that, like that, like that...' she chanted it until her voice broke and she screamed out his name.

And nothing had ever tasted better than Daisy coming on his tongue.

Chapter Thirty-Four

They'd collapsed in a heap and dozed off in a tangle of naked limbs. Elliot had pulled her close and now his ... sizeable ... cock was nestled against her ass, and his arms were banded around her waist. His face was buried in the crook of her neck, his soft breathing tickling her shoulder.

Daisy bit down on a smile.

Elliot had surprised her once again. For all his nerves, the man had nothing to be nervous about. At all.

The storm was over, and everything was peaceful and dark outside Elliot's windows. Daisy shifted a little and he murmured in her ear.

'You awake?'

'Yes,' she said. 'Sorry, I didn't mean to wake you.'

He rolled her over, so he was braced above her. He planted a kiss on her forehead. 'That was just a power nap. I'm not done with you yet.'

Daisy's mouth opened a little in shock and Elliot grinned.

'If that's okay with you,' he added and Daisy laughed.

'It's very okay with me.'

He leaned down to kiss her, his lips soft and warm. She smiled against his mouth.

'It was good? Before?'

'Very good. So good. Did you not hear me screaming?'

His grin grew. 'Just making sure.' He nudged her legs apart with his knee. 'Open for me again, Daisy. I want more.'

Daisy hummed in satisfaction. She was obliterating the hell out of this curse.

Elliot rolled on a condom and then pushed into her, slowly, letting her adjust to his size. Her breath caught and he froze.

'It's okay?'

'Elliot, you do know you have a really big dick, right?'

He breathed out a barely-there laugh, all while holding himself still. 'I *have* been in locker rooms before.' He leaned down and kissed her, slowly, softly, waiting until she relaxed again before he pushed in further.

'Okay,' she breathed, nipping his jaw, kissing down his neck. 'Give me all of it.'

He thrust the rest of the way in, and Daisy moaned. Full. She was so full of him, of *Elliot*.

'Holy shit,' she whispered, and Elliot pressed his forehead to hers.

'You're so beautiful,' he said, kissing her again, her lips, her neck. He devoured her, breathed her in until they were one moving part, one soul fused together. He started thrusting, tentatively at first, searching her face.

'It's good,' she assured him. 'More. Do more.'

He changed the angle of his hips, diving in deeper and Daisy's eyes rolled into the back of her head. She was so full, so hot, so … so … she clawed at Elliot's back, at his shoulders, his forearms … she needed … she needed…

'Talk to me,' he bit out, thrusting into her so hard, her head nearly hit the headboard, but then Elliot's hand was there to catch her.

'Harder,' she gasped. 'And maybe…' She tried to tilt her hips up and Elliot quickly caught on, stuffing a pillow under her butt. This man and his pillows. She loved it. 'Perfect,' she moaned. 'That's fucking perfect.'

Elliot's smile was quick and wicked before he picked up the pace again and at this angle with his hand padding her head with every ram into the headboard, Daisy fell apart so fast she didn't even see it coming before she was crying and shaking with the intensity of the moment.

He groaned, his cheeks flushed, and hair tumbled over his forehead. And he looked so damn beautiful like that, Daisy nearly confessed everything she was feeling.

'Daisy,' he sighed as he thrust into her one more time and Daisy felt his whole body tremble as he came, one hand still tangled in her hair and one holding tight to her hips.

'Daisy, that was…' he panted, his breath hot on her cheek. 'That was *everything*.'

Elliot's house was kind of a mess. Daisy was taking stock as she sat at his kitchen island while he made her a heaping pile of French toast. The bedroom had been tidy enough, other than the copious stacks of books, but the en suite bathroom didn't currently have a toilet or working shower, they'd had to use the one down the hall, and in the kitchen the tile back-splash behind the counters had been torn out, and beneath her stool was subfloor and nothing else.

It was the first time she'd been inside and since she was pretty distracted last night, she hadn't had a chance to look around, but now she had questions.

'You're redoing the kitchen?' she asked as Elliot poured her a cup of coffee.

'Pretty much always redoing something, yeah. It's what Caleb and I used to do before I moved here. We flipped houses.'

'Right. I know, but you're doing this house by yourself?'

He shrugged. 'I can manage small projects by myself.'

Daisy raised an eyebrow. 'Like tile and flooring?'

'I picked up a few skills along the way.'

'And plumbing?'

'Nah, I have a guy come in for that.'

'Hmm…'

'What's that *hmm* mean?' he asked with a smile.

'Nothing, I'm just always learning something new and surprising about you. Like that you're more than just a designs-things-on-paper guy.'

He leaned forward on the counter between them. 'And what else have you learned about me?'

Daisy tapped her fork against her lips like she was

thinking. 'I'm happy to say I finally got to learn about your impressive sexual prowess.'

He laughed and slid another slice of toast onto her plate.

'Thanks for noticing. You were pretty impressive, too.'

Daisy grinned, about to dig into her breakfast when Elliot stopped her.

'Wait, I didn't do the best part.' He grabbed a small sieve and scooped powdered sugar into it and then tapped the side until it sprinkled sugar over her French toast. 'Had to make it snow.'

'That's adorable.'

'My mom used to make it for us on snow days, but I feel like it works in June, too.'

'Totally,' Daisy agreed, around a mouth full of sugary bread. 'Delicious.'

Elliot grabbed a plate of his own and joined her at the island.

'Now I have to add amazing cooking to the new and surprising things about you,' she teased.

'Don't get too excited. This is my fanciest dish.'

'Still, a man who can do home renovations, make French toast, and give a woman multiple orgasms is a pretty good résumé.'

Elliot choked a little on his breakfast, his ears turning bright red. Daisy ran a finger over the rim.

'Oh, good,' she said with a laugh. 'I was afraid that after we'd done it, I wouldn't be able to make you blush anymore.'

He turned to face her, so their legs intertwined in the space between them. 'I don't think it's possible for me to stop having a face that alerts the world every time I'm embarrassed…'

'Or turned on.'

Elliot dropped his head with a laugh. 'Right. Or turned on. It's very inconvenient.'

'I still think it's cute.'

She'd slept in a pair of his boxers and one of his T-shirts, and Elliot's fingers were currently making circles on her bare knee. Sun slanted in through the windows over the sink and the air coming in was already warm. Goldie was sprawled out on her belly at their feet. It was going to be another summery day, but Daisy was sure that wasn't why her skin was heating.

'So, what's the plan for the renovation?'

'It's an old house, which was the main part of its appeal, of course.'

Daisy laughed. 'Of course.'

'I had originally planned to restore it and sell it, but now…'

'But now?'

Elliot's smile grew. 'Now I want to stay.'

Daisy leaned forward and kissed him. He tasted like cinnamon and maple syrup.

He ran his hands through her hair, gathering the strands at the nape of her neck. He twisted the elastic off his wrist and tied her hair back, giving that little piece back now that he had all of her. She kissed him again.

'Do you want to tell me what was in the diary that had you running over here practically naked in the middle of the night?' he asked, nipping at her lips as he said it, his hands wandering up her thighs.

'You live like two blocks away. I didn't run. I walked. Quickly.'

His delighted laugh made her smile.

'And I wasn't naked. I was wearing my PJs.'

'PJs that were completely translucent by the time you got here.'

Judging by the way Elliot's ears and cheeks were glowing, he was clearly picturing the whole scene. She squirmed a little on her stool, remembering how his hungry gaze had felt on her, and then his hands, his lips...

She shook her head, trying to stay on topic.

'That's all beside the point.'

'Okay,' Elliot straightened. 'Tell me. What was in there that was so urgent?'

Daisy frowned, remembering how frustrated and sad she'd felt reading her great-aunt's latest entries.

'I just got so mad at her. And then mad at myself for being just like her.'

'What do you mean?'

'She couldn't let the past go. She'd been hurt before, and it was clouding her judgment. It was making her push away a sweet, loving man because she was assuming it would end the same way.'

Elliot was very still, watching her. Waiting for her conclusion.

'And it made me wish I could go back in time and shake the damn woman!'

He cupped her face in his hands and traced the curve of her cheek with his thumb. She leaned into the touch.

'She talked about being cursed. She thought she was cursed to stay broken-hearted forever, but it was her own fault for not seeing what was right in front of her. I don't want to be like that ... I don't want to do that.'

'What do you want to do, Daisy?' he asked, his voice as soft as his touch.

'I meant what I said last night. I want to be with you. For real.'

He leaned forward and pressed his lips to hers, his fingers threading through her hair, and she felt safe. She felt adored.

'Daisy, I'm so in love with you.'

She wasn't expecting the tears. She wasn't expecting to crumple like she did, but Elliot scooped her up to his chest and held her close.

'Shh...' he crooned. 'It's okay. It's all going to be okay.'

'I'm so in love with you, too,' she sniffled. 'And I didn't mean to be, and I swore I wasn't going to do this again but'—she breathed, looking up at him—'I'm so in love with you. You made it impossible not to be.'

There was the lopsided smile she'd loved from the start.

'Sorry,' he said. 'But you didn't make it easy on me, either, you know. I came here to live like a hermit, alone with my history books, and look at me now! Spotted around town canoodling with the florist!'

Daisy's tears quickly turned to laughter.

'Well, you had to be sweet and understanding all the time and then you threw in French toast and a giant...'

He kissed her.

'Stop trying to make me blush,' he said against her lips and she giggled.

'It was just ... after I read those last few entries, I knew I was making a mistake keeping you at arm's length. I don't want to be cursed anymore. I want to be with you.'

'You're not cursed, Daisy,' he said, kissing her forehead. 'But'—he picked her up off the stool, and Daisy let out a startled squeak—'if we need to do this a few more times to convince you, then I'm game.' He tossed her over his shoulder, gave her ass a smack and carried her off to the bedroom.

Surprising her once again.

Chapter Thirty-Five

Daisy was feeling significantly less cursed in some ways, some very specific in-the-bedroom-type ways, but unfortunately that hadn't transferred into business-type ways.

It was the beginning of July, and she still hadn't booked a single wedding. She'd never been more in love or felt more secure with a man than she did with Elliot. They'd moved from fake to real without a hitch, but apparently, the town gossip chain hadn't gotten the memo.

Or they didn't believe that Daisy having a boyfriend for a few months was enough to trust her with their weddings.

She had been feeling so optimistic when she'd left his house that first morning she'd stayed over, so full of sweet breakfast treats and sporting a brand new orgasmic glow, but then she got to work and remembered her little curse wasn't just about her own love life, it was about how she was going to keep this damn shop running if everyone still thought she was going to destroy *their* love lives.

What the hell was a cursed florist supposed to do?!

Having her mother here today, drifting around the shop, replacing crystals and blowing cinnamon through every damn doorway was not helping.

'Mom, you're getting cinnamon all over the floor.'

'That's kinda the point, Daisy.' Her mother rolled her eyes like she was being ridiculous, closed the front door of the shop and wandered back in. It was hot outside, and the old shop didn't have the best track record with air-conditioning. The current window unit was making an awful lot of noise but not making much cool air. The tropical flowers loved it, but Daisy was melting.

'How's Elliot?' her mom asked, changing the subject entirely.

'Elliot is fine.'

'I heard you were in a hurry to get over there last week. I didn't know if there was some kind of emergency.'

Daisy winced. Of course her late-night jog in the rain to Elliot's house hadn't gone unnoticed. This damn town. Her mom knew there was no emergency.

'Elliot's good. I just needed...' *To get thoroughly fucked by a sweet man who loves me? Nope, not gonna say that.* 'I just needed to see him. And I felt like taking a ... walk.'

'In a storm?' Her mother waited with raised brows.

'I like the rain.'

Mom laughed.

'We had a nice night,' Daisy insisted. 'And that's all I'm telling you, *mother*.'

Her mom rolled her eyes again. 'We're all adults here, Daisy-girl. A few details wouldn't kill you.'

Daisy just shook her head and went back to poring over

the books. She wasn't in the mood to spill her guts to her mom. Especially not about everything she and Elliot had done that night. And nearly every night since. And most mornings. And yesterday afternoon... They'd been making up for lost time. And it had been amazing and wonderful and so freaking perfect that Daisy had been pinching herself every day.

She wasn't going to panic. She wasn't going to assume Elliot would eventually tire of her and leave. She was going to take what the universe was giving her.

Or at least that was what she told herself in the mirror every morning. Even when, deep down, this thing with Elliot felt so new and fragile that she didn't even want to breathe around it. She didn't want to talk about it for fear of jinxing it.

Breaking the curse was still a work in progress.

But Elliot showed up every day for her, and she was going to do the same for him.

Maybe she had to trust the universe more. It had brought her Elliot, maybe it would bring new business too. She just hoped it happened soon.

'Mom, give me some of those crystals.'

Her mother's face lit up as she reached into the deep pockets of her dress and pulled out a few crystals. 'I picked these for prosperity,' she said and Daisy couldn't help but return her smile. The women in her family had been running this shop for decades. Maybe it was time she trusted the process.

'Thanks, Mom.'

'Love you, Daisy-girl.' Her mom planted a kiss on her cheek.

'Love you, too.'

'Okay now let's think of the best placement for these.'

'Sure.' Daisy wiped the sweat from her brow and got to work.

'I can finally visualize everything!' Mary said as she wandered through the newly framed motel-style rooms. They'd gotten the asbestos taken care of, which had set them back about a week, but now they were actually starting to make progress.

'I'm glad,' Elliot said, following along behind Mary and Joseph. He wanted to point out that he'd shown them multiple 3D renderings of what everything would look like, but he was just happy that the owners were happy. He'd learned over the past few months that Mary had a tendency to spend a lot of time second-guessing herself while watching home reno shows. It was a bad combination. And Joseph agreed with whatever she wanted, even when she didn't know what she wanted. It hadn't exactly made things easy, but Elliot was excited to see his plans begin to come to fruition.

'I agree,' Joseph added, surprising no one. 'Things are really shaping up.'

He took Mary's hand and the two of them stood in what would someday be room number 7, beaming at Elliot. They were both younger than what he'd been expecting when he took the job. He'd pictured an elderly couple, but neither of them were over fifty and both considered running half marathons to be a good use of their time. A sentiment Elliot could not relate to. But they were full of energy and buying the inn had been their big new adventure when their kids went off to college. They'd only been running it for a few years now, and Elliot knew they were putting a lot of their hopes and funds into this renovation.

'I'm really glad you guys are pleased,' he said. 'It'll only get better from here.'

'Thank you for taking us through it,' Mary said. 'I'll sleep better now,' she added with a chuckle.

'Of course.' Elliot walked them out, feeling more than a little proud of himself for the successful meeting. He was still in a good mood when Caleb showed up an hour later.

'How'd the walk through go this morning?' he asked.

'Joseph and Mary are happy which is not something I get to say a lot, so nice work.' Elliot clapped his brother on the shoulder, and Caleb stopped in his tracks.

'What's going on with you?' Caleb asked.

'What do you mean?'

Caleb tipped his head like he was studying him. 'You seem different.'

'Different how?'

'Happy, I guess? Even more so in the past few days. Like something changed.'

Something like Daisy telling him she loved him. Something like officially going from a fake relationship to a real one. But he wasn't about to admit to his brother that this whole thing started out as a ruse concocted at least in part to keep him off Elliot's back.

'I am happy,' he said instead.

'Confident, too.'

A woman screaming his name every night did wonders

for his self-esteem. Another thing he wasn't confessing. He was close with his brother, but maybe not that close.

Instead, he just shrugged and kept walking toward the front of the inn. He was ready to be done for the day so he could go see the woman responsible for this newfound happy confidence.

'Daisy must be good for you,' Caleb went on. 'You weren't like this when you were with Leigh.'

'Really?' That gave Elliot pause. He'd been happy with Leigh, hadn't he? But had she made him feel confident?

'Yeah, I mean I liked Leigh, but you seem … better now than you have been in a long time.'

Maybe he'd been happy with Leigh at first, but his brother was right, it had been a long time since he'd felt like this. Those last few years of his marriage, he felt like he'd been clinging to something that just wasn't working.

'Thanks, I feel better.'

'Good.' It was Caleb's turn to land a hearty pat on Elliot's back.

'So, you can stop acting like a mother hen around me now.'

Caleb laughed. 'Maybe. But I'm not making any promises. Old habits die hard.'

Elliot just shook his head. He didn't really expect his brother to ever stop being a nosy bastard about his life, but maybe he could return the favor. 'What about you?'

'What about me?'

'You gonna ask Vivienne out?'

Caleb stumbled over his feet before shaking it off and feigning disinterest. Elliot was having a very hard time keeping a straight face.

'I don't think so.'

'Why not? She's cute.'

'She's fucking gorgeous.'

Elliot's eyebrows rose as a furious blush worked its way up Caleb's face. His brother never blushed. He didn't get flustered over women. Elliot was dying to tease him about it, but the man actually looked too pitiful to mock at the moment.

'But that's beside the point,' Caleb said, attempting to school his features and failing terribly. 'She wasn't interested and there's plenty of gorgeous women out there.'

'Mmm.'

If his brother felt like he had the first time he'd seen Daisy, then avoiding Vivienne would be a lost cause. He just hoped Caleb didn't fight it too hard. He was as stubborn as he was charming.

But a perk of being the younger brother was that Elliot didn't make a habit of worrying about his brother's love life.

'What does that mean? Why are you looking at me like that?'

'No reason,' Elliot said, heading out the front doors. 'Mom's wondering when you're going to settle down, though.'

Caleb followed him out, looking stricken. 'You're talking to mom about *me*?'

'Yep.' Elliot grinned. 'She's planning another visit for this fall.'

'She is?'

'She sure is.'

'Why?'

Elliot laughed. 'I don't know, to see us I would imagine. And'—he couldn't help adding—'probably to check up on you.'

Caleb scoffed. 'Why would she need to check up on me?'

'I told you, she wants to see you settle down with a nice girl. Or boy. Or any consenting adult, really. Your pick.'

Caleb snorted again, puffing out his chest like he was a big, bad man. 'That's not really up to her.'

Elliot patted him on the arm. 'Yeah, okay, buddy, good luck with that! I'll see you tomorrow!' He chuckled to himself as he made his way through the parking lot to his car, leaving Caleb scowling on the porch. It was nice to be on this side of his mother's concerns. Let Caleb deal with her worries for a bit.

A text vibrated the phone in his pocket. Daisy.

> Ice cream?! I'm melting!

Elliot smiled, his heart picking up speed just thinking about seeing his Daisy again.

> Sure. Meet you there.

It didn't take long before they were sharing a brownie sundae in the Apple Pie Ice Cream Parlor with several dozen of their neighbors. The place was packed, but Elliot wasn't really seeing anyone else but Daisy. The humidity had curled the hair at her temples, and her cheeks were rosy. She was wearing a dark gray T-shirt dress today that hugged all her curves.

Their legs were tangled under the small table, their

heads tipped over their shared sundae. Daisy's spoon disappeared between her lips, and Elliot was distracted by her mouth, by the thoughts of what he wanted to do with it later.

He wasn't sure if he'd been this happy with Leigh at any point in the past, but he knew for a fact his libido had never done this before. He couldn't get enough of Daisy. He wanted her all. The. Damn. Time. She made him insatiable.

She smirked around her spoon like she knew exactly what he was thinking about.

'What do you want to do after this?' she asked.

'I have a few ideas.'

'Do any of them involve keeping my clothes on?'

Elliot grinned. 'Nope.'

Daisy laughed, husky and sweet, and he was ready to ditch the last of their ice cream and drag her out of here when Jack and Gabe appeared at their table.

'Mind if we join you?' Jack asked. 'There's no more tables.'

Elliot looked up, noticing the crowd for the first time.

'Of course,' Daisy answered. 'We'll share.' She moved over and perched herself on Elliot's lap. He wrapped an arm around her waist, certainly not going to argue with this seating arrangement.

'Great,' Gabe said, sitting and pulling Jack into his own lap. 'We'll share, too.'

Jack's eyes went wide as he sat, and Elliot gave him a big smile. It was too hot for a vest, but Jack made up for it with a sunny button-down shirt. Gabe was in his usual grass-stained T-shirt and jeans. They were so different, but they looked like they fit together, like they just made sense.

'You guys are very cute together,' Daisy said, and Gabe grinned.

'Thanks. I had a crush on Jack for so long.'

Jack nearly choked on his milkshake. 'You didn't tell me that.'

Gabe kissed his cheek and Jack looked like he might melt into a puddle on the floor. 'Of course I didn't tell you. I was nervous.'

'You?'

'Yeah.'

'You were nervous?'

'Of course. Why does that surprise you?'

Jack sputtered. Apparently in all their sneaking away to make out they'd never actually discussed anything about their feelings for each other or when they had started.

'Because you're *you*. And you're beautiful.'

Gabe's smile grew. 'So are you, babe.'

Daisy clapped. 'Adorable. I guess you guys are official.'

'Sitting on a man's lap in the middle of the ice-cream shop usually does the trick,' Jack said, still looking a little dazed.

'So, I can call you my boyfriend now?' Gabe asked.

Before Jack could choke out a response, which wasn't really needed since the answer was clearly *yes*, Hazel and Noah appeared at their table. Elliot didn't think they could pile any more people on these two chairs, but Noah had managed to grab a couple and drag them over.

'Can we join you?' Hazel asked.

'Of course!' Daisy said, and Elliot gave her a little squeeze.

'How's everyone doing?' Noah asked as they sat.

He gestured to Jack and Gabe with his chin. 'You two are a thing now?'

'He's my boyfriend,' Gabe said, smiling around the straw of his milkshake. Jack just sighed, dreamily.

'Congrats,' Noah said with a grin.

'And you two look cozy,' Hazel said, directing her attention to Daisy and Elliot.

'We are *very* cozy,' Daisy said, 'So if you could spread the word that the curse is broken, I'd really appreciate it. Maybe your dad could make some sort of announcement.'

Hazel laughed. 'How do you know it's broken?' she asked, digging into her ice cream.

'Well...' Daisy launched into the story of her great-aunt's diary and the similarities between them, while Elliot just enjoyed holding her. Her ass in his lap was quite distracting... They hadn't had sex in this position yet, in a chair ... that might be something they should try, sooner rather than later...

By the time he had tuned back in, Daisy was passing around her phone to show everyone how much she looked like her great-aunt and Elliot was trying to reposition her, so it wasn't too obvious what he had been daydreaming about.

'This is crazy!' Jack was saying. 'Elliot, this man looks just like you!'

'It's wild, right? That's Elliot's distant cousin or something,' Daisy said. 'It's like we had to break this generational curse. Our ancestors couldn't figure out how to be together, but we did!' God, she was cute when she was talking about historical love curses that somehow brought them together.

Elliot didn't think he believed in fate but maybe...

Jack passed the phone back. 'Well, I'm glad you two found each other.'

'Me, too,' Daisy said with a smile. 'And I'm sure the next wedding I do flowers for will lead to a long and happy marriage.' She looked pointedly around the table.

Noah laughed. 'Don't look at us. We're already happily married.'

Daisy rolled her eyes. 'But you never had a reception. Don't you want a big party?'

'Not particularly,' Hazel said, and Noah dropped a kiss to her head.

'That's my little introvert.'

'Well, if you ever decide to let all your friends and loved ones celebrate with you, come to me for all your floral needs,' Daisy said, not letting them get away with avoiding a party that easily.

Gabe laughed. 'I like your style.'

'Don't think you're off the hook,' she said, wagging a finger at him. 'When you decide to be husband and husband, the same applies.'

'Jesus, Daisy! We just said *boyfriend* for the first time,' Jack said, appalled.

Daisy shrugged. 'Just putting it out there.'

Elliot chuckled and Daisy smiled at him.

'I love you,' he whispered against her ear as the others started talking about Gabe possibly volunteering for the fire department. 'Let's get out of here.'

Daisy grabbed his hand. 'Your place or mine?'

'Yours is closer.'

Daisy laughed as they waved goodbye and hurried out the door.

Chapter Thirty-Six

'You were right, this is the perfect spot.'

'I thought you'd appreciate it.' Daisy clinked her beer bottle gently against Elliot's, and he kissed the top of her head. They were propped up on pillows, lying on the air mattress she'd dragged up to the roof of the flower shop this afternoon. The Fourth of July fireworks would be starting any minute, and they'd have the perfect view without dealing with the crowd. In fact, if they stood up, they'd probably see Shawn and Greg sipping champagne on the roof of the pet shop, and Jeanie and Logan snuggled up together on the roof of The Pumpkin Spice Café. Annie, Mac, Hazel, and Noah were watching from the harbor on his boat, *Ginger*. And she was sure the rest of her friends were somewhere in the throngs of people headed to the beach to watch the display.

But Daisy was happy they were here, just the two of them.

Well, three of them if you counted Goldie who was

asleep on a beach towel beside them. She was unfazed by thunder, so Daisy assumed fireworks wouldn't scare her, either.

It had been another hot day, but the air had cooled off considerably once the sun finally set. The night around them buzzed with cicadas and crickets and the laughter of a few stragglers on the street below.

Earlier they'd grilled hot dogs on the little charcoal grill she kept up here and ate them with thick slices of watermelon on the side, listening to the *Hamilton* soundtrack on repeat, with Elliot chiming in with his own historical tidbits. The whole thing had Daisy feeling unexpectedly patriotic.

'Oh, they're starting!' she said with a little gasp.

They put their drinks aside and snuggled down under the blankets she'd laid out, Elliot's arm wrapped around her shoulder, as the sky over Dream Harbor lit up in red and blue and silver. Goldie lifted her head, looked around, and decided nothing was amiss. She yawned dramatically and then continued dozing. Daisy reached over and scratched her head for being such a good girl.

'I wonder how many of my relatives celebrated the Fourth of July up here,' Daisy said.

'Do you think Aunt D and Nate did?' Elliot asked, turning to face her. He was lit up by the fireworks, the colors reflecting in his glasses. She slipped them from his face and laid them carefully aside.

'I hope so. I hope they were happy at least for a while.'
'Me, too.'
'I wish they'd been happy for longer.'
'Me, too.' He leaned forward and kissed the tip of her

nose. 'It wasn't all on your aunt. Dear old cousin Nate could have given her more time, been more patient with her.'

'It was the era, I guess? They couldn't keep being the town scandal. They had to be respectable.'

'He didn't have to push her.' Elliot shrugged. 'But they made their choices, and we can make ours.'

'Yeah,' Daisy said, running her fingers through his thick hair and capturing his mouth with hers.

'You're going to miss the fireworks,' he said, smiling against her lips.

'We could make our own.'

'You did not just say that.'

Daisy laughed. 'I regretted it immediately.'

Elliot rolled them so she was on her back, bracing himself over her. 'It's a great idea, though.' He nuzzled against her neck, kissing and nipping.

'So, you weren't always like this?' she asked, breathless.

'Like what?' He tugged her tank top over her head. 'Pretty color, by the way,' he said, tossing the red shirt aside.

'Thank you. And like … this…'

'Hornier than a teenage boy?'

'Yeah!'

He grinned. 'No, this is all for you, Daisy. Only you make me like this.'

She sighed as he worked his way down her neck, kissing her collarbone, her chest, licking the tops of her breasts, his tongue dipping into her bra until she gasped. Her shorts were off before she knew what was happening, her underwear tossed lord only knew where. And Elliot was everywhere. His mouth on her breast, his fingers working over her clit, sliding through her wetness.

He groaned. 'And what about you?' he said, his mouth back on her throat, teeth scraping sensitive skin. 'Were you like this before? Was anything ever like this before?'

His fingers were inside her now, thrusting, his thumb still working her clit so perfectly, getting her so close so quickly she would have been embarrassed if she didn't know that Elliot was right there with her, his rigid cock straining against her thigh.

'No,' she gasped. 'Everything with you is different. Better. *More*.'

She could feel his smile imprinted on her skin as he rubbed her just right, holding her as the pleasure built.

'Can you be quiet?' he whispered, even as his fingers did wicked and wonderful things to her.

Daisy whimpered and shook her head. Of course she couldn't be quiet. Even if they were outside. Even if their neighbors were inconveniently close by.

Elliot put his hand over her mouth, and she gasped at the feel of his strong fingers on her lips. 'Come apart for me, sweet Daisy.'

She did. Writhing and whimpering and groaning against his hand. She gripped his forearm, keeping him there, holding her.

'You look so perfect when you come,' he whispered.

Dazed but not finished, she climbed on top of him. 'So do you,' she said, kissing his neck, tugging his T-shirt off and kissing down his chest.

'Did you bring any condoms to this little set-up?' he asked, his voice hitching when Daisy undid the button on his jeans. 'I would have, if I thought *come watch the fireworks* meant *come fuck me on the roof*.'

Her laughter coasted over his skin and he shivered.

'I didn't bring any.'

'That's okay, we can just…'

'I went back on the pill.'

'Oh?' He looked at her, his eyebrows raised, waiting to see what she said next.

'So, we can go without. If you want.'

Elliot squeezed his eyes shut with a groan.

'That's a yes?'

He laughed. 'Yeah. That's a yes.' He slid his pants and boxers down and kicked them off. Daisy gripped his length, and he thrust up into her hand like he couldn't help himself, like he couldn't wait any longer.

Lucky for him, neither could she.

She lowered onto him, slowly taking him all, taking him bare and it was all heat and pressure and *fuck*, was it good. She leaned forward, letting her mouth find his again, their kisses becoming a frenzied mess as she rocked.

Faster.

Faster.

Until her orgasm was building again with each thrust forward.

'Don't stop,' Elliot gritted out as her pleasure broke around her, pulsing right along with Elliot's. 'Holy shit,' he gasped, his hands gripping her face, their gazes holding as they both came.

She collapsed on top of him and may have briefly died.

But Elliot's heartbeat was steady beneath her ear.

It wasn't until she came to that she realized the fireworks were over. The air hung thick with the residual smoke. She could hear the cover band from the festivities playing 'Take Me Home, Country Roads'.

'I petition to make this the new national anthem,' she said, her cheek still resting on his chest.

'I'll see what I can do.' His voice rumbled through her.

She sighed. 'I've never even been to West Virginia, and yet, this makes me feel like I miss it.'

'You're a complex woman,' he teased and Daisy swatted at his arm, but she was so weak he probably didn't even feel it.

She rolled off of him, and they lay on their backs, staring up at the night sky, while the sweat on their body dried and left goosebumps behind. Gradually, the smoke cleared and the stars came back out.

'I've been thinking about the curse,' Elliot said after a while, surprising her. He'd always insisted there was no such thing.

She rolled to face him.

'Oh, really?'

'Yeah, I think maybe you've been thinking about it the wrong way.' He stroked her damp hair off her forehead.

'How so?'

'Maybe you just need to rebrand it. Maybe it's actually your power.'

'My power to break up marriages? You know I'm not actually a witch, right?' she teased, but Elliot was serious.

'Talk to the brides. Maybe they're happy to be out of those marriages. Maybe you did them a favor. Aren't you happy to be out of yours? Do you really want to be with Matthew? Or David? You don't need them and you don't need me.'

'Hold on, wait, what are you saying?' Daisy sat up, reaching for the blankets, her heart-rate ratcheting up to a million beats per minute. Where was Elliot going with this? 'Of course I don't want to be with Matthew or David, but I *do* want to be with you. I do need you.'

Elliot shook his head. 'No, you don't. Not to break the curse. Not to save the flower shop.'

'But...'

'I think we should fake break-up.'

'*Fake* break-up?' She was clinging to the word fake like it was a life raft in the ocean.

'You're not your aunt. This isn't nineteen-twenty-five. You don't have to be married to be respectable. You don't have to listen to your family or this town or anyone. It shouldn't matter if you're with me or not. So, people don't want to book you for weddings? Sell them something else. You have the power here, Daisy. Use it.'

She blinked. 'Damn,' she whispered. 'You really have thought about this.'

Elliot took her hands in his, kissing the backs of each one, flipping them and pressing his lips to her palms. 'I love you. I will be here for you however you want. I just don't want you thinking that your success has to hinge on our relationship. You can do this, Daisy. With or without me.'

'So we fake break-up?'

'To show the town your relationship status is irrelevant.'

'And then I—'

'Think outside of weddings. What other big events are out there? Graduations?'

Daisy thought about it, her heart ramping up for a different reason now. Excitement. Hope. She'd been so focused on weddings she'd lost sight of every other life event. People needed flowers for all sorts of things, didn't they?

'How about *quinceañeras*—baby showers?' she ventured, tentatively.

Elliot lit up. 'Perfect.'

'Milestone birthdays.'

'The big Five-O. Definitely.'

'Anniversaries?'

'Sure! You could do a million other things, and once people see how amazing your flowers are, they won't remember anything about this absurd rumor.'

'Maybe Kira could help me with the rebrand on social media. She's good at that stuff.'

Elliot smiled at her and her heart broke a little bit. He was so beautiful.

'So, we're fake broken up, but we keep doing this, right?' She gestured between them, Elliot's bare chest and the tangle of blankets covering their legs.

He tackled her into the pillows, and her laughter rang out into the night sky. 'Hell, yes,' he said, his face buried in her neck.

'Good,' she said, her fingers raking down his back. 'Because I love you, too.'

Chapter Thirty-Seven

'Sorry I'm late!' Iris said, rushing over to their table at the pub. Daisy and Kira were already working their way through a plate of nachos and their first round of margaritas. 'Owen was fussing and Olive was not at all convinced that I needed a night out with only other grown-ups. She said that sounded boring.' Iris blew out a long breath. 'But Archer practically shoved me out the door, so … here I am.'

'We are very glad you made it,' Kira said, scooting over in the booth to make space for Iris.

'And I only cried a little bit on the way here.' Iris grabbed a cheesy chip and stuffed it in her mouth.

'We're proud of you,' Daisy said and Iris smiled.

'Thank you. Okay, now, what did I miss?'

'Kira was just telling me that David and Hailey decided to go with a destination wedding, after all. So, they won't be getting married in Dream Harbor.'

'Good. We didn't want them here anyway,' Iris said and Daisy couldn't help her laugh.

'And now she's showing me my new and improved Instagram account. Look at how gorgeous this is,' Daisy said, passing her phone to Iris.

'They're all your designs. I just curated them,' Kira said with a smile. It was more than that. Kira had taken beautiful photos of her flowers all over town. Daisy had donated free bouquets and centerpieces to any business in Dream Harbor that wanted one. She'd themed them for each shop, and the owners and customers had loved them.

But the real luck had come when Kira booked a 50th wedding anniversary party at the farm. Apparently, no one was worried about Daisy breaking up a couple that had been together for a lifetime, so Kira managed to get her the job. Daisy replicated the couple's flowers from their wedding day right down to the bride's cream-colored roses and the woman was so happy she cried. And then Daisy cried.

Now she had to keep up the momentum.

'Wait, I didn't show you the best part.' Kira took the phone back and tapped on some of the comments. 'Look at this one.'

'Read it out loud!' Iris insisted as Daisy's eyes scanned the comments.

'Is this who I think it is?'

'Out loud!'

Daisy laughed. 'Okay, okay. It says, "Daisy did the flowers for my wedding, and even though the groom ended up being a cheating bastard, the flowers were stunning. I donated them to a nursing home after finding my ex in bed with my cousin! Thanks, Daisy, for being the bright spot on a shitty day!"'

'That's incredible!' Iris said.

'I know, right?!' Kira said, giddily. 'And don't worry, I confirmed with the nursing home that no cute little old people couples split up that day.'

'You didn't.'

'Of course I did! And there's another one.'

Scroll, tap, and Daisy was looking at another comment on a different post, one of a glowing Annie when Mac surprised her with a bouquet of peonies, her favorites.

'"My marriage didn't last but the wedding flowers provided by The Daisy Chain Flower Shop looked beautiful for weeks! My husband never bought me flowers but now I buy bouquets for myself and my friends whenever I'm in town."'

Daisy could feel the tears burning at the back of her eyes. 'This is crazy,' she whispered. 'How did this happen?'

Kira shrugged. 'I may have reached out to some of your past customers.'

'You did?'

'Yep. None of them blame you, Daisy. Obviously.'

'Obviously,' she repeated, a little breathless. But it wasn't obvious. By the way people had been avoiding her shop, she thought the poor couples who broke up must surely blame her bad luck. At least a little bit.

'People don't break up because of flowers, Daisy,' Kira reiterated like she needed to hear it. Because she did. 'People break up for a million reasons, but not flowers. I promise.'

'Thanks, guys. I really needed this, I guess.'

'Me, too,' said Iris with a grin. Her copper hair was piled on top of her head, and her cheeks were flushed with happiness. She looked like herself again. Or like a new stronger version of herself, and Daisy was so glad she came tonight. 'It feels good to be out.'

'Another round, ladies?' Mac asked, appearing at their table.

'One more couldn't hurt,' Kira said with a wink.

'A virgin for me,' Iris said.

'Of course. How is the little man?' Mac asked. 'Good sleeper?'

Iris scoffed. 'He'll sleep anywhere if he's strapped to me. His crib? No way.'

Mac winced. 'I hear it gets better.'

'We'll see.'

'How about another plate of nachos?'

'Now you're talking!'

Mac laughed. 'Anything else?'

'Yeah,' Kira said. 'Tell Annie she owes me twenty bucks.'

'For what?'

'Elliot and Daisy broke up.'

Mac's gaze swung to Daisy, who did her best to keep a neutral face.

He smirked. 'Well, Annie is never going to buy that, but I'll give her the message.'

'I told you!' Iris said as Mac walked away. 'No one is going to believe you two broke up.'

'Why not!' Daisy said, sipping her drink. She found it oddly romantic that Elliot wanted the town to see she didn't need a man to break her curse. But apparently, no one was convinced.

'It's the way he looks at you,' Kira said.

'How does he look at me?'

'Are you kidding me right now? Daisy, he looks at you like you are his entire reason for being. He has since long before you two were dating or fake-dating or whatever.' Kira waved a hand at her before grabbing another chip. 'That man has had it bad since day one and he's terrible at hiding it.'

Iris nodded. 'That's true.'

Daisy couldn't help her smile, the heat washing over her face. He *did* look at her like that. She knew he did. And she was sure she looked at him like a lovesick idiot, too, but it was really nobody's business but their own.

'Oh, well,' she said. 'I'm sticking to my story. We decided to be just friends.'

'Whatever you say,' Kira said with a smile. 'But let's get down to the real reason why we're here.'

'A brainstorming session,' Daisy said, pushing her empty margarita aside. 'Screw weddings.'

Iris and Kira's eyebrows rose.

'I need your help figuring out how we emphasize other big life events. And how to market that. Weddings are not the be-all-end-all of people's lives, right? I want to help people celebrate all the other stuff, too.'

'You are speaking to two happily un-married ladies,' Iris said with a smirk. 'We can definitely figure this out.'

Kira leaned in, her mind clearly already working. 'I liked what that one commenter said about buying her friends flowers. Maybe we could do something with that?'

'Ooh, yeah, and what about some kind of subscription service? Like monthly bouquets?' Iris chimed in.

'Yes, perfect, this is all good.' Daisy took out her phone again and started filling her notes app with all the ideas her friends were spilling out.

By the end of the night, they'd polished off two plates of nachos, several rounds of margaritas, and renewed Daisy's faith in herself to pull this off.

The Daisy Chain Flower Shop was not going down without a fight.

A real one this time.

Daisy wasn't hiding behind a fake relationship anymore.

Or a probably fictional generational curse.

It was time she made the long line of Daisies proud.

Chapter Thirty-Eight

Ten months later

Elliot's palms were sweating. So much so he'd nearly dropped Goldie's leash several times on their way here.

Which was absurd because he'd done this exact thing nearly every day for the past year. But today was going to be different.

He pushed open the door to the flower shop and Daisy beamed at him from behind the counter.

'Elliot,' she said, coming around to greet him. She wrapped her arms around his neck and planted a kiss on his lips. Goldie happily circled them until Daisy reached down a hand and scratched between her ears.

'Closest friends I've ever seen,' Marty muttered as he headed out of the store with his arms filled with wildflower bouquets.

'Friends with benefits,' Cliff stage-whispered beside him

carrying a new cactus for his windowsill. 'That's what the kids call it.'

Daisy stifled a laugh, pressing her face against Elliot's neck. 'See you next week, boys!' she called over Elliot's shoulder before straightening up. 'Hey,' she said, still smiling, and Elliot's stomach did a concerning swoop right down to his toes.

'Hey.' He ran a hand through his hair, unable to stop fidgeting. 'They can't possibly believe we're still broken up, can they?'

'You know the town lost interest in us months ago. I think those two just forgot what actually happened,' Daisy said, moving back behind the counter. Goldie followed, plopping down on the bed Daisy kept here just for that reason. 'Crazy old men aside, I'm glad you're here. Guess what?'

Elliot leaned on the counter. 'What?'

'We went viral. The shop, I mean.'

'Really?'

'Well,' Daisy shrugged. 'Mini-viral anyway, but yeah, we started a trend!' She was nearly squealing, her face glowing with excitement.

'I'm not surprised but tell me. What trend?'

'You know how we did that thing on our socials asking people to tell us why their friend deserved flowers?'

'Yeah, you got so many amazing responses.'

'I know, and we picked a few people to send flower arrangements to, but then people started calling the shop wanting to fill in the gaps, so *every* person that was nominated got flowers.'

'That's incredible.'

'I know! And then, an influencer-type person learned about it and amplified the whole thing and now people are posting online about the amazing people in their life and *other* people are buying them flowers. There's even a hashtag!'

'I think that might be the most wholesome thing the internet has ever done.'

'I know!'

'I'm really proud of you.' Daisy had put so much work in over the past few months and had come up with so many new ideas to keep the shop going. And none of them had to do with fighting a curse. In fact, he hadn't heard any curse gossip for a long time. All anyone wanted to talk about was the Dream Harbor glow up now that Daisy's flowers graced nearly every business's door, window, or counter tops. She'd taken over the whole damn town.

'Thanks,' she said with a grin. 'I'm really proud of myself.'

Elliot laughed, sharing in Daisy's excitement and nearly forgetting how nervous he was.

'Anyway, I'm almost done here and then we can go home.'

Home.

Daisy moved in months ago. Slowly.

First, just her toothbrush.

Then PJs and a pair of cozy socks.

The drawer he set aside for her gradually began filling up. Soon she had a favorite mug in his cabinet, an opinion on paint colors for the kitchen and a routine to walk Goldie every morning.

Elliot let her take her time.

When she rented out the apartment at the flower shop, he figured she was all-in.

But he was still nervous about what he was about to do. A year ago, he would have never considered it. He didn't think his heart could possibly love someone again. Not the way he loved Daisy.

But hearts were funny like that.

'Actually, I wanted to ask you something.'

'Oh? Okay. What's up?'

Elliot cleared his throat. 'Do you ever miss doing flowers for weddings?'

Daisy shrugged. 'I wouldn't turn away the business, but I don't know if I miss it.'

'What if I wanted to hire you?'

She wasn't looking at him, too busy tidying up for the day, tucking away receipts and ribbon bits and brushing stray leaves and flower petals into the trash.

'For what?' she asked, shutting down the register.

'For our wedding.'

She paused. Realization dawned on Daisy's face. 'Wait a minute ... wait ... are you ... is this?' She came around the counter, yanking her apron off and tossing it to the side. 'Are you really doing this?'

Elliot nodded. Swallowed. Nodded again.

Breathed.

'Daisy November Scott, will you marry me?'

Daisy's hands flew to cover her open mouth.

'You want to marry me?' she whispered between her fingers.

'Of course I do.'

'I don't have the best track record.'

'I don't care about your track record.' He pressed his forehead to hers. 'Daisy, if you want to stay fake broken up, or say we're roommates or best friends or enemies or whatever, I don't care as long as we're together. But I want you to know this is forever, for me.'

'It's forever for me, too.'

Elliot nearly melted with relief.

'So do you want to stand up in front of our family and friends and tell them it's forever?'

Daisy's teary smile shattered him.

'Yes.'

'Really?'

'Yes.'

'You do?'

'Yes!' Daisy said with a giggle as he lifted her onto the counter. She took his face in her hands. 'I want to marry the hell out of you, Elliot Milton Parker.'

'That makes me absurdly happy.'

Daisy leaned forward and kissed him. 'Did you really think I would say no?'

'I didn't know if you would want to do the marriage thing again, but I knew I wanted to be with you.'

'*Forever.*'

'Yeah.' He kissed her again, whispering the words across her lips. 'You put me back together, Daisy. Brought me back to myself.' Her hands were in his hair now, his thumbs swiping away the tears on her cheeks.

'Same,' she whispered. 'You reminded me who I was.' Her lips coasted across his cheeks, his nose, his lips, showering him with her love.

'I'm really glad you asked me to be your fake boyfriend a year ago.'

'I couldn't have picked a better one.'

Elliot grinned and the sun shone in through the stained-glass window, painting them in pink and purple and yellow.

He had not seen this coming, but he was really glad he walked into this pretty little shop all those months ago.

Maybe it was fate, or a long-gone ancestor whispering in his ear. Or maybe he just needed a house plant his mother couldn't kill too easily. But if he was being honest, he'd fallen in love with Daisy the moment he'd seen her, before he'd ever set foot in her shop.

He was just glad he was brave enough to stop hiding. And that she was brave enough to start over. Whatever it was that brought them together, he knew this one was going to last.

Daisy had pieced his heart back together and now all it wanted was her.

'Let's go home.' She hopped down from the counter and took his hand. 'Come on, Goldie.' The dog followed as they walked out into the warm air.

Daisy gave his hand a squeeze.

She was wearing yellow today and she looked perfect.

Like sunshine and flowers and summer days.

She looked like the future.

She looked like *his*.

Epilogue

Twenty years later

'We're going to be late.'

'We're not going to be late.' Elliot's calm voice came from behind her as she applied mascara at the mirror above their bathroom sink.

Daisy took a deep breath. 'I'm feeling emotional.'

'I know.'

She could feel Elliot's smile as he lifted her hair and kissed the back of her neck. She was in just her bra and panties, the dress she planned on wearing today was still laid out on their bed. His hand splayed across her bare stomach.

'Our first baby is graduating high school today,' she said, already getting weepy. 'I really don't know why I'm bothering with mascara. It's going to be a mess in a matter of minutes.'

'Who do you think is going to be worse, you because it's our first baby graduating or Iris because it's her last?'

They both thought about it for a minute before saying in unison. 'Archer.' Iris and Archer had already watched Olive and Owen graduate and Archer had been a mess each time, so Daisy could only imagine how he would be today when their youngest, Ophelia, would leave the nest.

Daisy laughed, shaking her head. Poor guy.

She relaxed into Elliot's body behind her. 'We definitely don't have time for this.'

'We always have time for this,' he said, kissing along her neck and down to her shoulder.

Daisy studied their reflection in the mirror. Elliot still looked good, handsome as ever with his salt and pepper hair and glasses. Aging had just made him look even more like a sexy professor.

She ran her fingers through her own hair. 'I should probably get these grays dyed.'

Elliot spun her around. 'They're not gray, they're silver,' he said, nuzzling further into the crook of her neck, pressing her back into the bathroom counter. 'I like them. They make you look perfect. Like a sexy witch.'

Daisy hummed her approval as Elliot kissed and licked along her collar bones, forgetting that they absolutely didn't have time for this until pounding at the door interrupted them. 'Mom!'

Daisy sighed. 'What?'

'Where are my shoes?'

'What shoes?'

Elliot just kept kissing right through this conversation,

eighteen years of parenting desensitizing him to insistent knocking and yelling through closed doors.

'My open-toe platform ones.'

'Probably in your closet.'

'They're not there!'

'Margaret Daisy Parker, just find some damn shoes to wear! We're leaving in fifteen minutes for your brother's graduation whether you are barefoot or not.'

A loud noise that could only be described as a growl came from the other side of the door, followed by stomping and a door slamming somewhere else in the house. In the meantime, Elliot had unhooked her bra and tossed it aside.

'We really don't...'

He cut her off with a kiss, hoisting her onto the counter. 'Shh ... this will take five minutes tops,' he said, dropping to his knees in front of her.

She *could* argue. She probably *should* argue. But she was so tense and emotional about today, maybe this would help take the edge off.

Her head dropped back against the mirror as Elliot pulled her panties aside and got right to work. Another perk of being together for so long, he knew exactly what to do. And he was right, it wouldn't take long.

She hissed his name, her fingers tugging at his hair as he licked and sucked. He reached up and rolled her nipple between thumb and forefinger until she whimpered. She rocked her hips and he hummed with encouragement.

'That's right, sweet Daisy. Come on my tongue,' he rasped, nipping at the inside of her thigh.

And then it was heat and pressure and pleasure building until it broke with this man she loved more than anything between her thighs. As soon as she came down, before she could catch her breath, he pulled her off the counter, turned her around and dove into her. His mouth was on her neck, one hand between her legs, thrusting, thrusting until they both came again.

He buried his groans in her shoulder, and she bit down on her hand, trying to keep quiet, until they were giggling at the absurdity of it all.

'How'd we do?' he asked, still panting.

Daisy glanced at her phone. 'Seven minutes. We're going to be late.'

Elliot smirked. 'We're not going to be late.' He kissed her shoulder one more time before turning around to clean up and get dressed.

And he was right.

At exactly nine o'clock her little family was dressed in their finest and waiting at the door. Maggie had found her shoes, apparently. James was in his graduation gown looking so much like his father that Daisy was fighting back tears already, and Elliot was there to shuffle them all out the door.

For twenty years, he'd been there. A steady and patient presence.

Today was just another reminder of how happy she was that she ran to his house one stormy night and broke the curse.

She was pretty sure Great-Aunt Daisy would be very proud.

❀❀❀❀

THANK YOU FOR READING
The Daisy Chain Flower Shop

IT WOULD MEAN SO MUCH IF YOU COULD LEAVE A REVIEW
ON ALL YOUR PREFERRED PLATFORMS AND SOCIAL MEDIA
TO HELP SPREAD THE WORD!

YOU CAN ALSO FOLLOW ME ON INSTAGRAM
@LAURIEGILMORE_AUTHOR

AND MY WEBSITE AT
WWW.THELAURIEGILMORE.COM
FOR ALL THE UPDATES ON MY LATEST WORKS.

❀❀❀❀

Acknowledgments

Book six! Phew! At the end of my thank yous for *The Pumpkin Spice Café*, I thanked readers for reading and said I hoped you would come back for more. Well, you certainly have. You've come back for more books and special editions and reader events! Your love for Dream Harbor continues to blow me away. So I'll just say, again, thank you. Thank you for reading and sharing and coming to events and chatting with me and being enthusiastic and just generally fabulous. You've made me an author and that's pretty freaking cool.

Much of this book was conceived on various train rides across the UK on my tour this summer with my incomparable editor, Jennie Rothwell. As it turns out, we do some of our best work on trains. (Sometimes there's even a snack cart! Rail travel is very exciting.) Anyway, a big giant thank you to Jennie for brainstorming anywhere we need to, for planning the best dinner stops, and for being the other half to this creative team. You are the best. I hope you all fell in love with sweet, nerdy Elliot as much as we did.

To everyone at One More Chapter and Harper 360, thank you for getting these books looking incredible and out into the world. To Charlotte Ledger for believing in this series. To Chloe for her marketing expertise and for escorting me around for the first part of my UK tour (and for teaching me about trendy things like Trader Joe's totes).

To Sofia for sending me so much fun mail. To Ashton and Aisling for getting these books out across the whole world at this point! To Emily and Jean Marie and everyone at Harper 360 for all your work (making the NYT's list was certainly a highlight for me!). To Kamrun for planning an amazing US tour! To Lisa and HarperCollins Canada, thank you for an awesome Canadian tour! There are so many more people who work on these books, so to everyone I'm forgetting or not calling out by name, I'm sorry and thank you!!

To my agent, Amy, thank you for all your work this year (important agent-y things but also even more important chats about *Love is Blind*)! Here's to even more fun next year.

A special shout out to my brother-in-law, Janzer, who helped me figure out the mystery component for this book. I knew I wanted Daisy to be cursed but it was during a chat on our family vacation (thirteen people crammed into one rental house leads to great conversations) that Janzer suggested some sort of doomed love affair that happened to one of Daisy's relatives, and so Daisy's love curse was born. Thanks for talking books with me, Janzer. Maybe someday I'll get to read one of yours.

Last but not least, always thank you to my family. An extra thank you this time around to my nephew Tommy and my niece Brooklyn, who while not being old enough to read these books, always manage to make me feel like a celebrity whenever one comes out.

To my kids for helping set up the new office (it's so nice and quiet up here for writing!) and to my husband for thinking my gray hairs are sexy. I'll probably keep you.

WELCOME TO THE SMALL TOWN OF MAPLE HOLLOW…

BIG BAD WOLF
Coming September 2026

Ruby Bellerose lives on the edge of the woods, in a cottage more akin to a fairy tale than modern day life. Her love life is basically non-existent, and she keeps away from the whispered gossip that travels through Maple Hollow. Until a chance encounter with Rafe.
As mysterious as he is brooding, Ruby is drawn to the woodsman, curious to find out more about the stranger who lives deep within the woods.
But Rafe is hiding a secret. And with something lurking in the shadowy forest, will Ruby find that Rafe is her knight in shining armor or something altogether more dangerous…

Available to pre-order in paperback, ebook and audio now!

DO YOU LOVE LAURIE GILMORE?

Why not become a Dreamer and be the first to hear from Laurie Gilmore about:

New books
Special and exclusive editions
Additional content
Events and signings

Sign up to the newsletter or follow her at:
thelauriegilmore.com

The author and One More Chapter would like to thank everyone who contributed to the publication of this story...

Analytics
Imogen Wolstencroft

Audio
Fionnuala Barrett
Ciara Briggs

Design
Lucy Bennett
Fiona Greenway
Liane Payne
Dean Russell

Digital Sales
Laura Daley
Lydia Grainge
Hannah Lismore

eCommerce
Laura Carpenter
Madeline ODonovan
Charlotte Stevens
Christina Storey
Rachel Ward

Editorial
Janet Marie Adkins
Rosie Best
Kara Daniel
Charlotte Ledger
Jennie Rothwell
Sofia Salazar Studer
Emily Thomas
Helen Williams

Harper360
Emily Gerbner
Ariana Juarez
Jean Marie Kelly
Kamrun Nesa
emma sullivan
Sophia Wilhelm

International Sales
Ruth Burrow
Bethan Moore
Colleen Simpson

Inventory
Sarah Callaghan
Kirsty Norman

Marketing & Publicity
Occy Carr
Chloe Cummings
Grace Edwards
Katie Sadler

Operations
Melissa Okusanya
Vanessa Coubrough

Production
Denis Manson
Simon Moore
Francesca Tuzzeo

Rights
Ashton Mucha
Alisah Saghir
Zoe Shine
Aisling Smyth

Trade Marketing
Ben Hurd
Eleanor Slater

The HarperCollins Contracts Team

The HarperCollins Distribution Team

The HarperCollins Finance & Royalties Team

The HarperCollins Legal Team

The HarperCollins Technology Team

UK Sales
Isabel Coburn
Jay Cochrane
Leah Woods

And every other essential link in the chain from delivery drivers to booksellers to librarians and beyond!